CURVY GIRLS CAN'T DATE BEST FRIENDS

KELSIE STELTING

For Tricia, thank you for caring so delicately for this group of friends. We are lucky to have you.

This is my wish for you;
Comfort on difficult days,
Smiles when sadness intrudes,
Rainbows to follow the clouds,
Laughter to kiss your lips,
Sunsets to warm your heart,
Hugs when spirits sag,
Beauty for your eyes to see,
Friendships to brighten your being,
Faith so that you can believe,
Confidence for when you doubt,
Courage to know yourself,
Patience to accept the truth,
Love to complete your life.

Ralph Waldo Emerson

ONE

TEN YEARS OLD

CARSON

"This is going to be a good move for us," Mom promised as the GPS told us we were two minutes from our new home.

The home I'd never set foot in.

The home away from my grandparents.

The home away from my friends.

But it would still be filled with the same people.

The same mom who worked eighty-hour weeks.

The same dad who didn't work at all.

The same sisters living the same nightmare as me.

My oldest sister in the front seat barely looked up from her phone. "Sure, Mom," Clary said. I didn't even see a glint of the hope in her face that I was afraid to feel in my chest. But there was a reason Dad was alone in the moving truck while we piled five people into a car that barely fit all of us, especially now that my sisters were older and had bigger hips that made less sitting room for me. (Mom said that was because they'd gone through puberty. Whatever that meant.)

"It *will* be better," Mom asserted, her eyes dark blue in the rearview mirror. They got that color when she was upset. Even darker when she cried. "Your father grew up his whole life in that small town. Around the same patterns and the same people. When he's in a new place, he'll realize that we're what matters. I *know* he will."

No one had talked to me about the Cook Family Curse directly—they thought I was too young—but every man on my dad's side of the family was abusive. Had been for generations. Clary said it was like they didn't know any other way to be. My sister Sierra, who was into witchcraft, took the curse part more literally. No one had ever said what that meant for me.

One thing I knew—our home life couldn't get worse. At least, I hoped it wouldn't.

"And you'll all be at a great school," Mom

continued. "The best school money can buy. You'll meet your best friends there; I just know it."

On my left side, Gemma rolled her red-rimmed eyes and leaned against the window. Her best friend had lived next door to us at our old house, and Dad had to peel her off the mailbox to get her in the car.

"Just stop, Mom," Sierra said, her body stiff on my right. "You married an abusive narcissist, and instead of leaving him, you're staying with him and taking us so far away from the only family we've ever known. It's *pathetic*."

I flinched at her words. I hated the fighting. I hated how mean everyone was to Mom. Especially since I'd seen how it felt to have some of Dad's anger directed at me.

Mom's eyes grew darker. "You'll just have to wait and see."

She turned onto a road at a sign that said *Rhodora Home Owners' Association*. The houses lining the wide street were nice—not as big as the ones in Texas; Gramps did always say, "Everything's bigger in Texas."

Each home had bright green lawns and big bay windows, and everything looked just as perfect as Mom wanted us to believe it would be. The moving truck was parked in front of a house painted light blue—like it had tried to blend in with the sky but missed a shade.

The house on the left was a boring brown color, but right next door there was a bright yellow home with the windows open, and I swore there was a pie sitting in the windowsill. I wished I could move into *that* house, with a perfect mom and a perfect dad and maybe even a brother and a sister who weren't so busy dealing with their own problems they forgot about me.

"This is it," Mom announced, putting the car into park along the curb. She got out and said, "Carson?"

After my sisters left, I scooted out of the middle. Mom waited for me by a white mailbox shaped like a swan. "Yeah?"

She knelt down and put her hands on my shoulders. "I want to thank you for staying so positive." She glanced over her shoulder where Dad stood by the truck, smoking, and lowered her voice. "I know Dad's been hard on you, but you keep being the bright, silly, fun, *good* kid I know you are, and great things will happen for you."

My throat stung like when I had to tell Grandma and Gramps goodbye. "Are you sure?"

"I promise. This move will be the best thing to happen in your life."

CALLIE

Through my bedroom window on the second floor, I watched a man who looked as old as my dad yank the for-sale sign out of the ground. He tossed it aside, and a laughing woman came and kissed him.

A boy bent over, pretending to throw up, while three older girls walked toward the front door.

"Joe!" I called to my older brother. "They're our age!"

He came into my room and pulled his headphones around his neck. "Any hot girls?"

"Ew," I said, even though the girls were pretty. They each had long blond hair like their mother that rippled down their backs.

I didn't focus on them for long. My eyes were on the boy. He straightened, and sandy blond hair covered his forehead, brushed over his dark eyebrows. Was he in my grade? He could have been. What was he like? I couldn't tell anything about him from his plain T-shirt and khaki shorts.

Only that he looked like he was my height. But again, that was hard to tell from up here.

I wished I could open my window and lean out to get a better look, but it was the middle of August, and Dad would be so upset if he knew I was letting out all of *his* cold air. Apparently, all of the house was his and Mom's...until it needed cleaning.

From downstairs, my mom called, "Joe, Callie, come here!"

Joe and I gave each other a look. Mom always made us greet new neighbors, but I was only wearing basketball shorts and a T-shirt from practice earlier today...

"One second," we yelled at the same time.

Joe ran out of the room, and I had a distinct feeling he was doing the same thing I was: primping.

I ran to my dresser and dug through the bulk of my jeans and T-shirts until I found the ones that looked best on me. I tugged them on and started toward the stairs. Joe came out of the bathroom smelling like way too much cologne.

Fanning my hand in front of my nose, I said, "You smelled better before!"

"Really?" He put his armpit in my face, and I nearly fell down the stairs.

"Stop!" I cried, hurrying to the bottom before I could get more hairy armpit in my face.

He finally gave up, and when we reached the kitchen, Mom gave us an exasperated look. "You two," she sighed. Then she reached for a carafe of her special homemade strawberry lemonade and handed it to me.

I adjusted the sweating pitcher in my hands as she gave Joe a round glass pan full of cinnamon rolls. She'd been experimenting with different flavors lately, and through the glass, these looked strawberry flavored.

"Can I have one?" Joe asked.

"You don't think they'll notice one missing?" she said, turning to get the plastic plates and cups decorated with tiny flowers.

"I just don't care," Joe retorted. "They look so good, Mom."

I rolled my eyes. Flattery was his strong suit. "Kiss up."

"Callie," Mom admonished. "No name-calling."

"Even when it's true?" I said sweetly.

Smiling, she shook her head. "Let's get going."

We marched out the front door and down the sidewalk. Last time we'd done the neighbor greeting, it was for the house across the street where an old couple lived with their creepy cat. It had a scraggly coat and two different colored eyes and curled around my legs the entire twenty minutes we were there, like it had an evil plan to trip me. This family already seemed more promising.

Their front door was open, and we could hear girls arguing inside about who got which room.

"See? You're not the only siblings who argue." Mom looked over at us pointedly and knocked on the door frame. "Yoo hoo, neighbors."

My cheeks reddened. Not only was I standing here with a sweaty glass of lemonade, my mom said *yoo hoo*.

The woman I'd seen earlier stepped from the direction of the garage. I'd been in this house when it was still listed for sale—it looked a lot like ours but like someone had flipped it the opposite direction and painted it in bright, coastal colors unlike the beige that covered all of our walls.

The woman smiled wide and said, "Hi there. Come inside."

Mom walked a couple of feet into the living room, and as we followed, I thought we might as well have been standing on the porch.

A crashing sound came from the direction of the garage. Shattering glass.

I flinched, and the Mom said, "Whoops. Must have dropped something."

It didn't sound like dropping. The next crash that came sounded like something had hit the wall.

The boy came running out of the garage and ran out the back door. His mom's eyes trailed behind him for a moment before turning back to us, looking tight around the corners. "It was nice to meet you, but we better get back to unpacking."

"Of course," Mom said, a smile pasted on her face like she hadn't seen what I had. "I'm Anne, and this is Callie and Joe. My husband is Robert, but I'm sure there will be plenty of time to meet him once you get settled in. Where would you like us to set the snacks? I'm sure you'll need them!"

She nodded gratefully. "We will. Here on the floor should be fine."

Mom seemed to hesitate before bending to set the plasticware and plates on the dusty ground. Joe dumped his cinnamon rolls, and I carefully lowered the carafe to the floor.

As we turned and walked out, I heard a door slam and a man's voice grumbling something about lazy and ungrateful.

After the door closed firmly behind us and we heard the heavy clicking of a lock, Joe said, "That was weird."

"Shh," Mom said.

"It was," I said, my throat tight. "Do you think the dad was throwing something at the boy?"

"I'm sure it's okay." Mom smiled at me, but there was still a troubled look in her eyes. "Why don't you get some time outside? Maybe hang out in the green belt."

The message behind her words was clear. *Find him.*

I cut across our lawn to the gate that opened to the expanse of grass that cut through the neighborhood. There were a few parks dispersed through the place, and I didn't see him on the one closest to our houses.

Trying to stall the worry rising in my throat, I shucked my flip-flops, hooking the straps between my fingers. I always felt better with the grass forming and molding to my feet. Even so, the sense of dread lingered.

This time of summer, it was too hot to be at the park, I reminded myself. Everyone was probably at the pool or the beach. Or watching TV in the *air conditioning*. Having fun instead of bringing food to grumpy neighbors. Maybe the boy had found a tree to hide out under.

I rounded a corner and saw the next park. The same boy from earlier sat on one of the swings, dragging his feet over the worn-down path of gravel underneath. His head hung low, sandy hair falling around his face. I opened my mouth to greet him, but he lifted his arm to his face and used the back of his forearm to wipe his eyes.

He was crying.

It felt like a hand had reached around my lungs and squeezed. I both wanted to run to him and make him feel better and dodge behind a tree to let him have some privacy. The war of the two options held me firmly to the spot, unable to move.

Like he sensed me watching him, he looked up and immediately began wiping at his face, trying to hide his feelings. Before I could speak, he said, "You live next door, don't you?"

My chest ached even more at the sight of him trying to hold it together, but maybe that was what he needed—for me to pretend nothing had happened.

"Yeah, in the yellow house," I said with a smile, going to the swing next to him and sitting down. "What grade are you in?"

"I'm going to Emerson Academy. I'll be in sixth grade."

"Me too," I said. "Do you play sports?"

"Swimming. But I want to try football too."

I nodded. "Our school does flag football in sixth grade."

"What about you?" he asked. "Do you play sports?"

"Everything I can," I answered. "I'm in a summer basketball league, but I'll play volleyball when school starts. Where'd you move from?"

"Texas." He said the word bitterly, like Texas was just as bad as sitting on the bench a whole game or something. He pumped his legs and started picking up height. "Want to see who can jump farther?"

I nodded and began swinging my legs too. "I'll warn you though. I've been practicing on these swings my whole life."

"Well I have natural talent."

I snorted, working even harder. "Good luck."

We were both high now, the chains squeaking harshly as we worked to best each other.

"Ready," he said.

"Set," I yelled.

"Go!" we shouted at the same time.

We flew through the air, weightless, soaring, and then the ground came toward us. I touched the ground and rolled, him doing the same beside me. As I skidded to a stop on the gravel, I looked over to see the boy at the same distance as me.

"Tie," he said.

I grinned. "I'll win next time."

A woman's voice yelled in the distance, "Carson!"

His expression soured. "That's me."

That tight feeling was back in my chest. "See you later?"

He nodded. "Race?"

"You're on."

We sprinted back toward our houses, neck and neck the entire way. When we reached the back gate, one of his sisters was standing there with her arms folded across her ample chest. "Looks like you're fitting right in," she said drily, extending her arm for him.

He ducked under it and started inside.

As I walked toward my house, I couldn't get the boy and his hidden tears out of my mind. Not during supper when Joe told Dad what happened. Not when our parents sent us upstairs and I could hear my parents whispering downstairs through the bathroom vents, and not at bedtime as I sat at my desk, carefully braiding my hair so it would be crimped the next morning.

Not when I heard something tapping at my second-story window.

With my eyebrows furrowed together, I went to the window, pushed it open, and looked down and around. There were bright little pieces of something on the ground. And then one pegged my head.

Across the gap between our houses, I could see the boy, *Carson*, leaning out his window, holding on to a handful of Legos.

Before I had a chance to speak, he said, "I didn't hear your name."

"Callie," I answered.

"Same place, same time tomorrow, Callie?" he asked.

I nodded, a smile growing on my face. "You're on."

TWO

ELEVEN YEARS OLD

CARSON

Mom's promise only lasted three months before the fighting started again.

My parents yelled back and forth downstairs, just like they had at the old house. Even worse. They'd been at this for at least an hour, and there was no hope of slowing down anytime soon. The words they flung at each other made me sick to my stomach. Usually Dad was the one who got physical, but Mom could be just as hateful with her words, calling him a deadbeat and a waste of skin.

My chest was tight, and I had trouble breathing, much less sleeping, even though my alarm clock said it was 2:53.

Clary's window had slid open for her to sneak out half an hour earlier.

Gemma's music was loud—but not loud enough.

I had no idea what Sierra was doing. Was she okay? Should I check on her?

Something heavy slammed against the floor downstairs, and I cringed, stuck somewhere between leaping out of bed to protect whoever it was that had been hurt and running away as far as I could get.

My door cracked open, and I scrambled back on my bed.

"Shh, shh," Gemma soothed. She came into my room, fully dressed in day clothes. "Let's get out of here."

"Where?" I asked. Not that it mattered. Anywhere would have been fine.

"I have an idea." She quietly opened my dresser drawers, then flung clothes at me.

I threw them on over the underwear I'd gone to bed in and followed her down the hallway. She paused before the staircase, making sure the yelling was farther away, toward the garage, before continuing to Sierra's room.

"Won't Sierra be mad we're going in her room?" I whispered.

Ignoring me, Gemma pushed through the door where I saw Sierra waiting for us, looking down at her phone. At the sound of the door opening, she jerked away, but seemed to relax when she realized it was us. She walked straight to the open window and began climbing down the lattice on the side of the house.

Gemma easily followed out the window, and I looked back toward the stairs. The yelling had stopped. Maybe it was over? But then other sounds came from downstairs, just as disturbing, and I hurried toward the window.

Sierra sprinted across the grass toward the green belt, and Gemma and I followed. They went past the first, smaller park next to our house, past Callie's house, and stopped at the bigger park.

"I'm so sick of them," Sierra gritted out as she climbed the stairs meant for much younger children.

Gemma followed after her. "They should have just left us with Grandma and Gramps. Mom and Dad clearly don't want kids anyway, and Clary's gonna wind up pregnant before she even graduates."

My chest ached at their words about our sister. About our grandparents. I missed them too. Gramps was the only guy in my life who actually cared to have me around. Dad would order me around to get tools when he worked on the car or yell at me to find the remote, but he never taught me anything like Gramps had. Gramps was the one who showed me how to fish, how to set up a tent and start a fire. Without him, I was lost. The only time I felt like I knew what I was doing in our new town was around Callie. Being with her was as easy as it had been with Gramps. I felt like I could just be myself around her, even if we didn't talk about how horrible things were at my house.

I got on the stairs and walked up to where my sisters lay on the platform. Gemma had a bottle of Mt. Dew in her hand, and I realized I was thirsty too.

"Can I have some?" I asked her.

She tossed me the bottle, and I waterfalled some into my mouth. She usually didn't mind sharing if I didn't put my lips on it.

Sierra busied herself, spreading out her glittering gemstones. "Should we call the cops on them?"

"No," Gemma said immediately. "They would

blame us. Remember what happened when Clary called them at the old house."

I shuddered against the screaming and yelling and punishment our parents had given her.

"Hey, Sierra?" I asked.

She looked up at me, her eyes glittering like her stones.

"Can you..." I bit my cheek, tasting blood with the leftover Mt. Dew. "Can you break the curse in me?"

She and Gemma exchanged a look before Sierra said sadly, "I'm sorry, Cars. It doesn't work that way."

No, there was no one coming to help me. There was no way out. There was just a way *through*. As I lay beside them and looked at the few stars dotting the sky through the city lights, I thought Clary had it figured out.

She had an escape, and I needed to find one too.

CALLIE

"Callie, can you take the trash out?" Mom asked. It was just the two of us in the dining room this morning since Dad had already left for work and Joe was catching up on his assigned reading—much to Mom's chagrin.

I finished rinsing off my breakfast plate and put it in the dishwasher. "This is what I get for doing my homework?"

Joe glared at me over the top of *War and Peace.*

"Just be careful not to get anything on your uniform," Mom said, stacking up the rest of the dishes.

I tied off the kitchen trash bag and carried it to the front door. The trash cans were hidden beside our house, and this was the closest way. I pushed the door open and walked through, then saw the drip on the sidewalk.

"Shoot," I muttered and hurried off the concrete, holding the bag as far from myself as possible. I carefully lifted the trash can lid and lugged the bag into it. Something about swiping my hands together to free them of invisible germs made me feel better. I didn't know why.

A scuffing sound came from a few feet over, but I didn't see anyone walking around me. Then I looked up and saw Carson climbing in through a bedroom window that wasn't his. My eyebrows drew together. Hadn't we already talked about training for *American Ninja Warrior* together? Was he trying to one-up me again?

As I went back inside to finish getting ready for school, I promised myself to confront him at lunch time.

When I got to the cafeteria and had my tray, I found Carson sitting at our usual spot. We always took the end of a long table, that way we had at least one side free.

He waved at me as I approached, but he looked exhausted.

"Are you sick?" I asked as I set my tray down.

"No. Why?"

"You look terrible," I said, taking him in up close. Even his hair was rumpled, like he hadn't had a chance to comb it. "Do you need my extra brush?"

"No." He yawned and set his cheek in one of his hands. "Maybe food will help."

I remembered my own food in front of me and dipped a chicken nugget in some ranch. "I saw you climbing in the window this morning."

His back stiffened. *Guilty.*

"I knew it!" I accused.

Putting his hands up, he said, "It was Sierra's idea, honest."

"Oh, sure, blame your sister," I said, shaking my head. "That's fine. I'm still going to win."

His eyebrows drew together. "Win?"

"Don't play dumb," I said. "*American Ninja Warrior*. You're trying to train."

Suddenly, he burst out laughing, so loudly that the people around us noticed and were turning our way with incredulous smiles that said they wanted in on the joke. Well, I did too. "What's so funny?" I asked.

"You're so innocent," he said, finally cooling down and wiping tears from his eyes.

I hated when people said things like that. If I had a dollar for every time someone called me naïve or gullible, I could have bought plenty of duct tape to shut them up. "Tell me then."

Just as quickly as his features had lit up, they fell, making him appear more exhausted than ever. He looked to the side to make sure no one was paying attention, then to the right to make sure no one was walking by.

"You know why we moved?" he whispered.

We'd been best friends for almost a year, and he

was asking me if I knew why he'd moved in? "Of course. Your mom got a new job."

He shook his head.

"What?" I asked, confused. "But you said..."

"It's a lie," he said bitterly, then he looked away and took a deep breath, his shoulders heaving from the force. "My parents have a...bad marriage."

My mind flashed to the time we brought them cinnamon rolls, and the way I was never allowed at their house, only outside. "What do you mean it's bad?"

"They fight," he whispered. "Things get broken, and when Dad's drinking...people get hurt."

My heart felt like it had stalled in my chest, every bit as heavy as a boulder. "He's abusive?" I breathed. Even the word felt wrong in my throat. I knew he was mean, but not in that way.

Carson nodded. "Last year it got so bad Clary called the cops. Of course, when they showed up, Mom and Dad said it was a misunderstanding. Said Mom tripped down the stairs and that Clary had a nightmare. After the cops left, Dad..." He cringed and took a breath. "He hurt Clary. Mom threatened to leave him, but he said he would do anything —even move away from his family and his friends —if she would stay with him."

The weight of what Carson told me struck harder than anything of the individual words. It made all of the times he was sent away from the house, the way his mom worked so many hours, the way his sister was always gone—make sense. But none of it should have made sense. Parents weren't supposed to hurt their kids. They were supposed to love them.

"Carson, I'm..."

"Sorry?" he finished for me. "Don't be. I just didn't want you to think I was trying to cheat to win at American Ninja Warrior. If I win, it'll be 'cause I'm awesome."

I rolled my eyes. How could he joke at a time like this? Having said what he'd said? I just reached across the table and touched his hand. "I'm here for you."

His lips quivered for a moment before he bit them together. "Best friends forever?"

I smiled and nodded, wanting to just take him into a hug and make all of the hurt go away. Instead, I repeated his words and meant them with all of my heart. "Best friends forever."

CALLIE

Carson and I sat in the two bucket seats of Mom's minivan on the way to our first boy-girl party at Merritt Alexander's. Her family lived in a mansion, and her big brother, Ryde, was probably the *cutest* guy I'd ever seen. Even cuter than my favorite movie star. I wondered if he'd be there. If he'd like the bejeweled party dress Mom had bought me especially for this party.

Carson said, "Anne, do you have any more of that hard candy?"

His lips were already blue from "taste testing" the batch of candy Mom had made. She'd been on a real candy-making kick lately.

"They're going to have food there," I reminded him.

Dad chuckled from the front seat. "Carson's a smart man. There's no telling whether the food will actually be *good* or not."

I rolled my eyes. "We're not going there for the food."

"Speak for yourself," Carson said, taking another piece of candy from the tin Mom passed back.

Mom and Dad laughed, but I just shook my head. "Pass me one then." If you can't beat 'em, join 'em.

Carson extended the tin, and I put a piece in my mouth. They actually tasted kind of like Jolly Ranchers. But instead of buying a pack, Mom had spent all afternoon in the kitchen making them. Seemed like a waste of time if you asked me.

Out the window, a long, tree-lined driveway came into view. Balloon bouquets were strung along the path, along with big signs saying HAPPY BIRTHDAY MERRITT.

Carson's mouth fell open, showing half a piece of candy. "This is where Merritt *lives*?"

I nodded. "You should see the treat bags."

Mom and Dad gave each other a look, then turned back to the road.

"What?" Carson asked, not hiding his excitement at all. "What's in the treat bags?"

"Last year, they gave everyone a smart watch."

His eyes lit up. "Seriously? I don't even have a phone."

Dad coughed. "They didn't pay for service, though, did they?"

"I can still listen to music on it though," I said.

"Do you think they'll do that again this year?" Carson asked.

I shook my head. "It's usually different. But this is the first party boys will be at, so who knows."

Dad stopped behind another car letting out kids and turned back to us. "Okay, son, here's what you need to know about a boy-girl party. You be the man, pull back chairs, hold open doors, pick up the extra plates."

Carson's eyebrows drew together. "That sounds so lame."

Dad chuckled. "Not lame, chivalrous."

"I don't know, Dad," I said. "Have you seen the guys in our class?"

"Someday," Dad said, "stuff like that will matter."

Mom smiled at Dad and said, "You'll want a guy like that, Callie."

"Like Carson?" I sputtered. "Ew, he's like my brother!"

Mom and Dad laughed, and Carson got red.

"I wasn't saying Carson specifically," Dad said. "Just someone *like* him."

Okay, now I was blushing. "Can we go?" I asked before they could turn their dating advice on me.

"Have fun," Mom said. "We'll be back at nine to get you."

My hand was already on the handle, pushing the button to let us out. I climbed out of the car, careful to be modest with my dress, and started toward the door, nerves jumping through my system. What would a boy-girl party be like? Would we play Spin the Bottle? Would I have my first kiss? Was I ready for that?

We reached the front door, and Carson held it open for me.

I gave him a look. "You're seriously following my dad's advice?"

"It's better than my dad's advice," he said as we stepped inside.

I didn't get a chance to ask him what that advice had been before Merritt's mom greeted us and told us the party was upstairs. Like we needed that knowledge. I could hear the music blaring from here.

As we walked toward the massive marble staircase, Carson whispered, "Merritt's mom is hot."

I elbowed him in the gut, and he doubled over, but it relieved me a little bit to be back to normal. Dad's advice was weird. I didn't like him telling Carson how to "get girls" just as much as I disliked him telling me what kind of guy I should go for. As far as I was concerned, Ryde Alexander was the dream guy.

We topped the stairs and followed the music to a massive room with a pool table, foosball, air hockey, a few pinball machines, and giant speakers blaring pop songs.

One of Carson's friends, Beckett, came over and said hi. Carson asked him about the food, and within seconds, they were off to the tables filled with different foods and desserts.

I rolled my eyes at him, and Merritt came and slung her arm around my shoulders. "Hey, girl," she said. "You killed it in the game yesterday!"

Tinsley and Poppy were beside her, and they nodded in agreement. "That spike was amazing."

My cheeks felt hot. I loved volleyball, and I

worked hard in the games, but I wasn't used to getting compliments all the time. "You did great too, Merritt," I said. "Your setting was awesome."

She smiled and pushed some curls over her shoulder. "Aw, thanks." I took in her outfit now, her sparkly dress and the tiara that said BIRTHDAY GIRL atop her head.

"Love your outfit," I said, grinning. "We almost match."

"We do!" she said and held out her phone, already on selfie mode. "Let's get a picture."

I held up a peace sign and stuck out my tongue while she pursed her lips together and made a duck face.

"Okay, now a smiling one," she said.

I grinned into the camera, liking the way I looked in the makeup Mom let me wear. I hoped Ryde liked it too.

After Merritt left to hang out with some of her other friends, I looked around and found Ryde leaning against a wall with a couple of his friends. They were all in high school, and they looked like royalty, even though they weren't dressed up like the rest of us.

Rumors had started going around that Ryde was going to get a big role in a movie soon. I hoped he would—then I wouldn't just have to stare at his pictures on social media.

The music stopped, and I looked around to see Merritt standing on the air hockey table holding up a glass of punch. "Time to play Seven Minutes in Heaven!"

The blood drained from my face, and nerves danced in my stomach.

"And since I'm the birthday girl, I get to pick," she said. Her eyes narrowed in on the cutest boy in our grade. "Me and Beckett."

Beckett's cheeks were bright red as Merritt's friends helped her down from the table and she walked to him. She took his hand and led him through double doors into what looked like a bedroom.

After the door closed, I beelined to Carson, who held a plate piled high with snacks.

"Oh my gosh," I said.

He had to work to swallow the massive bite in his mouth. "What happened?"

Carson could be so oblivious sometimes. "Merritt and Beckett! Seven Minutes in Heaven!"

Rolling his eyes, he said, "Five bucks they don't do anything."

I raised my eyebrows. "Not even kiss?"

He shook his head.

"Make it ten."

"Who do you think she'll pick next?" Carson asked, looking around.

"Probably Tinsley and someone." I glanced around, trying to figure out who the cutest guy in the room would be after Beckett.

My cheeks flushed as I realized it would be Carson.

"Maybe Dugan?" Carson suggested.

"Sure," I said, not wanting to share my revelation. "But he's kind of a jerk."

"What?" he asked. "Are you okay?"

I nodded, glad he was so oblivious despite my red face.

"Want a pig in a blanket? They're like *heaven*."

He held one out, and I took a bite. "Why are you so hungry all the time?"

Beating his chest with his free hand, he said, "I'm a growing boy."

The double doors opened, and the room grew hushed. I took them in, Merritt's disheveled crown and Beckett's lips smeared with lipstick.

"Ten dollars," I said to Carson. "Hand it over."

"You don't know—"

"Next up," Merritt yelled, "Callie and Carson!"

"Oh no," I said. "Why don't you let someone else have a turn?"

Merritt marched over to us, put her hands on our backs, and began shoving us toward the bedroom. "You score on the court, time to score in real life."

The doors banged shut behind us, and Carson and I stared at each other, white as the messed-up sheets on the bed.

Merritt yelled through the door, "If you don't do anything, we'll know!"

Carson gulped. Like out loud.

"Same," I said.

He looked from me to the door. "We don't have to," he whispered.

"We're *not*," I said, my heart racing. "You're like my brother."

"I'm glad you noticed. I always try to ask myself, WWJD: what would Joe do?"

I rolled my eyes and shoved his arm. Using the momentum of my push, he turned and sat on a bench along the foot of the bed, then extended his plate.

I looked at the picked over food and saw a

chocolate-covered strawberry. Picking it up, I took a bite, chewing nervously. "That still doesn't solve the problem though. How can we make it look like we..."

Merritt banged on the door. "Timer won't start until you do!"

Carson's lips turned up in a grin, and he stood and did something I never thought he would: set his plate down.

"Come on," he said and tugged me toward the bed.

My eyes flew open, and I held back. What was Carson doing?

He climbed onto the bed and pulled me up with him. Then he started jumping.

My laugh was soft and breathy. Relieved. And I started jumping with him.

Cheers erupted from outside the room. Carson still held my hands as he jumped with me, and then he flopped to his butt and pulled me on top of him, rubbing my head with his fist.

I groaned and pushed him off of me.

More cheers sounded outside the door.

A wide grin spread on his face. "I'm a genius."

Shaking my head, I got off the bed and straightened my dress. "You're something, alright."

"But you love it," he said, following me.

"What's not to love?"

From outside the door, Merritt yelled, "Time's up!"

I walked to the door and put my hand on the handle, but Carson stopped me, his hand atop mine.

My breath caught, and I looked at him, trying to figure out what he was doing.

His green eyes sparked as he smiled. "A man always opens a door for a lady."

Catching my breath, I stepped back and let him open the door.

We walked out of the room like heroes. A bunch of guys took Carson in and held him up on their shoulders. The girls crowded me, asking me what it was like. I looked at them and grinned. "Fun."

CARSON

When Callie's parents stopped in their driveway, my house's front porch light was off and Mom's car was gone. She'd picked up a night shift again.

"Need a light?" Callie's dad offered, reaching for his phone.

"I'm good," I said. Gemma, Sierra, and I were

getting pretty good at navigating around our house in the dark.

I waved goodbye and crossed the grass to my house. I put my key in the front door and tried to be as quiet as possible as I opened it. Unfortunately, Dad was wide awake on his recliner, the TV's blue light reflected on his surly face.

"You're back late," he spat.

I felt caught—between the truth and what my dad expected me to say. The truth was that my mom knew Callie's family was taking me to the party and bringing me back—she hadn't given me a curfew. Dad expected me to apologize. To give in to whatever he said.

I decided to avoid a fight. "I'm sorry," I said, locking the deadbolt behind me, even though it felt like sealing my own fate.

"I'm sorry's not gonna cut it," Dad sneered. "What happens when you get a job and you show up late?"

As if he had a job or knew what it was like to be held accountable to anything except a La-Z-Boy recliner. I stayed still like a deer might in the road.

Dad shook his head and leaned back in his chair. "Get out of here."

He didn't need to ask me twice. I hurried toward the stairs and took them two at a time. The second I reached the top, Clary whisper-yelled to me from her room. "Carson!"

I followed her voice and leaned against the open door. She was sitting on her bed, her computer in front of her and countless papers around her.

"What are you doing?" I asked.

"Oh this?" She began scooping up the papers and patted at the bed. "College applications."

"I didn't know you were going to college," I said honestly.

She shook her head. "I have to get out somehow. Rex's not about to get me out of this house and somewhere better."

I looked toward the ceiling, thanking whatever God might be out there that she was seeing her jerk of a boyfriend wasn't the guy she thought he was.

"What's your plan?" she asked.

"What do you mean?"

"To get out."

Her words hit me like a sack of bricks. I didn't have a plan to get out. Did that mean I'd be stuck here forever like Dad?

"Here." She handed me a red folder. "Stanford

has a swim team. I think you could get a scholarship if you keep working at it."

"What about you?" I asked, feeling the smooth paper under my fingers. "Where are you going?"

She held up a purple folder. "TCU. Grandma and Gramps said I could live with them to save money. They have a good child development program." She shrugged. "I don't know. Maybe I can help kids like I wasn't able to help you guys."

My chest had that tight feeling again. Because she was right. Trying to help us had only hurt her.

"Enough about me," she said. "How was tonight? Did you get your first kiss?"

My shoulders sagged. "I did what you said to do. I tried to act like I wasn't interested, but I just ended up eating the whole time."

She laughed and rubbed my shoulder. "Oh, Carson. You're too sweet."

"What does that mean?" I asked. "Callie's dad said women like polite men."

She shook her head. "Maybe when they're older. Like out of college and ready to settle down. Girls your age want a guy they can't get."

"That doesn't make any sense."

Clary glanced toward her window, seeming sad. "I know."

"So what do I do?" I asked. "I don't want to be in the friend zone forever."

"You be yourself," Clary said and brushed some hair out of my eyes like Mom used to do. "If she doesn't see how amazing you are, she doesn't deserve you."

FOUR

THIRTEEN YEARS OLD

CALLIE

The shouting was getting worse at night. Ever since Clary left for college across the country, things had seemed to fall apart more than ever. I left my window open to let the spring air in while I slept, but it also let in the hatred coming from next door.

It was well past ten, and there was crashing, shattering, banging, yelling, screaming. Each new sound made me flinch, and even though I should have been afraid for Carson's mom, I worried most about him.

I got up from my bed and went to the window. We usually kept our blinds open—unless we were changing or something—so we could talk at night if we needed to.

I couldn't see him, and his room was dark.

"Carson," I whispered. "*Carson.*" I picked a Lego from the bag he had given me and threw it at his window. It sailed through the opening and into his room.

His face appeared in the window, a dark outline, but from the light in my room I could see the circles under his eyes. Haunted.

A scream sounded from downstairs in his house, and Carson closed his eyes, his body rigid. "I hate him."

I wanted to take away all of Carson's pain, to never see the defeated look on his face again. "Come over," I whispered, desperate to help.

His eyes widened for a moment, then another crash sounded.

"How?" he finally asked.

"The back door," I whispered. "I'll shine a flashlight when it's clear."

He nodded. "I'll be down."

With a racing heart, I grabbed my flashlight from my desk drawer and tiptoed down the stairs. I could hear Dad's snoring coming softly from their room, and heat stung my eyes. I was so lucky to have them, to not have to deal with the horror Carson did every single day.

I crept past the stairs to the next set of stairs that led to the walkout basement. The TV was on, but Joe wasn't here. He must have forgotten to shut down his game console before going to bed.

Actually, the music on the pause screen could help us get to my room without being detected. Passing the TV, I walked to the sliding door and looked into the dark backyard. There weren't any lights in the green belt, not that it would have helped me see Carson waiting outside our privacy fence.

"Callie?" Joe said.

I jerked, holding my flashlight to my chest. "I-I thought you went to bed."

"Nah." He pointed his thumb over his shoulder at the open bathroom door where I could hear the toilet water running. "Pit stop."

"Going upstairs soon?" I asked hopefully.

"As if." He plopped onto the couch and put on his headset. "Yeah, I'm back. No, you're going down, man."

I turned my eyes toward the ceiling. This was risky. But Joe's back was toward the sliding door. And if we were quiet, maybe he wouldn't notice.

Joe looked at me suspiciously over his shoulder. "What are you doing?"

"Um... just getting some fresh air."

He lifted his eyebrows and pushed his headset back. "You're meeting Carson, aren't you?" he accused, making kissing sounds. "You *are* in love with him!"

My cheeks flushed red.

"You are!" he hissed. "My, my, my, perfect little Callie is sneaking out?"

Overwhelmed with embarrassment and frustration, I shushed him. "Can you not hear his parents fighting?"

Joe's smile immediately fell. "Is he in trouble?"

"He might be," I said, my chest aching all over again. "I offered him to stay in my room until it blows over... unless you're gonna snitch."

To Joe, a breech in loyalty was the worst betrayal imaginable. He acted offended at my suggestion. "I'll do one better. I'll help you get him in."

Now that surprised me. "Seriously? You'd do that?"

"Of course," he said, shrugging. "Carson's practically the brother I wish I had."

I narrowed my eyes at him. "Fine. Just don't mess it up." I went to the door and flashed my light outside a couple of times. In the dim glow from the basement, I saw Carson's body move quickly over the grass. He was getting stronger—quicker.

I slid the door open and looked back at Joe. He went back toward our parents' room, with a promise to run interference if needed.

Carson's eyes were frantic, but I grabbed his hand and pulled him as fast as I could toward the stairs. I flew up the steps, practically dragging him behind me. We rushed into my room, closing the door behind us and sliding down against the wood.

My chest heaved from the speed and the adrenaline, and when I looked over at Carson, his chest was doing the same.

He rolled his head over and looked at me, then offered his fist for a bump.

With a small smile, I tapped my knuckles to his. Then, I looked back at my closed window with the curtains drawn. Worry creased my brow. "Will your parents be upset if they find out you're gone?"

He shook his head. "Sierra's at her boyfriend's almost every night, and Gemma practically lives at her friend's house. And, well, Clary hasn't come home from college since it started." A rare look of deep sadness covered his face. Carson didn't get sad —he got distracted, filling his time and thoughts with happier things. But now, he wore the ache of his parents' fighting on his sleeve.

I leaned my head against his shoulder. "You've got me."

His lips lifted at the corners. "This is my first boy-girl sleepover."

"Please." I stood and rolled my eyes. "You can have any patch of floor you'd like." I walked to my closet and reached for the sleeping bag shoved way at the top.

"It's pink," he said.

"And princess," I added, rolling it out to show Cinderella's face. "It might be a little short, but..." I shrugged.

"It's a quiet place to sleep," he said. He nodded toward the window. "Can you hear them fighting at night?"

"Only when the window's open," I answered softly, turning off the light before going to sit on my bed.

He moved from the door, slipped off his shoes, and lay down in the sleeping bag. It only went to about halfway up his waist, so I tossed him a throw blanket too. He covered up with it and laid his head back on the pillow I gave him.

"Comfy," he said.

I frowned. "I'm sorry I can't do more."

He put his arm under the pillow and lay on his side, facing me. "You're amazing, you know that?"

My cheeks felt warm for the second time that night. "I'm not. I just love you...as a friend," I felt the need to add.

"As a friend," he repeated, closing his eyes.

I lay down too then, tucking myself under my blanket in my warm bed, where I could sleep every night without being woken by my parents' screams.

"Hey, Callie?"

"Yeah?"

His eyes opened, green orbs right on mine. "What are you doing when you get out of here?"

"What do you mean?" I asked.

"Where are you going—when you're eighteen and you can leave?"

I honestly hadn't thought about it. So I hedged. "Where are *you* going?"

"Stanford. I'm going to get on the swim team to pay for it."

He said it with such surety, it took me aback. But his next words surprised me even more.

"Will you go with me?" he asked.

"Yes." I answered with my heart before I did

with my mind. Because I couldn't imagine ever being more than a window away from Carson.

"Do you mind if I sleep?" he asked. "I haven't been resting well."

At that moment, I realized how deep the shadows had gotten underneath his eyes. He'd always hidden them so well with his smiles and jokes.

"Goodnight, Carson," I breathed, and within minutes, he was asleep.

CARSON

I slept better on Callie's floor than I had for weeks in my own bed. Until I heard her bedroom door creak open.

I jumped to my feet and watched in horror as her dad stood in the doorway, his eyes going from me to his daughter.

"What..." he asked, like he couldn't even finish the sentence.

Callie slowly rolled. Then, like she realized her dad was right there, she practically leapt out of bed, stammering unintelligible words.

"Mr. Copeland—" I began

"No, Carson," Callie said, finding her voice,

then stood to face her dad. "Carson's parents were fighting last night, and I was worried about him. I said he could sleep on my floor. Please don't be mad at him... Be mad at me."

The tightness in my chest was back in full force. Callie had given me my first full night of rest in weeks, and she was trying to take the fall for me? It was so wrong, but it also made me feel cared for in a way I hadn't been since staying at Grandma and Gramps's for Christmas. It was like having a piece of them here.

Her dad's frown deepened, and he did something so surprising, I almost couldn't believe it was real. He pulled Callie to his chest, then extended his hand and looped me into the hug as well.

He was *hugging* me? Not beating me to a pulp? Was he ill?

When he was done squeezing us, he got to his knee and looked us both in the eyes. "Callie, you have the biggest heart, but you are not allowed to have boys in your room."

She hung her head, tears already glistening in her eyes. "But Dad—"

"No," he said. "Carson, if you ever need a place to stay, our guest room is yours, no questions asked." He looked from me to Callie. "Is that understood?"

My eyes stung at the meaning in his words. I had a place to go. A place to stay. Somewhere safe. "Yes, sir."

"Now," Robert said with a smile. "Come downstairs for breakfast. Mom made waffles."

As I followed them down the stairs, I thought maybe if Callie was only my friend for the rest of my life, it wouldn't be so bad. At least she could be my family.

FIVE

FOURTEEN YEARS OLD

CALLIE

The back of my neck felt itchy and bumpy when I woke up, and I went to the bathroom to see if I'd been bit or something. I pulled my hair away from my skin and angled my head until I had a clear view of the irritant. A red, splotchy, scaly patch of skin about the size of my fist spread from my hairline to the spot behind my ear.

My eyes widened. What was that? I'd never had a rash like that before...

"Mom!" I yelled down the stairs. It was a weekend morning, and I could already smell the fudge she had cooking. She'd gotten super into making different types of fudge these last few weeks, and it did nothing good for my sweet tooth or the weight that was beginning to appear on my hips and midsection.

"What, honey?" she called up the stairs.

"Can you come look at this?"

As I heard her footsteps come near, I continued examining the spot. It didn't look like just dry skin, but maybe some lotion would help?

"What's up?" she asked, stepping into the bathroom.

I turned to show her the patch of irritated skin. "I don't know what this is. You don't think it's eczema, do you?"

She took my shoulders and gently turned me to get a better view. "I don't think so. Does it itch?"

I nodded. "It's painful."

"Let's get some hydrocortisone on it and I'll take you to urgent care to get it checked out before your tournament."

I nodded, even though that was the last thing I needed. I had wanted to spend the day resting and preparing myself for the first basketball game of the year. This would be my last season before high school. But I could center myself on the drive as long as we figured out what this was.

I pulled the mirror back on the medicine cabinet and found the small green and white tube labeled hydrocortisone. The white lotion felt thin on my fingers, and I spread it over my neck, hoping for some relief. None really came. Hopefully the doctor could figure it out today.

As I got my bag ready for the game, I found a big headband to cover the spot, and then Mom and I left for the doctor. Dad and Joe would be coming later to watch me play.

At urgent care, Mom and I had to sit with all the other people coughing and emptying their sinuses into twice-used Kleenexes. They couldn't call us back soon enough.

When they finally did, I was antsy and ready to figure out what it was so I could get back to thinking about the game. But the PA took his sweet time looking at the spot, and finally he said, "It looks like psoriasis to me. For now, keep hydrocortisone on it and schedule an appointment with your primary care doctor as soon as possible."

Mom thanked him, but my eyebrows drew together. That was it? It seemed like such a lazy thing to do—just shove it off on another doctor while I had a scaly, painful patch of skin on my neck.

On the way to the game, Mom tried to soothe me, but I just kept looking up psoriasis on my phone. It sounded awful. The page I was reading said it could spread down from my scalp, cover my neck and even my arms, and lead to other worse autoimmune issues like debilitating arthritis.

I tried to keep my mind off of it during the game, but it was hard to focus. I missed shots I shouldn't have, made careless mistakes with my passes, and it made my teammates mad.

"Get your head in the game!" Merritt yelled at me as we ran down the court.

I kept my eyes on the hardwood and continued ahead.

Carson tried to comfort me after the game, but I wasn't okay. I just wanted this to be over—for the growing patch of itchy skin to go away. But when I woke up the next morning, it had spread, reaching to the base of my neck. Even my knees and elbows felt uncomfortable.

I slathered lotion over it all, and Mom promised to take me to the doctor on Monday—she said we could show up at eight and wait in the lobby until they let us in. I was so embarrassed about the spot, I dodged Carson on Sunday—I couldn't see him like this until I at least knew what it was for sure.

Monday morning, the itchy spots on my knees and elbows looked even worse. As promised, she called RWE Medical and convinced them to squeeze me in first thing in the morning.

Besides us, there was another girl from my class at the Academy in the waiting room—Rory, I think her name was—but I kept my eyes down while our moms made small talk. I didn't feel like talking. I just wanted to figure it out.

A girl named Chloe led us back to an open room, and Dr. Edmonson came inside. "Callie, I hear you're having some issue with rashes."

I nodded and extended my arms to show him the fiery red spots on my elbows. He extended his hands and held my arm to examine it better.

"We went to urgent care," Mom said, "and they seemed to think it's psoriasis. It's not contagious, is it?"

"I agree," he said, going to the cabinet and removing tools from a drawer.

"What does that mean?" Mom asked. "We don't have anyone in our family with psoriasis."

He finished putting the tools on a tray and then leaned against the cabinet, folding his arms over his chest. "Basically, psoriasis means your skin cells are shedding faster than other people's. It's not something that goes away, but there are treatments to help manage it." He frowned. "I'll be honest with you. This looks like it's in the early stages, but it could get worse. It could stay the same and respond to treatment, but I want you to be prepared."

Mom nodded, while my mind went blank.

Worse? Worse than this constant discomfort and the unsightly sores?

"I want to send a biopsy to the lab to see for sure what type we're dealing with," Dr. Edmonson said. "Until then, I'm prescribing a strong topical steroid cream. Call me back if you don't feel it making a difference within three days."

He said it so matter of factly, like he wasn't diagnosing me with an incurable autoimmune disease at fourteen years old. Didn't he know I was an athlete? That I ran around in tank tops and shorts and there was no way to *hide* this?

The biopsy was painful, but it didn't hurt anywhere near as much as my worries about what life would look like with skin like this.

Mom was quiet on the way out, and I said, "Mom, what am I going to do? The girls on the team are going to think I'm contagious."

"They're good girls," she said. "They'll understand."

I looked out the window, hoping she was right but knowing deep in my gut that she was wrong.

At school, I kept my blazer on all day to make extra sure my elbows were covered up and kept my hair down over my neck. Carson asked me how the doctor's appointment went, but I only shrugged. It was embarrassing, knowing there was something wrong with me. What had I done to deserve the constant torment of these rashes? Hadn't I always been a good person? I'd always tried to help others when I could—did the chores Mom asked of me, never cheated on an assignment even when presented with the opportunity.

But here I was, dressing in my practice gear with big red splotches on my neck, arms, and knees.

Merritt's gym locker was next to mine, and she did a doubletake. "What happened to you?"

Poppy laughed next to her. "It almost looks like you're a burn victim." She sobered. "Did your house, like, burn down, Callie?"

I narrowed my eyes and shut my locker. "No, my house didn't burn down. I have psoriasis. And it's not contagious."

"Good," Tinsley said, "because I don't want to catch crocodile."

Merritt snorted. "Good one."

My eyebrows drew together. Seriously? Merritt

wasn't my best friend or anything, but she'd never been this outright rude to me.

"Sorry," she said, "but my brother's a movie star now. I can't have The Thing ruining my image."

She walked away, but I stared after her, my mouth open. Tears were already in my eyes, and the last thing I felt like doing was going to practice. The few girls left in the locker room gave me sympathetic looks as they walked out, but that was it.

I tried to breathe deep against the pain spreading in my chest, but my scalp just itched, my knees itched, my elbows too. I shook my head and wiped at my eyes. I had practice to get to.

With Coach around, the girls were better. They kept their distance and only said mean words when she couldn't hear. But the game was worse.

On Thursday, I suited up in my blue and white uniform and looked in the mirror. My skin was bright red, and even though some of the flaking had gone down, Dr. Edmonson was right. It was worse. It hurt, and it was unsightly.

I threw myself into the game, playing harder than I ever had. I stole the ball from another girl and went down the court as fast as I could before sinking a three-pointer.

The crowd burst into cheers, and I grinned at

the numbers being added to my team's side of the scoreboard. That was, until I heard what they were chanting.

"THE THING. THE THING. THE THING."

Merritt jogged by me and slapped my back. "Nice move, Thing."

Tears stung my eyes, and I was frozen, right there on the hardwood floor. The ref was saying something to me, but I couldn't hear it. My vision was starting to look like I was seeing through a tunnel. Everyone sounded so far away.

A strong arm wrapped around my shoulders and began hauling me off the court. I heard Carson's voice saying, "It's going to be okay. I'm right here. I'll always be right here."

CARSON

I hung out in Callie's room before the first swim meet of the season. Her parents had offered to drive me to the Brentwood pool where I'd be competing.

"Are you sure you don't want to be on the swim team?" I asked her, tossing a tennis ball against the wall and letting it bounce back to me.

She gave me a look from her desk, where she

was rubbing cream onto her elbows for her psoriasis.

"Seriously," I said. "They make full-body swim-suits, and I'm sure if you said you had a medical reason, you'd be able to wear one. And don't they say sunlight is good for people with psoriasis?"

She shook her head and capped her lotion. "Even if it wasn't too late, I just don't want to. Can you imagine all the jokes I'd get for having scaly skin *and* being in the water?"

The thought distracted me so much, I missed my tennis ball and had to go grab it under her bed. When I lifted her dust ruffle, I caught sight of a pair of skimpy underwear, and my stomach did a somersault.

Callie wore thongs?

I tried to clear my mind and redirect my blood flow before scooting out from under her bed. When I had, I resumed my drum of the tennis ball against the wall. Finally, I said, "Who cares what anyone else thinks?"

"What do you mean?" she asked.

"Why do you care if they make fun of you?"

She stood and went to the laundry basket on her bed, sorting and folding the clothes. My mind wondered if there were more thongs in there, but I quickly shut down that thought. She shook her head and let out a sigh. "I know you don't understand because you're popular and athletic and have perfect skin, but trust me, it's not worth it."

"But you loved basketball," I argued. "Don't you miss competing?"

"Not really," she said, setting down a neatly folded shirt. "You know what I miss?"

I held on to the ball, waiting for her answer.

"I miss not worrying what people thought of me. Not feeling like people were staring at me everywhere I go, you know?"

"Yeah," I said softly, but my heart hurt for her. Callie was so pretty. She had this long blond hair that was softer than silk and big blue eyes as deep and beautiful as the ocean on a sunny day. Her smile was enough to take my breath away. Not to mention the way her body had been changing— adding curves in the best possible places.

I'd been in love with her before, but seeing her like this—a woman, a *goddess*, was making it hard to keep my mind in the right place. But if it was so hard for me to keep my thoughts off how stunning she was, why couldn't she see it for herself?

It was like my sister Sierra who dated losers even worse than the ones Clary used to. Didn't she know she deserved better? Or Gemma, who dyed her hair black and cut it in layers so half her face was covered. I missed *seeing* her. I miss the Gemma who wanted to be seen.

I *hated* that people did this to girls. I'd do anything to make them see how beautiful they were. It made them hide the light inside themselves.

"What's your new thing going to be, though?" I asked Callie. "You were always running around to games and stuff, but now you don't have that. What's the...game plan?"

She rolled her eyes. "That was a bad joke."

"You're still smiling," I said, tossing the ball against the wall.

"I'm not like you," she said. "You've always had a plan, known what you've wanted. What if I just want to help people?"

I mentally added that to the list of things I loved about Callie. She had the biggest heart of anyone I knew. There was no meanness or hate in her. Not even for the people who had crushed her love for sports and made her afraid to be seen.

"What about dating?" I asked, dipping my toes into the metaphorical water. "Your boyfriend's going to know you have bumpy skin." Especially if it's me.

"No way I'm dating," she said, pointing at her bare arm and the white flaky skin there. "This doesn't exactly say datable."

"Come on," I said, gutted for her and myself. "You can't just stop living your life."

"Really?" she argued. "Who's going to want to date this?"

"I would," I breathed. "I do." It was my heart, out there on my sleeve. I was telling her I loved her, open to the possibilities. And yeah, maybe I hadn't planned it this way, but what in my life had gone as planned? I hadn't wanted to move here, but look where it brought me. Right next door to Callie Copeland, the most beautiful girl in the world, inside and out.

"Of course you would," Callie said. "You have the best heart. But I don't exactly see anyone else like you hanging around."

Ouch. She hadn't even considered what I was saying. Considered *me*. "I seriously would," I said, trying to make my point clear.

She smiled at me and rolled her eyes. "We all know Carson is the sweetest guy ever and follows all of my dad's chivalry rules. Now if he could just train someone else for me."

"Kids!" Mom called up the stairs.

"Coming," Callie yelled back, grabbing a thin sweater from her chair.

As I watched her cover up all that embarrassed her, my heart sank. I'd put myself out there, told her I would date her, and nothing. Maybe it was better to stay in the friend zone. Better to stay where I belonged.

SIX

CALLIE

I looked at myself in the mirror, trying to stir up the confidence I needed to tell Carson I liked him. But it was hard with fresh acne and my parents' scale telling me I'd gained fifty pounds since my last doctor's visit. The one where he'd called me in and told me I had plaque psoriasis and gave me a laundry list of treatments to do.

In the last year, I'd gotten my period. My cheeks had gotten rounder. My stomach fuller. My chest bigger.

Mom said gaining weight was a normal part of puberty, but if I'd known my period would come with fifty pounds and acne, I would have said no thank you. On the other hand, puberty had worked so well for Carson. While I'd become plump, he'd filled out, gotten taller. His voice had deepened, and his face had lost the soft curves of youth.

He was attractive, and other people noticed it. Other girls. Me. I wanted to run my fingers over the hard edges of his jaw and kiss his lips until the world disappeared around us.

A knock sounded on the door. "Callie?" Carson called.

I jerked back, stumbling off the scale and nearly crashing to the ground.

"You okay?" he asked.

"I'm fine," I said, steadying myself and putting the scale back in the cabinet. *Just daydreaming about your face.* Hurriedly, I tamed stray hairs into place and double-checked my makeup. "Why are you in my parents' room?"

"I used my key," he said. "Are you the only one home?"

"I was," I said and stepped out of the bathroom.

"Gross. I didn't hear you wash your hands."

I rolled my eyes. "Maybe that's because I wasn't actually using the bathroom."

"Sure." He didn't believe me.

"What's up?" I asked, not wanting to argue

about poop. That was so not attractive. If telling Carson I liked him was going to have any chance at working, we needed to get off this topic.

"Thought you might want to hit the mall?" he said.

"Sure." Actually, that could be the perfect place to bare my feelings to him. Our outing at the mall could turn into our first date before the day was over. My stomach fluttered and not just because I'd been craving the edible cookie dough from one of the stores there.

"You ready to go? Gemma said she'd drive us, but she needs to leave in ten."

"Yeah. Let me grab my bag." I tried to hide my nerves as he followed me up to my room. When I peaked the stairs, I asked, "How was football practice?"

"Being a sophomore on the team is better," he said. "At least I'm not scared ninety-nine percent of the time."

"Scared? You?" I teased.

He shook his head. "You know, the guys don't outweigh me by fifty pounds now."

I knew. I *definitely* knew. Every female at our school knew.

"Are you really not doing volleyball?" he asked.

"You just missed a year. It wouldn't be too hard to pick it back up."

"No." I brushed by him and started down the stairs. I so was not in the mood to have this conversation, again. Especially not now that I was fat *and* had psoriasis.

"But you love it," he argued. "You shouldn't give it up just because Merritt and her crew are jerks."

At the bottom, I turned on him. "You didn't have everyone in the school and half the town calling you 'The Thing' at a game. So yes, I *loved* volleyball, but I love not feeling like crap even more."

The words scraped my throat as they came out, because part of me knew giving up meant that Merritt had won—that she had power over me. But I could find a new passion. Something else I loved just as much as volleyball that wouldn't make me feel so bad.

Carson looked down at the stone entryway floor. "Okay," he said softly.

"Okay?" I asked, my voice harsh in contrast to his.

He nodded and pulled me under his arm. "You know I'm here for you, Cal Pal."

I shook my head and pushed away from him in an attempt at playfulness. "Good thing it's not contagious."

"No, but you got a little dandruff on my shirt."

My heart froze, and I searched his navy-blue tee for a hint of flaking.

"I was just kidding!" he said.

I punched his arm and opened the front door to see Gemma sitting in her car, making out with her sleazy boyfriend.

"I hate him," Carson said.

"Same," I agreed and walked to her car.

As I opened the door, her boyfriend looked back at me and winked. I ignored him and buckled in. "Hey, Gemma."

"Hey, girl," she said with a grin. "Being a mall rat today?"

I shrugged. "I prefer mall mouse."

She laughed. "Thanks for helping me hang up that picture yesterday, by the way." She glared at her brother. "Since someone was too busy being a bigshot football player."

Her boyfriend turned toward Carson now and raised his eyebrows, making his nose ring wobble. "You play football?"

Gemma rolled her eyes and put the car into gear. "I've only told you a thousand times."

He smirked and turned forward. "Guess I was too busy looking at your mouth. I love your lips." He leaned across the console and nipped at her ear, making her giggle.

Carson pretended to throw up. I felt exactly the same way.

"Stop it!" she said, "I'm trying to drive."

"Driving me crazy," the guy groaned.

When we reached the mall, we couldn't get out of the car fast enough.

"Remind me to never ride with Gemma again," I said, watching her peel out. "I'd rather spend all my babysitting money on an Uber than watch Jake eat her throat at a red light."

"His name's John," Carson said, tucking his thumbs in his pockets. "Jake was the last guy."

"Seriously?" I asked. "They all look the same."

"Like douche?" Carson said, starting toward the mall.

"Language," I hissed, glancing around and realizing we were thankfully not within earshot of any children.

"That's tame," Carson argued and started through the rotating door to Emerson Shoppes.

The stores opened up before us, and he asked, "What should we do first?"

"Cookie dough," I said. A girl's willpower could only take so much. Especially after a ride like that. Besides, what could be sweeter than telling him over dessert? If it went well, the cookie dough shop would always be our place. If it went poorly, I had comfort food at the ready. Win-win.

"That's why I love you," he said, tucking me under his arm. "You have the best ideas."

"I mean, is cookie dough ever a bad idea?"

"Genius." He pulled me to the side so we could dodge another couple walking by. Carson had been putting his arm around me since we were kids, but I noticed it more now. Felt it. Like the new muscles he had were electric charged.

"You get us seats, and I'll order?" I suggested, just to get away from the brain-fogging charge.

"Sure," he agreed.

I went to the counter and ordered a small chocolate chip for myself and the largest, most chocolatey thing on the menu for Carson. He was ridiculous that way—he didn't like just a little of a good thing; he went all in.

I paid in cash, then turned, holding the two cups with tiny spoons, in search of my friend I hoped could be more. I didn't see anyone sitting at a table by themselves in the expansive food court, but then I realized: Carson wasn't sitting by himself.

A girl from school named Sarah was sitting with him. And she was laughing, flipping her blond hair over her shoulder.

And he was laughing too.

My stomach clenched in a confusing way, and I started toward them. Why would I be upset about another girl talking to Carson? Even if she was pretty? What did that matter? Girls tried to talk to Carson all the time now that he'd hit puberty. That didn't mean I didn't have a chance.

I steeled myself and walked to where they were sitting. The problem? They didn't even realize I'd approached until I set the cookie dough down on the table.

Carson and Sarah jerked back like I'd snuck up on them, not like I'd walked across the room in broad daylight with something I'd told Carson was coming.

"Oh, hi, Callie," Sarah said, looking disappointed.

Carson's eyes widened at the chocolatey mess in front of him. "This looks amazing."

Sarah smiled. "Maybe we should get some together sometime?"

This was quickly going from bad to worse. I was clenching the world's tiniest spoon as I dreaded and prayed for his answer.

With a grin, Carson said, "Definitely. I'll text you. Can I have your number?"

My legs swayed, and I fought to stay on my feet.

Sarah nodded and bit her lip before extending her hand for his phone. He swiped it open to a new message, and she entered her number, then handed it back to him. "See you around, Carson." As if realizing I was there for the second time, she said, "Callie."

My heart had stalled in my chest, and my joints worked about as well as steel as I sat down across from Carson and his dopey grin.

Everything in me wanted to run away and cry, but I stayed for my friend. Tried to be as happy for him as he clearly was for himself.

He looked up at me from his phone, his mouth full of chocolate, and pointed at my cookie dough. "Are you going to finish that?"

I shook my head and pushed it forward. For once, I wasn't hungry.

. . .

CARSON

Sarah's house was perfect. Not in the same way the Copelands' house was. Callie's house felt like home. Sarah's house felt like there would be a realtor walking in at any moment to show a trendy couple all the cool features that could be theirs if they just wrote a check. It made me feel like maybe I didn't belong here.

Sarah pulled me past the entryway to the living room, where her parents sat in front of a big-screen TV watching what looked like a home improvement show. An old white dude on the screen was making lame jokes while his wife smiled and shook her head.

"Mom, Dad," Sarah said, squeezing my hand tightly. "This is my boyfriend, Carson."

I loved how easy things were with Sarah. I'd never even asked her to be my girlfriend. She just assumed, and I rolled with it. Simple. Not like with Callie, where I could put my whole heart out there and have it ignored.

Her dad lowered his reading glasses to examine me, making them hang so low on his nose I worried they'd fall off. But her mom, she practically jumped from the couch and came to greet me. "This is

Carson?" She sent her daughter a massive wink, and Sarah's cheeks grew pink.

"Yes, ma'am," I said, extending my hand. "It's nice to meet you."

"And polite?" she said. "Swoon."

Well, I had Callie's dad to thank for that. I definitely hadn't gotten any kindness from my father.

"Mom," Sarah admonished.

"Oh, it's fine." Her mom brushed my shoulder. "He can take a little teasing. You know, Carson, we've been begging her to bring you over ever since that adorable first date you took her on."

Now my cheeks were starting to feel hot. Taking Sarah to play mini golf had been Mom's idea, but we'd actually had fun. You know, aside from the fact that I was too tall for those stupid clubs and Sarah couldn't make a hole to save her life.

"Cute," her dad said, still staring me down.

Honestly, it was hard not to laugh. He had no idea what I dealt with at home on a daily basis. I simply stuck my hand out to him and said, "Pleased to meet you, sir."

He looked at my hand for a moment like he might not take it, and I'd be lying if I said I didn't feel a little sweat beading up on my forehead. But finally, he grasped my hand. He must have liked my handshake because he pushed up his glasses and said, "Nice to meet you too."

"Soo, we're going up to my room," Sarah said.

Her dad frowned, but her mom said, "Have fun!"

As we walked upstairs, I could hear her parents muttering back and forth. Part of me worried they'd start fighting because of me, and I didn't want Sarah to go through that. I didn't want anyone to go through that.

"We can stay downstairs," I whispered to her.

"No way." She tugged my hand, practically yanking me up to her room.

This space was just as perfect as the rest of her house. She stood near her frilly pink bed and tucked her hands into her tight jean pockets. "What do you think?"

I knew what I was supposed to say now. That I loved it. That it was perfect. That I was glad she had me over. With Sarah, things were easy. No guesswork when it came to how she felt or what she wanted me to say. I picked one of the phrases, and she grinned at me like I'd made her the happiest girl in the world.

Was it that easy?

"I can't wait to see your room," she said, walking to a mini fridge near her desk.

I swallowed. My room? No way would I have her over. My sisters would live and die to humiliate me in front of a girlfriend. And my dad? Sometimes he made creepy comments to my sisters' friends when they came over. If he said something like that about Sarah or Callie, I wouldn't be able to control myself, even if it was a losing fight.

"What?" she said, sounding hurt. "You don't want me over?"

Now I knew what I needed to do next—comfort her. I stepped closer, taking the can of soda from her hand and setting it down. Then I wrapped my arms around her slim body and held her to my chest. She was short enough I could rest my chin against the top of her head and completely enclose her from the world. From her self-doubt.

Sarah may have been thin and on the cheer-leading squad, but she seemed just as insecure about her looks as Callie. Couldn't they both see they were beautiful, even if it was in different ways?

"I like you," she said into my chest, and I just held on because here was everything I'd ever wanted Callie to say, and it was coming out of another girl's mouth.

I needed to let go of something that was clearly never going to happen because my childish idea of what could have been was ruining the possibility of what was happening now. I might not have Callie, but I had Sarah, and feeling wanted was something I never wanted to give up.

SEVEN

SIXTEEN YEARS OLD

CALLIE

Sarah settled into Carson's lap on my basement couch. "Can you believe we've been dating for *five months*?"

I could. These had been five of the longest months of my life, having to share my best friend with his girlfriend. Trying to shove down my feelings for him while supporting him while also hoping his relationship would fail. I was a mess, and my psoriasis was showing it.

I continued flipping through the movie options, trying to find something that wasn't violent but also wasn't romantic—and failing.

"No way, babe," Carson said. "Feels like it hasn't been long enough."

A loud smacking sound came from right next to me as she kissed him. "Thanks, babe, but I was asking Callie."

My hand froze on the remote as everything inside me cringed. Good thing I'd gotten five months of practice hiding my thoughts. Especially about the number of times they used the word "babe" in regular conversation. "Is today your anniversary?" I asked, even though it was completely ridiculous to celebrate an anniversary before the year-mark hit.

"Tomorrow," she said, then nuzzled her nose against Carson's. "What are we going to do to celebrate, babe?"

I watched his reaction, trying to tell if he was happy with her—really happy. I'd do anything for Carson to be happy, even if it meant having his obnoxious girlfriend at my house half the days of the week. Even if it meant keeping my mouth shut about how I felt about her.

Even if it meant staying quiet about how I felt for him.

He grinned at her and said, "Whatever you want, babe."

His smile seemed genuine... his voice was doting. And they were celebrating their five-month anniversary. Maybe it was time to give up, move on, find someone else I might actually have a chance with. I was sixteen, and the closest I'd ever gotten to a kiss was sitting next to Carson and his girlfriend.

While they made plans for an especially sappy date the coming day, I finally settled on *Stepbrothers*. Usually I wasn't in the mood for such crass humor, but I could use the distraction tonight.

As the opening scene came on, I heard my brother's voice on the stairs saying, "Cal Pal *chose* this movie? Who are you and what have you done with my sister?"

I grinned at the sound of his voice. He'd started college a month ago, and I hadn't seen him in weeks. "Joe!" I jumped up from the couch and began running toward him. Until I saw the guy behind him. The *cute* guy behind him.

Oblivious to my pause, Joe hugged me and said, "Maybe I should leave for college more often. You'll actually get some taste."

I rolled my eyes. "If you consider *Stepbrothers* tasteful, you've learned nothing at Brentwood U."

"Fair," said the guy behind him, and man, his voice was even better on my ears than his appearance was on my eyes. He had close cropped brown hair and pitch-black eyes that intrigued me almost as much as the pale smattering of freckles across his nose. His chin had the cutest dimple, and his height...he had to be at least a foot taller than me. Maybe even taller than Carson.

"This is Nick," my brother said. "My room-mate," he added for Sarah's benefit.

My family had heard all about Nick—or at least my mom had during her daily calls with Joe. Of course, I wasn't supposed to know about those calls or how homesick he'd gotten while trying to adjust to college life.

Joe introduced each of us, and when he said my name, Nick gave me a smile so warm, it turned my knees to melted butter. Someone needed to bring me a fainting couch. Stat.

Mom called down the stairs, letting us know she had a new test round of eclairs up for grabs.

"I'll get it," Joe offered, then said to Nick, "make yourself at home." As he rushed up the stairs, he called, "Pause the TV, Cal. This is the best part."

I glanced at the screen and winced at one of the guys putting his private parts on a drum set. Really? This was comedy? But then again, it was better than yet another romance that would just leave me weeping at the end.

Nick sat on the couch far away from Sarah and Carson, whose lips seemed to be glued together at the moment. To dull the growing ache in the pit of my stomach, I sat near Nick with my back to them. "What are you studying? Are you in videogame design like Joe?"

"Nah." He shook his head. "Poetry."

My eyes widened. He was cute *and* he could write? Where was that fainting couch again?

"Joe and I are actually going to my first poetry slam tomorrow. You should come."

"Where is it?" I asked. It might be hard to swing a ride to Brentwood and back home. Dad usually had an event for the non-profit he managed on Saturdays and spoke to churches on Sundays about ways to get involved. That left Mom to go with him and take care of the house.

"It's actually at an animal shelter not too far from here," he said.

"A shelter?" I asked, dumbfounded. Didn't poetry readings usually take place in angsty coffee shops?

"It's a benefit—to try and get people to adopt dogs."

The list of reasons I liked him just kept growing. I'd been begging Mom for weeks to get a dog I could take on walks. Maybe this could be my chance? Not only for a dog, but for a boyfriend of my own.

But as Joe walked downstairs with a plate full of chocolate and cream eclairs, I couldn't help but feel disappointed. Joe would never let me date his best friend. Not that Nick would be interested in his roommate's kid sister. Nothing said unattractive to someone fresh out of high school like two and a half more years before graduation.

"Those look incredible," Nick said, staring at the plate Joe set on the coffee table.

"Dig in, dude," Joe said, grabbing four for himself. He jerked his finger at Sarah and Carson. "Do they ever stop doing that?"

"Sometimes. When they need to come up for air." I glanced at them for as long as my heart could take it, lamenting the fact that I'd wanted that same obliviousness for Carson and myself.

Joe said, "Good for him. Thought he was going to hang out in your friend zone forever."

Well, that stopped the kissing. Sarah pulled back from Carson, her lips red and her cheeks redder. "Friend zone?"

Joe chuckled. "Yeah, we all thought Carson had it bad for Cal. Apparently we were wrong."

"You're one to talk," Carson said. "Gemma ever call you back?" He reached for just as many eclairs as Joe had taken. Now that each of the guys had their fill, there was only one left on the plate.

"Take it," I told Sarah. "It's yours." *He's* yours.

Nick and Joe went back to their dorm that night, leaving just Mom, Dad, and me at breakfast the next morning. I had convinced Mom to let me take her car to the poetry reading. She said it would be good for Joe to see family there.

"What about adopting a dog?" I asked. "Maybe I'll find the dream dog. Hypoallergenic, low shedding. It could be good for me, you know, give me a reason to get out and exercise again."

She pressed her lips together in that way that told me I'd made a good point but she didn't want to admit it. "You know a dog's average life span is somewhere between eight and sixteen years."

"And?"

"You have two and half years before you go to college. It might feel like a lifetime now, but it will fly by. And it's not like you'll be able to sneak a dog into the dorms at Stanford."

I loaded my fork with a bite of biscuits and gravy and eggs as I thought over my next angle. "You and Dad wouldn't want to have a dog? What about empty nest syndrome?"

Dad laughed. "We've had kids in our house for nearly twenty years. We're ready for a break!"

Mom nodded. "So unless you can find a dog that'll be around for two years, the dog days are over."

"Ouch," I said, pushing back from the table. "I thought you loved me."

Dad extended his arm and rubbed my shoulder. "We do. Your furry friends? Not so much."

"Yeah, yeah," I said. "Have a good day at the convention."

Mom patted my other shoulder on my way to the kitchen. "Have a good time at the poetry reading. It sounds so fun. And get your doggy pets in while you're there."

I went upstairs to pick out my outfit, even though I had a good six hours until I needed to be there. Nerves were starting to fill my stomach, and for the first time, they weren't about Ryde Alexander or Carson Cook. No, they were about possibility.

A knock sounded on my door, and I looked up

to see Carson, a sad smile on his face. "What are you getting ready for?"

"Hey," I said. "I'm thinking about going to a poetry reading with Joe and Nick..." I held up two shirts. "Which one is better?"

He shrugged and sat on my bed. "The red one?"

I looked toward the ceiling. "This one isn't even red; it's coral."

Rolling his eyes, he said, "I'm bad at this."

Putting the black shirt back in my closet, I teased, "How does Sarah deal with you?"

He flexed his biceps, making the muscles bulge and my stomach swoop. "These bad boys help." He stuck out his tongue.

"You're crazy," I said, because my mouth had gone dry and my mind was numb and I couldn't think of any other words.

"You're not going to ask what I'm doing tonight?" he questioned.

With a sigh, I sat on my desk chair and gave in. "What are you going to do tonight?" He glanced at the door, and getting his message, I shut it. Now I was really curious. "You're not in trouble, are you?" I asked.

"No." His laugh was breathy, so not like him. "I'm not in trouble."

"What is it?" I asked, my chest tight.

"Tonight's going to be my first time," he breathed, his voice rough.

My mouth parted, and the blood in my veins turned to ice. Carson was going to have sex, with Sarah. Moisture sprang to my eyes for a million reasons I didn't understand and one I did.

I'd been holding on to Carson, on to the possibility of a crazy story that he and I could somehow be meant for each other. But I'd been wrong, and now I was crying, and he was looking at me with a doubtful look, and I never wanted my best friend to look like that after telling me such big news.

"I'm sorry——" he began.

I shook my head, not wanting to know why he felt sorry for me. He deserved a friend that would celebrate him. I launched in to hug him. "Don't be sorry," I said through my tears. "I'm happy for you."

"You don't think it's a mistake?" His big arms held me close, and it felt like home.

I pulled back, wiping away my tears. "You love her, right?"

He nodded. Another knife through the heart.

"And you'll be careful?"

Another nod.

His phone dinged, but he ignored it.

"Then it's your decision," I said. "Whatever feels right."

His lips twitched, and he nodded. The reminder chime went off, and he glanced at it. "Sarah's ready." His eyes searched mine for a moment. "Are you okay?"

I forced a smile and nodded. "I'll see you around?"

He nodded, then stood. Before walking out the door, he said, "You're still my best friend, Callie."

My smile trembled. "You're mine too."

After he left, I cried and cried for everything Sarah had that I didn't. I cried for all the memories I had with Carson in here. For the "first time" everyone at school thought we had when we were too young to even know what that meant.

But then I picked myself up because what was the alternative? Carson had moved on, and I needed to as well.

I got in Mom's minivan and drove to a shelter called Nature. And I cried some more as Nick recited a poem he wrote about losing the person you used to call home.

EIGHT

SEVENTEEN YEARS OLD

CARSON

Sarah's parents were out at some home goods show, looking for ways to make their already perfect house more perfect. Sometimes when they were gone, we just sat on the couch and watched TV. They had a giant screen, and Sarah seemed happy to just sit tucked under my arm and just be. Which sounded perfect, but honestly, it was just kind of boring.

Sarah moved from her spot under my arm and lay down on my lap. "What do you want to do later?" she asked.

I shrugged and began playing with her hair. "We could go hang out at Callie's?"

"Ugh. We're always hanging out at Callie's. All we do is watch her brother and that guy play video games."

She wasn't wrong. Sarah and I didn't talk a lot nowadays. We were either watching TV or making out. And yeah, I was a guy, so I wasn't about to complain about kissing my girlfriend, but it wasn't all that I wanted out of a relationship. Especially not with Sarah constantly reminding me she was ready for the next step after I'd backed out last time.

We'd been set to do it on our five-month anniversary, but it just didn't feel right. And maybe it was the Cook Family Curse at work, but it felt like there was something missing. A piece of me that was gone when Sarah and I were together, and it made me feel like a piece of crap. Because I liked Sarah. So why did it all feel wrong?

"What do you want to do instead?" I asked, trying to change the subject, to focus on something different.

"We could go hang out at Poppy's? Maybe hot tub?"

I looked toward the ceiling, trying to hide just how awful that sounded. First of all, hot tubs were gross. Second of all, Poppy's mom always hit on me. Always. And her daughter was no better. Poppy tried playing footsie with me in the hot tub every time Sarah wasn't looking.

"Why don't you ever want to spend time at *my* friends' houses?" Sarah's question was loaded, and from years of watching my parents fight, I knew we were about to get into one. I just wanted no part in it.

"I think I better head home."

"Why?" she asked, sitting up and narrowing her eyes at me. "Because you don't want to admit you just like hanging out at Callie's because she's there?"

"Of course that's why I like hanging out there. She's my friend." I kept my tone measured, even though my frustration was mounting. Sarah had been getting more and more jealous of Callie for months now, no matter how many times I told her that Callie was just a friend.

She raised her eyebrows. "Oh really? So you're saying you've followed Callie Copeland around like a stray dog for years and never had a crush on her?"

Each of her words hit me like a truck. Stray dog? Was that how Sarah saw me? Worse, was that how Callie saw me?

Sarah continued on her rampage like she didn't

even need to hear my answer. "Everyone thinks Callie's *so sweet* and *so innocent* and they ignore the fact that she's been leading you on for *years*!"

I grew up in a home listening to my parents fight and break things every night. Hearing my sisters sneak out to meet terrible boyfriends. Feeling terrified of continuing the Cook Family Curse when I grew up. I even took a few hits from my dad. But I would never take anyone talking bad about the Copelands.

"They've been there for me through everything, Sarah," I snapped, standing up and sucking in deep breaths just to keep my cool. "And ever since we've started dating, Callie's family has welcomed you into their home with open arms. She's never said a mean word about you."

"Answer the question, Carson."

"What question?"

"Do you like her?"

CALLIE

I texted Carson and asked him to come over. My newest foster dog was the cutest thing I'd ever seen but in the ugliest of ways. She had scraggly brown hair, eyebrows that stuck up, big round eyes that protruded from her face, and crooked teeth that stuck out from her mouth at every angle.

Lorelei, the owner of Nature, said she didn't know the dog's name, but I'd started calling her Gertrude. Gertie for short.

She sat on my lap as I waited for him, letting me pet her back. When my hand stalled, she growled at me, like she was grumpy I'd gotten lazy.

"Sorry, Gert," I said and resumed my petting. I was just so excited for Carson to meet this one. He'd absolutely loved my last foster dog, Sanderson, a Lab mix that loved nothing more than to chase his tail and eat only left shoes.

I knew Carson probably couldn't stay all evening and play with her, but maybe he could get some good ear scratches in to give me a break before he went to hang out with Sarah.

A soft knock sounded on my bedroom door, but Gertie barked loudly all the same.

"Shh, Gertie," I said, trying to soothe her.

Carson smiled sadly at Gertrude. "Another one? You cried for a month after Sanderson left."

I touched my fingers to my lips and patted the picture of him and his new family on my desk. "At least I still get to see pictures of him online. And my shoes haven't been eaten for a while."

He came to me and lifted Gertrude from my arms. She relaxed into his grip like she'd known him her whole life.

"How did you do that?" I asked, shocked. "It took her hours to warm up to me."

His smile seemed even sadder as he sat on my bed with her nuzzling her face in his chest. "Guess I just have a way with the ladies."

Something was off. I wheeled my desk chair closer to him. "What's wrong?"

He cast a sardonic smile toward my window where the blinds had been closed ever since the first time I saw him and Sarah making out in his room. I didn't want to chance seeing where it might lead.

"Sarah broke up with me," he said emotionlessly.

My mouth fell open, and my heart froze. "What? You guys have been dating for like nine months..."

"Eleven," he said, scratching Gertie's neck. She rolled onto her back, and he rubbed her belly.

"What happened?" I asked.

"You mean what's been happening," he said.

"Ever since your brother made that comment about you putting me in the friend zone, she's been jealous of you, thinking that I'm only dating her because you won't date me."

Now my heart shifted into hyperdrive. "You told her that was ridiculous, right? Joe's always saying the dumbest stuff."

"I would have," Carson said, "but I would have been lying."

I placed a hand on my desk to steady myself. "What?" My heart dreamed what my brain wouldn't dare. Did Carson...like me?

He leaned back against the wall, absently stroking Gertie's coarse fur. "Do you remember when we went to that pumpkin patch for Halloween last year? We dressed up as M&Ms, and you told me I was the best friend you ever had."

I nodded slowly. That had been one of my favorite days ever. "I remember." I'd never forget.

"I think that's when I realized all you'd ever see me as was a friend. And I moved on. I was idiotic to think I'd met my soulmate at ten years old."

His words sent a knife twisting through my heart. Because the feeling had been mutual, and I'd been too afraid to tell him the truth. But I could now. Now that he didn't have a girlfriend, I would tell him that I'd been feeling the spark as well—that it wasn't all in his head. But the second I opened my mouth to speak, he sat up and continued.

"I don't even know if I had a crush on you as much as I did on your life. I think I just saw how great everything was here and wanted it for myself."

My soaring heart crash-landed, shattering. "Everything here *is* yours," I breathed, my voice coming out strangled. Everything I had was his.

He smiled sadly. "I know. I guess I was just afraid it might be taken away somehow?" He shrugged. "I don't know. I'm just glad I have you as a friend." He extended his arms for a hug.

My joints moved like cinder blocks as I rose from my desk chair and leaned into his embrace. I let myself melt into him, pretending just for a moment that this alternate universe could exist where you could meet your soulmate at ten years old and that I wasn't sitting here, hugging my best friend, and wishing that being just friends was enough.

Gertie growled, making us split apart, tears shining in both of our eyes.

Carson wiped at his cheeks and then pet Gertie

for a moment before turning his gaze back on me. "Best friends forever?"

I smiled and returned the phrase. "Best friends forever. No matter what." Even if it breaks my heart.

NINE

EIGHTEEN YEARS OLD

CALLIE

"Callie!" Carson's voice came through my open window. I shoved aside the curtains, getting a full breath of the fresh evening air, and looked out at him where he leaned from his second-story bedroom window across our property lines.

"What's up?" I asked, tucking loose strands of hair under my shower cap. Putting psoriasis cream on my scalp and covering it with yellow vinyl was not sexy. At all. But it helped, and Carson had seen it before. Still, I checked to make sure no one was watching us from the street. All clear.

My psoriasis had been better this last year, probably because I'd clicked with a great group of girls, and having friends aside from Carson was amazing.

But the stress of graduation and of what I was about to ask Carson had my skin dry and flaking. I hoped I'd caught it before the flare-up got too bad.

"I'm bored." Carson's forearms flexed as he leaned on his windowsill. "Wanna watch a movie?"

"Great start to our last summer break before college," I retorted. "Stay inside and watch a movie while everyone else is out living their lives."

He chuckled, his laugh almost as warm as the evening sun. "You do look like you were ready for a night out on the town."

My cheeks went red. "Caught me."

"So..."

Mom's voice sounded from downstairs. "Come over, Carson. Joe isn't here yet, so you two can pick the movie before they get here!"

I looked down and saw my mom leaning out the open kitchen window, waving across the way at Carson. She must have been in the dining room with the windows open downstairs. Anything for Dad to make the most of these last cool evenings. Shaking my head, I grinned at Carson and said, "See you in a few."

"See you!" my mom called.

I checked in the mirror to make sure I didn't accidentally have any ointment smeared on my face and then picked up Franklin, my old, blind, grumpy foster dog. He growled until he settled snugly in my arms. Once I had his bed and stuffed animal, I started down the stairs.

Carson came inside about the time I reached the landing. He hadn't knocked, but Franklin's hackles rose, and he howled at the top of his little lungs.

At the disturbance, Dad looked up from his laptop where he was working, and Mom set her frosting bag down on the counter, clearly disgruntled.

"Franklin," I soothed, "it's just big bad Carson."

"Yeah, buddy," Carson said, coming closer and scratching his ears.

Franklin quickly relaxed and scratched to get in Carson's arms. Carson held the dog close to his chest, whispering calming words. How he had such a way with animals, I didn't know. The only person I knew who was more of a natural was my boss, Lorelei.

"Hey, kid," Dad said to Carson. "Can you convince her to get rid of this one? The blind bat wakes all of us up every time a car door shuts." Or your parents argue, my dad didn't say.

Carson shook his head. "You know she's a lost

cause just as much as I do." He nodded toward my shower cap. "Flare-up?"

A corner of my lips pulled down in response.

"Need me to grab the humidifier from your room?" he asked. "I can get it going in the basement."

"Sure," I said, going to examine my mom's latest creation. Today looked like pirate-themed sugar cookies.

Carson passed Franklin back, and I tucked him to my side. As Carson easily thudded up to my room, I used my free finger to swipe some frosting off the edge of a bowl.

Mom gave me a chastising look.

"It's delicious," I said, savoring the sweet flavor filling my mouth. "Want me to run QA on this batch?"

Carson's voice boomed from the stairs. "If Callie gets a test cookie, I do too!"

Franklin gurgled in agreement, and I stroked his back. "Isn't that right, sweet boy?"

Mom's lips spread into an exasperated smile. "I guess my cookies aren't too bad since you two are always such willing taste-testers."

Dad chuckled. "More like willing victims.

Carson, have you already forgotten the nightmare batch?"

He came into view, holding my humidifier, and shuddered.

Mom waved a wooden spoon through the air. "One time I use baking soda instead of flour and everyone's a critic."

Dad rose from his spot at the table and walked toward the fridge, kissing my mom on the cheek on the way. She smiled at him lovingly, and Carson and I gave each other a look. How pathetic was it that my parents had a better love life than me? But if Carson agreed to my idea, that could all change, and soon.

"So," Carson said, "about that taste test."

Mom and Dad both chuckled, and Mom handed each of us a sugar cookie. I barely got a look at Carson's skull and crossbones before he shoved the whole thing into his mouth.

"Gross," I said. Focusing on the dumb guy things he did made it easier to move on. That and knowing we were about to go to Stanford, where the college girls would be all over him and his swim-team friends.

I took a bite of my cookie, if only to drown the unpleasant emotions growing within me. It was a yellow circle, much less elaborate than Carson's. "What is this supposed to be?"

My mom put on the worst fake pirate accent ever and said, "It's me booty, matey."

Carson guffawed. "You just ate your mom's butt."

I didn't want to, I swear I didn't, but I burst out laughing, as did both of my parents. Franklin growled and demanded to be let down.

The front door opened, and my brother and his best friend, Nick, walked through the door, carrying bags full of takeout from our favorite Chinese restaurant.

As Franklin barked madly, my gut dropped, and I hissed, "What happened to Nick not coming over?"

Of course everyone was laughing too hard to have heard me. I picked up Franklin, trying to settle his nerves.

Joe set his bags on the table and said, "What's so funny?"

Carson answered, "Cal just ate your mom's butt."

Joe gave us a funny look, and Nick's beautiful pitch eyes took on an amused expression as he studied me.

It was then that I realized I was holding a half-eaten sugar cookie, wearing a yellow shower cap, and probably had crumbs all over my face. Not to mention my dog was still barking wildly at all the commotion. My eyes widened, and I slowly stepped backward, trying to keep hold of the squirming dog in my grip. I was *mortified*. I had made extra sure that Nick never saw me like this, opting to stay in my room instead of going downstairs when he was around if I had to wear my cap.

But now, there was no avoiding it. I was in my jammies, my shower cap, and my slippers. At least I'd put on a bra.

Joe and Nick walked into the dining room and set the takeout bags on the table. While Joe began taking out boxes, Nick walked toward us. "New batch of sugar cookies, Anne?"

Carson seemed to stiffen beside me, which was strange because I was having the same reaction, even though my mind was screaming at me to *move*. But apparently the part of my mind that controlled movement was too preoccupied with the embarrassing image of myself that was sure to be seared into Nick's brain for the rest of time, labelling me as completely undatable. Even more than being his best friend's little sister already did.

"Here," my mom said, walking past me and extending a cookie to Nick. "Pretty sure there's no baking soda in this one." She shot Carson and me a look over her shoulder, pretending like she wasn't amused.

Nick took it with an easy grin and popped it in his mouth, just as Carson had. Humming low, he closed his eyes. "Man, this has to be your best batch yet, Anne."

My mom's eyes lit up. "You think?"

"Oh yeah." He put his hand on my shoulder and patted. "I could see why Cal Pal would want to eat the pirate's booty."

In an ideal world, I would have replied with something witty and humorous and preferably something that kept his hands on me. But my brain was still too busy short-circuiting. The electricity from his hand had my mind going haywire, and clearly even forming a coherent sentence was too much to ask. Because all I did was stand there like a big dope, my mouth hanging open, probably revealing a half-chewed cookie. RIP whatever was left of my self-respect.

Franklin barked at Nick, who quickly backed up and continued toward the table where Joe had already opened all of the boxes.

"Thanks," I grumbled to the worst wing-dog ever.

Carson had caught sight of the food and of course forgot to be embarrassed for me. Trailing Nick to the table, he asked, "Mind if we take some downstairs, Anne?"

Mom shook her head, admonishing him. "Carson, you know this house is just as much your home as it is ours."

Carson smiled sheepishly. "In that case"—he reached out and took one of the boxes and then looked back at me—"General Tso's?"

Still unable to find my voice, I nodded. He came back to where I stood rooted to the tile and handed me a set of chopsticks and a cardboard box.

Joe looked at us from the table and talked around a massive bite of egg roll he'd taken. "What are we watching?"

"Well," Carson said, "if Callie picks, it'll probably be some sappy chick flick."

I elbowed him in the stomach.

"I mean a delightfully hilarious romantic movie."

Everyone chuckled at him, except for me. I was too busy thanking my lucky stars I could move again.

"I'm definitely feeling an Adam Sandler romcom," I admitted.

Carson groaned and bent over the counter in a dramatic display of disappointment.

"Please," I said. "You know you cried at *50 First Dates* just like I did."

Joe and Nick looked at each other, and Joe shrugged.

"I'm down for *50 First Dates*," Nick said.

Was it just me, or was he looking at me only? I needed to stop letting my mind get away from myself. It was just those dark eyes. They seemed to take in everything, especially me. Which was kind of a problem right now, considering my appearance.

"Let's go watch it," I said casually, even though I felt anything but. My heart was racing, and I was trying not to read too much into the fact that he had vouched for my movie choice. "Carson and I will go get it set up."

I used my shoulder to push Carson toward the stairs. We had to hurry before the other two came down. I needed to ask him for help, and we were running out of time before the boys would finish ransacking the boxes.

"What's the rush?" he asked at the bottom of the stairs.

"I need to ask you a favor," I hurried out, setting Franklin on the ground. He jumped onto the couch and took his favorite spot on Mom's biggest throw pillow.

"What?" Carson asked, seeming concerned. "Is everything okay?"

I looked up toward the ceiling, toward my yellow shower cap. "I'm beyond mortification, but I think I'll be okay."

He shook his head. "I've seen you in your shower cap before."

"Nick hasn't."

He rolled his eyes.

"What?" I asked.

"Nothing," he said too fast. "I just don't see why you're so embarrassed about the shower cap. It's medical. It's not like you're trying to make a fashion statement."

I shook my head. "We're getting off topic. I need you to help me with Nick."

His eyebrows came together. "With Nick?"

Was this really that big of a secret? "I like him," I hissed, glancing toward the stairs, "and I need you to help get him to like me."

His jaw went slack. "You want me to *what*?"

"Don't seem so surprised," I said, trying not to feel hurt. "Is it so far out there that Nick could like a girl like me?" I said it in a joking tone, but his answer really mattered to me. Carson knew me better than anyone else, and if he thought I wasn't worthy of Nick, I didn't have the slightest chance.

"No," he stuttered, "it's not that at all. It's just the fact that... *Nick*? Really?"

I glanced toward the stairs again where I could hear him and my brother laughing. They were always having so much fun. And I loved Nick's laugh. It was low and happy. Kind of like Carson's. "What's wrong with Nick?"

Carson shook his head. "It's not about Nick. I'm not going to *try* and get anyone to like you. That's crazy. They should like you on their own."

Desperation spread through my chest, a feeling I needed to stop being so familiar with. "Please, Carson?"

"No," he said, resolute. After setting his food on the coffee table, he put his hands on my shoulders. "Look, you don't want to be dating a college guy."

"Why? I'll be going to college in less than three months."

"And? You don't want to date college guys then either."

"You'll be a college guy," I pointed out, stepping to the table to put down my own food. "Should no one date you?"

He brushed off my comment. "College guys only want one thing, and they know how to get it."

Cue the world's biggest eye-roll. "Carson, it's not about sex. It's about the fact that I just graduated high school, and I *still* haven't even had my first kiss yet. The closest I've ever gotten was jumping on the bed with you during Seven Minutes of Heaven. Don't you see how pathetic that is? I've been so busy being the 'good girl' that I haven't even had a chance to have an adventure of my own. I've been watching my friends fall in love, get dates, have *fun*, and what have I done? Played my piccolo in the marching band and hung out in my shower cap."

Carson frowned, shaking his head. "There's nothing wrong with you, Callie." He reached out and tucked a loose strand of hair into my shower cap. "Except maybe your taste in movies."

Heavy feet landed on the stairs, and Joe said, "Agreed. Let's start the misery."

TEN

CARSON

Callie picked the movie, and yeah, I actually liked it. But I couldn't focus on any of it with her question ringing through my ears and Nick sitting feet away from me. From her.

I didn't have a problem with Nick, per se. He was nice enough. Played video games. But he wrote poetry. And he was so pretentious about it. Like stringing a few words together that didn't even rhyme all the time somehow made him an artist. And what did he think he was going to do after he graduated college? I hope he had luck rhyming with "do you want fries with that?"

Okay, maybe I was being rude, but seriously. Callie deserved so much better. Someone strong, who could protect her when people said mean things, who'd stick with her no matter what, not just write her a few sappy poems and move on.

But she kept glancing over at him like he'd personally discovered love rhymes with dove. And the worst thing was, it didn't seem like he cared. Didn't he realize what a gem he had sitting across from him? Sure, Joe was his friend, but Joe was the most laid-back guy I'd ever met. He probably wouldn't flip about it.

Definitely not like I was right now.

Callie wasn't the kind of girl who gave up on what she wanted. Not when she wanted to start fostering dogs, not when she wanted to learn the piccolo after quitting sports, and she wouldn't break that pattern now.

The problem was, we were about to go to Stanford together, and part of me had always dreamed we'd leave for college as a couple. The timing had always been off before. I'd been too afraid or dating Sarah, but now was the time, and she wanted me to seal my own demise?

Callie didn't know what she was asking me to do, not really. Still, if I said no, it would break her heart. But if I said yes? I might just break my own.

"I need to get something at my house," I announced and got off the couch.

"Hurry up," Callie said. "You don't want to miss their last first kiss."

I chuckled. That was her favorite part. "I'll be back soon."

I walked through the sliding doors and crossed their backyard to the other side of the privacy fence. As I walked toward the park closest to our houses, my fingers hovered over my phone.

One by one, I'd watched my sisters leave—go to college, get married, have children, and start lives of their own as far away from our parents as possible. As far away from *me* as possible. Clary was busy looking after her three kids, Gemma had a big job in New York, and Sierra had just started backpacking Europe with her husband to get inspiration for her next art installation. I couldn't even get ahold of her if I tried.

It was hard not to feel sorry for myself as I called my friend Beckett's number and hoped he wasn't too busy with his new girlfriend, Rory, to answer.

It went to voicemail, and I sent him a text.

Carson: I'm desperate. Pick up?

I dropped into the swing like I had all those years ago, not knowing the girl in the swing next to mine would become the center of my universe. Within a few seconds, a call came in from him.

"Sorry, Cars, I was in Spike. Hold on," Beckett said. The club's music quieted on the phone like he'd stepped outside or something.

Suddenly, I felt like crap for taking him away from his night when I was the one who'd put myself in this situation. If I'd just been brave enough, spelled out for Callie exactly how much she meant to me, maybe we wouldn't be in this position right now.

Maybe I did need to study poetry.

"What's up?" Beckett asked, in a quieter spot now.

"I'm screwed," I said, bending over in the swing and dragging my fingers through my hair.

"What happened?" He sounded concerned— but not panicked like I was.

"Callie wants me to help her brother's best friend fall in love with her, and I'm losing it. I can't do that. It would mess everything up! This was supposed to be *our* summer, and now I'm gonna watch her fall in love with some other guy? And not only fall in love, but orchestrate the whole thing? It's sick."

"Whoa, breathe," Beckett said. "That's a lot."

"You're telling me." I straightened and kicked my feet over the worn-down gravel, even though it felt like my rib cage was splitting in half. "I don't know what to do."

Beckett swore low. "Can't she see she's in love with you?"

I snorted. "That's a funny thing to say considering *she just asked me to help her land someone else.*"

"Don't ask me to read her mind. I barely know what Rory's thinking half the time."

"Well, thanks for the help, Becks." I wasn't mad at him, not really, but the hopelessness inside me was growing, and I didn't know what else there was left to hang on to once my hope was gone.

"Do you want me to ask Rory for help?" he offered.

"No, she'll just tell Callie, and then I'd look even more pathetic than I do now."

"And you can't just tell her how you feel?"

I squinted my eyes against the sunset and shook my head. "She likes him."

"Then I don't see any other option," Beckett said.

I hung on to one of swing chains and leaned my head against the cool metal. "What is it?"

"You have to help her," he said gently, but his words hit me like daggers.

"What do you mean?"

"When you love someone, you'll do whatever it takes for them to be happy, even if it means breaking yourself in the process."

My eyes stung and my throat felt thick, and God, I just wished hearing the truth didn't feel like this. "Thanks, Becks," I choked out, not sure if I could follow through on this.

"Call me if you need me," he said.

"I will," I promised, even though he'd already done more than enough by being honest with me.

"Don't give up," he said. "If there's one thing I learned from Rory, it's that love is messy, and sometimes you think it's all going to hell, but then you figure out it was just a part of your story. Someday, it will all make sense."

There it was, that little spark of hope I needed to hold my head up high and walk into the Copelands' house to see the girl I loved in love with someone else.

ELEVEN

CALLIE

I could hardly focus with Nick sitting just feet away from me. He'd gotten a new haircut, and I was trying to decide whether I liked his hair shaggy or close-cropped better. Either way, it was easy to see his angular cheekbones and the constantly sparking light in his eyes.

Without any dating experience to go off of, it felt like I was lost at sea. I hoped Carson would agree to help me. To be my anchor. The thought of going to college without ever taking my chance with Nick—without ever having a first kiss—was a dismal one at best.

The screen door slid open, and Carson sent me a halfhearted smile before coming to sit by me on the couch. I leaned my head on his shoulder. No matter what, I was lucky to have him as a friend.

When the end credits rolled on the movie, Joe and Nick went upstairs for more food, and Carson said, "I have to be up early for work tomorrow. I better get home."

"You don't want to stay over?" I asked. "We could stay up later and hang out that way."

He shook his head and said quietly, "Dad's started making comments."

"What kind of comments?" My heart clenched. "Are you okay?"

Understanding the meaning behind my words, he gave half a nod. "I will be in August."

"And until then?"

His shoulders lifted in a heavy shrug.

Feeling just as heavy, I said, "I'm sorry."

"Don't be." He shifted toward the door. "See you tomorrow?"

"See you," I said, "and think about what I asked."

"I won't," he replied with half a smirk. He paused with his hand on the sliding door handle. "Want to go shopping with me for work stuff tomorrow afternoon?"

"Sure." My internship at the animal shelter

wouldn't start for another week, so I had to find something to fill my time until then.

With a friendly wave, Carson left. When he disappeared through the gate to our privacy fence, I turned back to the living room. Joe was already in front of the entertainment center, flipping through video games. He looked back at Nick. "Call of Duty?"

Nick shrugged, sitting up to put his phone in his pocket. "Works for me."

Joe popped the disc into the gaming console and said, "I'm going to get my extra headset from my room."

Nick nodded and sat back on the couch. I suddenly realized that it was just him and me, and even though I wanted desperately to say something, I couldn't think of anything worthwhile. Talking with Carson was so easy, but when it came to other guys, I just froze.

Somehow, "Hey, I think you're cute, and I want to go out with you even though my brother would hate it" didn't seem right. But I couldn't help but worry about who he had been texting. Was it another girl? Had I lost my chance? I could already feel the clock of summer ticking down, and I would soon be at Stanford with Carson, and Nick would still be here, with my brother.

I leaned back against the sliding door with a quiet sigh. I would be able to come back for weekends if I wanted to, but only after football season was over. The marching band was sure to take up most of my time.

"Are you going to play with us?" Nick asked, twisting on the couch to see me better.

I shook my head slowly. I had never played with them before, and being yet another girl who didn't get video games probably wouldn't work in my favor.

"Why not?" Nick asked.

Was that a hint of disappointment I heard? I hoped I wasn't making it up in my mind because it sounded so real to me. My smile was already growing way bigger than it should have. Nick was asking me to hang out with him. *And my brother.* I needed to remember that part. "I'm not exactly a Call of Duty kind of girl," I said at last.

His lips quirked. "And what kind of girl are you?"

I was definitely the kind of girl who could be into him. But I didn't know if he was the kind of guy who could be into a girl like me. I tried to breathe normal and shrugged. "I guess the kind that likes General Tso's chicken."

He laughed. "I wish my real little sister was as funny as you are."

Ouch. So he thought I was like a little sister. Worse, like his preferred little sister. Not a great start.

Joe came down the stairs, holding another headset, and said, "Callie, what are you still doing here?"

Franklin jerked upright out of his sleep, barking at him. I scooped him into my lap and smiled innocently at Joe. "What? You don't want your little sister to hang?"

"More like my little sister *can't* hang," he said, going to the gaming console.

"Yeah," I said, "pushing buttons on a console is really difficult."

"Oooh," Nick said, laughing. "Burn."

Joe rolled his eyes. "Is that my little sister, Little Miss Perfect, being... rude?"

I shook my head and started up the stairs with Franklin in my arms. It was far past time for me to retreat into my room and forget the fact that Nick ever saw me in my shower cap.

"Buh-bye," Joe said.

I rolled my eyes and held my hand up in a wave.

"See you," Nick said, making my heart flutter.

I continued up the stairs, trying to keep my gaze forward. It was hard not to look back at where I knew Nick would be sitting, his strong arms taking ahold of the controller and his eyes focusing as he got into the game. But I needed to remember that college guys and curvy girls didn't date—not without divine intervention. If Carson wasn't going to help, I needed all the backup I could find.

In the upstairs living room, Mom and Dad were snuggled together, watching a baking show on TV. At the sound of my footsteps, Dad said, "Cal, can you close your window tonight? I'm going to run the AC."

"Sure," I said distractedly and continued to my room. When I got there, I looked at Carson's room across the way but didn't see him inside. He must have gotten caught up downstairs. I closed my window, drew my blinds, and went to my bed.

Feeling restless, I got out my phone and texted the girls.

Callie: Anyone want to grab breakfast tomorrow at the bakery? I need help making a game plan.

Immediately, my phone began chiming with new messages.

Zara: I'm down.

Jordan: Same. I need to leave at 10 though.

Ginger: I can stop by before I go to the boyfriend's. :)

Rory: I'll come! Are you bringing Carson?

Callie: No, just me.

Ginger: Girls only? :)

Callie: Exactly.

Zara: So… 9?

Callie: Perfect.

I turned my phone to play the sound of chirping crickets and fell asleep hoping my friends could help me have the summer—and summer love—of a lifetime.

TWELVE

CARSON

When I walked in the back door, Mom was actually sitting at the breakfast nook, drinking a glass of wine. She usually preferred to work the late evening shift to avoid Dad at his grumpiest, which meant we hardly saw each other.

She looked up at me and a smile spread on her lips. "Carson, come sit with me. I miss you."

Sure, I wanted to say. That was why she made sure she was never around the house when I was. But deep down, I knew it was less about me and more about my father. The Cook Family Curse was just as alive and well in California as it had been in Texas. This move hadn't been "better" for any of us. Sure, Mom and Dad had managed to stay married, but that was about all they'd accomplished.

I grabbed a plastic cup from the cabinet—most of our glassware had been shattered—and filled it with water from the tap. As I sat across from Mom, it felt like there was a heavy weight on my chest. I didn't want to be mad at her for Dad's transgressions, but she didn't have to stay. She was the one with a job—with a degree—that had allowed us to move out here in the first place. One word and she could have him out of all of our lives, but she'd chosen him over her children, over and over again.

"I have news," she said, knotting her hands on the table. They were practically shaking.

"Are you okay?" I asked, feeling unsettled. Even her eyes had a spark of something I couldn't put my finger on.

Nodding, she took a deep breath and said, "I got a new job as a traveling pharmacist."

My jaw went slack. "What?"

"I'll be going to pharmacies all over the country —wherever they need me—and they'll put me up in hotels and give me per diem for food, on top of my regular salary."

Feeling lighter than I had all day, I grinned. "Mom, that's amazing!" She was *finally* going to get away from Dad, and I would be out of the house, and maybe we could all start moving on from the hell of the last eighteen years.

"When do you start?" I asked.

Her smile faltered. "Next week."

It felt like all the water in my cup had been doused over my head. She was leaving next week?

"I have an assignment in Phoenix," she rushed out. "And your grandma and gramps said you could stay with them until the summer's over." She reached across the table and took my hands. "Let's get out of here."

My heart rate sped, and I wildly looked around. It was one thing to dream about this happening, but to have it sprung on you out of the blue? "Does Dad know about this?" I whispered. Her face paled, and understanding crossed my mind. "You weren't going to tell him before you left."

She opened her mouth to speak, but glass shattered on the wall above her head, exploding into a thousand dark brown shards as amber liquid fizzed and slipped down the wall.

My head snapped in the direction the bottle

came from, and my eyes locked on Dad's, his nostrils flared wide and his eyes wild. A string of expletives flew from his mouth as he advanced on us.

Mom scrambled back from the table, terrified, and just the fact that she was scared sent a bout of rage through me so strong, I rose to my feet, shoving the table out of the way.

"Get out of here," my dad snarled at me. "This is between your mother and me."

He didn't account for the fact that I was bigger than him now. Stronger. And madder. "Get away from my mom," I said low but just as deadly.

For a moment, his eyes stayed on mine, his pupils pinpricks and his jaw clenched tight.

My muscles were coiled, ready for him to try something, because now that the girls were gone and Mom was leaving, he had nothing left to lose.

Whether he saw the fight in my eyes or gave up, I didn't know, but he turned and began walking away. My shoulders relaxed, and I let out a breath, realizing how close that had been. How much worse it could have ended.

Then Dad spun on his heel and swung his fist at me, his knuckles crashing squarely into my temple.

In the distance, I heard Mom scream, but spots were flaring in my vision as realization struck. Dad had hit me. Anger sent fire through my veins as blood dripped in my eye, and I advanced on him, swinging twice as hard as he hit me until I had him pinned to the ground. He scrambled against the tile floor, trying to gain purchase, but I wasn't letting up.

"Carson!" Mom screamed.

I pinned him down, one forearm against his neck. His breath came out in wheezes, slower and slower. I slammed my fist into him, hitting him for all the times he'd hurt Clary, for the way he sent Gemma and Sierra running to all the wrong guys, for the pain he'd put my mom through with all his violence followed by broken, empty promises.

But then fingers dug into my shoulder, and Mom tugged on my arms, screaming, "Carson! You're going to kill him!"

Something in me realized my dad was losing consciousness, and I pulled back. He scrambled to his feet, stepping away, and Mom and I ran out to her car. I held my head in my hands and she drove away, telling me we were driving to a hotel to stay the night.

None of that mattered, because I realized I'd

fulfilled the Cook Family Curse. The anger flooding through my veins, acting in my fingertips, that would have let me kill my dad meant I could never be the kind of guy Callie deserved. I had to help Nick fall in love with her because I was the kind of guy who wasn't going to stop.

THIRTEEN

CALLIE

I got to the bakery early, not wanting to waste any of our strategy time. I had a big goal, I wasn't sure whether Carson would help me, and the clock was still counting down.

The owner of the bakery, Gayle, greeted me with a big grin. "Hey, girl, how you doing?"

"Great." I smiled at her. I loved how much care she and her husband put into knowing each of their customers. I hoped I could make people feel that special and heard someday.

Her husband walked by and patted her on the butt before going back to the kitchen. Her cheeks (the ones on her face) glowed bright pink, and she said, "He is such a child."

I laughed with her, because he kind of was, but he reminded me of Carson. It seemed like Gayle and her husband were more than man and wife; they were best friends. "How do you guys keep your relationship so good?" I asked. I needed all the advice I could get.

She smiled over her shoulder at where he had gone inside the kitchen. "The best advice I can give you is to marry your best friend."

The thought of marrying Carson made me laugh. That might have been good advice for her, but if I married my best friend, I would just have a life full of pranks—waking up with frogs in my flour tins or my hand in a warm bowl of water didn't exactly fit my expectation of "happily ever after."

Instead of telling her that, I asked, "How did you and Chris meet?"

She leaned over the counter and rested her chin in her hand, like she was deep in thought. "Well, he would tell you that we met in sixth grade when I was a new student at Seaton Middle School, *but* I honestly don't remember talking to him until he asked me to the seventh-grade dance."

I raised my eyebrows in awe. "You guys have been dating since seventh grade?"

She smiled. "There were a couple of lost years in there, but if I know anything, it's that love always finds a way."

I smiled, hoping that would be true for me too because playing the piccolo in boxy marching band uniforms didn't exactly tip the odds in my favor.

A guy in a military uniform entered the store, and Gayle picked herself up from the counter. "Better get you checked out. What can I get you, honey?"

I put in an order for each of us and then went to look for a table where we could have at least a little privacy. There were a few older people situated around the dining area, along with an excruciatingly cute couple splitting a heart-shaped donut.

Out the window, I could see Zara's new car, well, new-to-her car, pulling into the parking lot. Since her dad had admitted to their production company's challenges, she'd downgraded to a more standard SUV. She looked just as fashionable getting out of that car as she had the Rolls-Royce. Even though she didn't start work at Bhatta Productions until later this morning, she looked exactly like a movie producer should in her gladiator sandals, stylish khaki joggers and tight black tank.

I looked down at my striped shorts and band

camp T-shirt, feeling a little insecure. I didn't usually get jealous about other girls—everyone had their own talents—but I couldn't help feeling like Nick might be more interested in me if I had Zara's sense of style.

She walked inside, and I waved her over to the table I had found. Grinning, she came over to me and gave me a hug before setting her purse down and taking a seat. Each of my friends came into the bakery one by one until we were all sitting, eating our breakfast and sipping from delicious beverages.

"Could Gayle get any better?" I asked. "The food is amazing, and she and Chris are so nice."

"I know!" Jordan cried. "I miss coming by here every day since we moved to our new place."

"They are definitely hashtag goals," Ginger said with a grin.

"They're great," Rory agreed, "but quit stalling." She banged her fist on the table like a gavel. "Let's call this meeting to order. What's going on, Callie?"

My cheeks heated, being put on the spot, and I almost considered telling the girls that I just wanted to hang out, but I sucked it up. Playing it safe was what got me to senior graduation without ever having kissed a boy.

"I need your help getting a guy to fall in love with me."

Their eyes immediately lit up, and Ginger said, "Are you finally going to tell Carson you like him?"

"What?" I asked, stunned. "No. No. Definitely not." I was even more shocked at the disappointment on their faces. "You guys think I like Carson?"

Jordan and Zara gave each other a look, and Zara said, "I'm pretty sure you're the *only* one who doesn't know that you like Carson."

I shook my head. There had been a time when I dreamed of a happily ever after for Carson and me, but it just wasn't realistic to think that way. Why would I risk a friendship that close, that precious, on something as volatile as romance? I cared about Carson like he was family, and that was exactly why I'd moved on to someone else. "I like Nick. Remember?"

Jordan raised her eyebrows. "Are you sure you're not just aiming low because you're worried about what Carson would say if you told him how you feel?"

"I would have to feel a certain way to be worried about whether or not Carson reciprocated the feelings," I said, exasperated. "And going for Nick is hardly aiming low."

Zara pursed her lips together. "Mhmm."

I raised my eyebrows, beginning to feel frustrated. "Can you just help me?"

Rory shook her head. "You know how well you guys setting me up with Beckett went."

"Yeah," I said. "You fell in love with him and are still dating and now moving to New York together. I *definitely* want the group's help."

"You're forgetting the part where I had cupcakes showered all over me and I nearly lost the love of my life," she pointed out.

"Minor details, right, Cal?" Ginger said with a teasing grin.

I put my head in my hands. "I'm hopeless. I know. Maybe when I go off to college they'll need a sacrificial virgin or something."

Rory glanced at the other girls, communicating silently with them, then turned to me. "Callie, I don't know how to say this, but you really don't need our help. You're amazing the way you are, and if Nick doesn't see that, then he's just a half-witted, video-game-addicted, stupid college boy."

I groaned. "You guys are starting to sound like Carson."

"Like Carson?" Jordan asked. "You told him you like Nick?"

I wished I hadn't, considering all the embarrassment of the night before. "I asked him if he would help me get Nick to fall in love with me, and he said no. I'm still hoping I can convince him tonight."

Zara wiggled her eyebrows. "Tonight? What are you guys doing?"

"Don't get too excited," I said, staring sadly at my bagel. "We're just going shopping for his work clothes."

"Wait," Rory said, holding up a finger. "He's a lifeguard. You're going *swimsuit shopping* with him? Hubba hubba!"

Ginger fanned herself, and Jordan whistled.

Zara elbowed my arm. "Get some good looks in."

"You know it's not like that," I said, my cheeks feeling hot. "He just doesn't want to go by himself."

"Shopping actually sounds like fun," Ginger said. "I wish Ray was into that kind of thing."

Shopping with Carson *was* fun. He was an amazing friend, and I couldn't imagine my life without him. Apparently, my friends couldn't either. Maybe that was part of the problem.

"So will you help me?" I asked, desperate.

Rory reached across the table and patted my hand. "You don't need us. You've got this."

The problem was I really, really didn't. As I fought my disappointment, I held out hope that somehow, some way, Carson would take pity on me and agree to help.

FOURTEEN

CARSON

Mom and I spent the night in a pair of connected rooms. She took one and I took the other, but honestly, I just wanted her to lie with me like she used to when I was little and having nightmares. I wanted her to tell me that there was something special in me. That I was good. That I hadn't just been about to kill my father.

But that would all be a lie. I tried to justify my actions a million ways in my mind—he hurt my sisters, he hurt my mom, he'd slung fists at me, but the truth was I was just done with him. I was done with the way he made all of us feel. Done with him driving people away from me. Done with the fact that his family's curse, his blood, ran in my veins.

Maybe that was the real reason why nothing had worked with Sarah. Not because of my feelings for Callie but because of who I was. Maybe that part of me was too big and Sarah had been repulsed by it. Maybe Callie should be too. I didn't know how my mom was even in the next room. If she just left in the middle of the night and never came back, I wouldn't have blamed her.

A soft knock sounded on the adjoining door, and when I didn't respond, it creaked open and Mom poked her head in. "Hey, baby. Breakfast is going to be over here in a bit. Want to go down with me?"

My throat felt tight, and I swallowed. "No."

She paused for a second, but instead of leaving like I'd expected her to, she came and sat on my bed, by the tangled sheets around my feet. After flicking on a lamp, she gently rested a hand on my calves and said, "I'm sorry about last night."

My eyes opened wider. Out of all the things I'd thought she would say, that was the last. "What do you mean?"

She shook her head, her blond hair curling around her shoulders. "I never should have put us in that position. I just thought your dad was asleep, and I—I..." She put her head in her hands, her shoulders shaking. "I've put you kids through so much."

I sat up, shocked by her admission. Her words hit me hard because I'd wanted to hear them all my life, but they fell flat, missed their mark. What good was an apology from a flame when everything had been singed to ash?

"Can you ever forgive me?" she asked.

"I don't even know if I can forgive myself."

"What do you mean?" Her eyebrows creased together so much like Clary's did. It made me miss my sisters that much more.

"Mom," I breathed, haunted. "I could have *killed* him." I looked down at my fingers, so innocuous, but last night...

She took me in her arms and squeezed me tight. "Don't you ever blame yourself for defending yourself or the people you love."

"What's the difference between defense and revenge?" I asked, because I had crossed the line last night, wherever it lay.

She thought for a moment and finally said, "The difference is in how you feel about yourself. Defense says I love myself more than I hate you. Revenge says I hate you more than I love myself."

She paused and stood. "Come on. You need some food."

Feeling like I had a boulder on my chest, I got out of bed and slipped my T-shirt back on. We hadn't had time to get anything the night before, but I hoped we'd get a chance to grab some things later on. Like my car—my computer, the things I'd worked for and bought for college coming up soon.

We went down to the dining area and chose from the picked-over buffet. I could tell the food was good for a hotel breakfast, even though it tasted like cardboard going into my mouth.

Mom passed me a cup of coffee and then a bag of ice. "Put this on your bruise."

My eyebrows came together. "Bruise?"

Her sad eyes fell on mine, then shifted slightly to the right. I lifted my fingers to my left temple, to the throbbing spot I'd thought was a guilt-induced headache. It was tender to my touch. For the first time, my dad had left a mark where it couldn't be covered.

Good, let there be a bruise to remind me what I was getting away from. What I didn't want to become. I set the ice to the side, wanting the wound to look as bad as possible, and continued eating. I might not have loved myself as much as I hated my dad, but I loved Callie more than all of that.

"What do you have going on today?" Mom asked.

I swallowed a gulp of orange juice and then wiped at my mouth. "I have a shift at the pool, and then I'm hanging out with Callie."

Her smile seemed genuine. "I'm glad you have such a good friend." Her lips fell. "We need to talk about what you're going to do while I'm gone."

The boulder grew even bigger, and I had to force myself to take a deeper breath. The night before, she'd said I could stay with Grandma and Gramps.

But I didn't like that option. No matter how much I missed my grandparents or hated my dad, Emerson was my home. *The Copelands* were my home. Leaving Callie behind would be a thousand times more painful than the bruise blossoming on my face. That was why I'd asked her all those years ago to escape with me. There was never a version of my future that didn't have her in it. As my neighbor. As my friend. As more.

But the last twenty-four hours had changed everything. Should I leave? Get as far away from Callie as possible to save her from myself?

"I need some time to think about it," I told my mom.

She put her hand on my arm. "We have a little time."

One week to be exact. One week in this hotel before she left for Phoenix, before I was on my own.

FIFTEEN

CALLIE

Carson texted me and asked me to meet him at the pool so we could leave from his work to go shopping. I told Mom I was leaving Franklin in the backyard for some exercise and slipped out the back gate. It was about a twenty-minute walk from my house, so I put in my headphones and listened to some music on the way.

This time of year, there were little kids playing in the small parks along the way. Seeing them made me smile as I thought of two ten-year-olds trying to swing higher than the other.

Through the pool fence, I caught sight of Carson pacing the perimeter of the water with his float. He wore board shorts only, avoiding a farmer's tan like the one he got his first summer guarding. Across the water, a couple of college girls sat in the lounge chairs, ogling him. They kept giggling and glancing over their sunglasses, trying to get his attention.

Couldn't they see he had more important things to focus on—like saving lives? Okay, to be fair, there were only three kids in the shallow end and an older lady who looked like she'd fallen asleep on a float, but still.

I approached the pool cabana and entered the code to get in.

"Hey, Cal," said the pool manager, one of the moms who lived a few houses over from me.

"Mrs. Mayes, how are you?" I asked.

With a smile, she shrugged. "Can't complain. Caden is actually lifeguarding this year."

"You're kidding!" I said. Her daughter had just finished her freshman year at Emerson High.

"Nope," Caden said from behind me.

I turned to see her smiling with a full set of braces.

"Good for you!" I said. "How are you liking it?"

"It's my first shift," she said. "Carson gave me a few pointers though."

I glanced at him, his whistle between his lips.

He blew a few short bursts and then called, "Safety break!"

"He's the best," I said.

As the people in the pool made their way to the edges, Caden walked to the rack of life-guard supplies behind her mom's manager desk and grabbed a float. She looked so cute in her bright pink one-piece. Part of me thought it might be best to avoid swimming while someone so petite was responsible for saving my life.

Carson didn't meet my eyes before hanging up his float.

Why did he seem so off? Usually I could count on him for a smile and a wave.

"Ready to go?" he asked.

I nodded.

He went back to the locked room where they kept their things and the lost and found. When he returned, he had his keys in hand and a T-shirt halfway over his head. He slid it over his abs and pushed out the door without even saying goodbye to Mrs. Mayes. Something was seriously wrong.

I followed a few steps behind him to his car and got in. He shut his door a little harder than usual. Where was my happy-go-lucky friend?

"What happened?" I asked, realizing he wasn't going to divulge anything on his own.

He looked at me, and I jerked away from the bruise spreading around his eye with veins of purple and blue. A gasp escaped my lips. "Carson... what happened?"

His hands clenched on the steering wheel. "My mom took a traveling pharmacist job. She's leaving my dad."

My mouth fell open, my mind reeling with all that came along with that news. "She's what?"

Carson's gaze darkened, and he pulled out of the parking lot, starting down the road. In the lines of his face and the whiteness of his knuckles, I felt each ounce of his pain as if it were my own. With each sister that left, things had gotten harder. His mom worked more hours, his dad began leaning on alcohol again for comfort at night, and Carson had been left to navigate life on his own. Still, his mom had always been at least a phone call away.

"But the bruise..." I covered my mouth. "Your dad was upset."

"Their marriage has been over since before we moved here."

For a moment, I realized how lucky I was, just to have the parents I did. And none of that had been due to anything but sheer fortune. What would my life be like if I'd been the one his parents had taken home from the hospital?

"What about your bruise?" I asked. It looked bad, and the fact that Carson was avoiding the topic scared me even more. Was he afraid to go home?

Carson's jaw tightened. "He acted like he was walking away, then he threw a fist at me."

My stomach churned. How was Carson driving right now? Keeping the car between the highway lines? I could barely sit up straight. "Are you okay?"

The second the words left my mouth I realized how dumb they were. Of course he wasn't okay. The one person who should have been there for him no matter what, who should have kept him safe, had injured him. Now Carson had to wear the evidence of that betrayal on his face.

"I'm not," he said. "But I will be." He didn't even sound like he believed the words.

There was something he wasn't telling me. I could see it in the tightness around his eyes. In the hesitancy of his voice. "Carson, what's going on?"

Instead of answering me, he silently pulled into Emerson Shoppes and stopped in a parking spot. Once the car was off and his seatbelt undone, he turned to me and said, "My mom said I could go with her or stay with my grandparents."

His words practically opened the ground underneath me. "You're *moving*?"

"I can't stay with him."

The ache in his voice hit me straight in the chest. "Don't go," I said, scrambling for ideas. "Stay with us. You know the spare room's yours."

He took a deep breath and met my eyes, his a dark, stormy blue. "I don't want to ruin your last summer at home."

I blinked, not understanding him. "You know what would ruin my last summer at home? Not spending it with my *best* friend. You *have* to stay."

So much of my heart was on the line here. I may have had a crush on Nick, but Carson was *everything* to me. He'd been there for me, right next door or even in our house, since I was ten years old. Losing him would be like losing a part of myself.

"My dad will be mad—he'll know I'm next door. I wouldn't want him taking it out on you guys."

Anger flared within me at the way that man had made my best friend's life so miserable, but he was right. Staying with us would just put him more at risk. "There has to be a solution. Can you stay with Beckett?"

He shook his head. "They just have a two-bedroom, and I'm pretty sure they wouldn't like me bumming it on their couch for three months."

"Think about it," I said, reaching across the car and holding his hand. It was big and warm inside both of mine, but he still seemed so vulnerable. "I don't want to lose you, but I don't want to see how far your dad would go either. He's evil to put you through this. What kind of person would lay a hand on another..." I shook my head in disgust. "It's awful."

His jaw trembled, but only for a moment, and he nodded. With a sniff, he looked out the car window and said, "Now, let's go get me some new board shorts."

I wanted to talk to him more about everything, to let him know I was here for him no matter what, but there would be time for that eventually. There had to be.

As I got out of the car, my leg stuck to his leather seats, and I cringed. So not sexy. Not that I was really worried about Carson thinking I was sexy, but it was just a reminder of how unattractive I was. How much I really had to lose if Carson left.

We walked quietly across the parking lot and into a big department store. The line of doors let us into the women's section. I scanned the scanty summer pieces and shook my head. The thought of wearing something like that, showing the scaly skin on my neck and arms, made me feel ill. I could almost hear people at the pool calling me the Loch Ness monster and making fish faces at me.

Carson didn't seem to notice my expression as we walked toward the men's section of the store, which was buried so far back I almost thought it didn't exist.

We passed a big display of purses, and I paused, running my fingers over a silver buckle.

"Oh no you don't," he said, gripping my fingers and pulling me away.

"But it's so pretty!" I reached for it, but it was a losing fight.

"You told me you were trying to cut back!" he said, ignoring my longing looks over my shoulder.

"I need one for college."

He lifted his eyebrows. "One of the thirty you already own won't work?"

"No." I sniffed. "None of my purses say 'college girl' like that one."

"A talking purse?" he asked. "We better go back and get it."

Barely keeping a straight face, I shook my head. "Now you're just being rude."

"Step away from *the precious*," he said, making some people walking past us giggle.

Blushing furiously, I gave him a glare and began marching toward the illusive men's section. "Let's get this over with."

He laughed the entire way. Being with Carson was so easy. He had this amazing skill to smile through the hard times. To make the difficult look easy. I loved that about him.

"So," I asked, standing in front of a rack of board shorts. "Are you looking for anything specific?"

"Mrs. Mayes is fine as long as it doesn't have any words." He shrugged. "I wouldn't get more, but the ones I have are just a little tight."

I patted his firm belly. "Growing up, are you?"

He shoved me off, and I couldn't help but giggle.

"So what are you in the mood for, cabana boy?" I teased. I was still laughing about the summer an elderly lady had come to the pool every day and referred to him exclusively as "cabana boy."

"Have your laughs," he said, shuddering. "I still need therapy about that."

I saw a floral pair of shorts that looked really cool and pulled them from the rack, along with a striped pair I knew he would like better, and handed them to him. If you wanted a guy to try something out of his comfort zone, you had to give him a practical option with it.

He raised his eyebrows at the floral pair. "Seriously?"

"Just try them on, cabana boy," I said, pushing him toward the dressing room.

Shaking his head, he did as I asked, and I continued flipping through the racks, looking for more options for him to try on.

I heard a couple of guys talking nearby and glanced at them out of the corner of my eye. They were cute, but I didn't recognize them. They probably went to one of the local public schools because I'd never seen them at Emerson or any games at Brentwood.

One of them caught me looking at him and snorted. "Are you checking me out?"

My cheeks got even redder than they were before, and I quickly shook my head. "No, I—"

"She totally was," the other one said. "Ew. Why don't you flirt with someone your own size?"

Suddenly I felt like a whale, ballooning to twice my weight. I wanted to tell them to stop, to stand up for myself like I should have back in middle school, but I couldn't bring myself to do it, to say anything. I was just as frozen as I'd been on the basketball court, listening to everyone chant at me.

The other guy laughed. "Why are you shopping in the guys' section anyway? Can't find anything that fits over there?"

My shoulders sagged. I wanted to melt into the floor, to disappear into the heap of garbage I felt like.

An arm snaked around my shoulder, and Carson leaned low, brushing his lips against my cheek. "Hey, baby. Anything wrong?"

I still couldn't bring myself to speak, maybe because of the fact that Carson had *kissed* my cheek.

He sent a steely glare at the guys who had been picking on me. "If you say one more word to my girl, I'll put your lips over your head and force you to swallow them. Capisce?" Carson was standing at his full height—every six feet, two inches of it—and in his swimming trunks, it was easy to see the muscles he constantly worked to build.

"We were just kidding man," the loudmouth said.

"You weren't, and that's not okay," Carson said just as firmly as he held me at his side. "Now, get out of here before I consider introducing my fist to your useless face."

The guys hightailed it away from the men's section, and Carson stepped back from me, making me feel cold in his absence. He gestured at the floral shorts. "I'm getting them."

I shook my head distractedly. "You don't have to do that."

"I know." He put his hands on my shoulders and looked me straight on. "Are you okay?"

Tears stung my eyes as the reality of what had happened settled in. I'd been called out for my appearance and had done nothing to defend myself. I felt like a failure, but mostly, I felt fat. "Can we just get out of here?"

He held me to his chest and hugged me tight. "Of course."

SIXTEEN

CARSON

Shopping with Callie had made me feel like my regular self. Until those two jerks decided to pick on her. And for what reason? She weighed more than their blow-up dolls at home? The same kind of rage I'd felt with my dad had started welling inside of me, but I willed it down. I could control it around Callie—I had to.

I took her to Waldo's Diner to have her favorite —fries and a strawberry milkshake—but I could tell she was still down. But maybe that had to do with my news as well. We were only a few days into our last summer before college, and it was off to a dismal start.

"Can you quit looking at me like I'm a sad puppy?" she asked.

I set down my hamburger. "Can you stop looking like one?"

She managed half a smile before it faltered, and she shoved her milkshake away. "It's been four years since I got psoriasis, and I swear every time someone picks on me, I feel like I'm fourteen years old again."

My mind flashed back to seeing her on the court, the anger that had rushed through me when everyone chanted at her, calling her The Thing. Maybe the Cook Family Curse had always made me an angry person, and I just couldn't see it. But then again, the anger toward the people who hurt Callie seemed to be justified. She was the nicest person ever, and for people to humiliate her like that because of a skin condition she had no control over or because of her weight? It was despicable.

Callie had changed that day at the game. She'd gone from the competitive, vivacious person I knew to someone who was afraid to put herself out there in any capacity. Even in band she wore a uniform that covered everything, and she never took a solo if she could help it. Becoming friends with the other curvaceous girls in our class had been a godsend for her.

Now that she had a good set of girlfriends, I had to find a way to push her toward a better guy as well. Someone who wouldn't feel such a massive, uncontrollable surge of anger at a moment's notice. Someone whose hands weren't capable of doing what I'd contemplated the night before.

Someone like Nick.

She shook her head. "I can't believe I didn't say anything to those guys. I should have stood up for myself."

"Why are you mad at yourself?" I asked, bringing myself back to our conversation. "Those guys were being jerks."

"I'm not fourteen anymore. I'm about to go to college. I should be able to stand up for myself. You're not always going to be around to save me."

The ache in my chest grew bigger. For her and for me. Because her words were completely true. "Those guys should have known better."

"But they didn't," she argued, pushing her fries away too. "And why would they? No one wants to date me. It's not like I have guys lining up."

I hated it when she talked like this. No matter how much her friends adored her, no matter how stunning she was with her blonde hair and Barbie-doll eyes, she couldn't see herself as she was. "Callie, you're beautiful."

She raised her eyebrows at me and muttered, "You have to say that. You're basically my brother."

An exasperated sigh escaped my lips. "I'd say it no matter what. Besides, it's not up to you to make other people see your worth."

She swirled her straw in her melting milkshake. "Yeah, but no one does."

I reached across the table and stilled her hand. "I do."

"I do too," rattled an older voice from behind me.

Chester was sitting in his usual booth, and his hearing aids must have been working because he'd overheard our conversation. I said over my shoulder, "Thanks for the backup, Chester."

With a smile in his voice, he said, "If I was sixty years younger, I'd be first in line."

"I'd be first to say yes." Callie laughed, and the tinkling sound made my chest feel lighter.

But why was I suddenly jealous of an old man? Under my breath, I muttered, "Should I give you two some privacy?"

Callie reached across the table and hit my arm.

"Ouch." I pretended to be wounded, rubbing my shoulder. But then something clicked. When I had pretended to be Callie's boyfriend earlier, those guys had completely changed their tune. I could practically pinpoint the moment their eyes saw Callie in a new light.

Callie rubbed a napkin over her lips. "Do I have something on my face?"

I must have been staring as I considered my idea...but it could work. The problem was it might just destroy me in the process. But Callie was worth it. She was always worth it. "Go out with me," I said.

"What?" Her eyebrows flew up her forehead.

I'll be honest, that didn't do great things for my pride. Still, I repeated my wish. "Go out with me."

Her mouth opened and shut in the most adorable way. Well, it would have been adorable if I couldn't see the clear war of emotions crossing her face. Just another nail in the coffin of my heart. But that was good for me to see. Maybe if I could watch how little she wanted to be with me, it would make it easier to do what I had to.

"Carson," she finally breathed.

I shook my head quickly, not wanting to hear what came next. "Hear me out. Did you see what those guys did when I pretended to be your boyfriend?"

Slowly, she nodded. "They went away."

"They reacted *differently*."

"And?" She seemed confused. I had to get this through to her. Help her understand so it seemed like her idea.

"What motivates men?" I asked.

She shrugged and gestured at my half-eaten burger. "Food?"

A short laugh peppered out my lips. "That's a close second, but no. *Competition*."

"But what does that have to do with me dating you?" Her eyebrows were drawn together.

"Fake dating," I clarified, as much for me as for her. "If Nick thinks I'm dating you, he'll be jealous. And you know what jealousy does?"

"Turns you green?" she teased, shifting uncomfortably in her seat.

"It makes you *move*," I said, waiting for the idea to find purchase.

"So you think if I *fake* date you, Nick will suddenly be interested?"

I nodded, my stomach churning no matter how much of a good idea this was for both of us. "Nick will see what he's missing out on, and he'll have to make a move."

"He'll know we're just friends, though," she argued, clearly not sold on the idea.

"Friends become more all the time." I shrugged. I'd been hoping for just as much myself. "I don't see why it would be impossible for us to do the same."

"I don't know. It just...doesn't seem like a good idea."

I leaned forward, catching her blue eyes in mine. It made my heart stutter, stumble, but I pressed forward. "You wanted me to help. Now you have to decide. Do you want it?"

She chewed on her bottom lip. "You really think it will work?"

"I know it will." Because I had to make it work. There had to be a way for me to excuse myself from Callie's life before we became just another couple ruined at the hands of the Cook Family Curse.

She reached across the table and extended her hand. "Deal."

Ignoring her hand, I stood and slid into the booth next to her. If this was going to happen, I would make the most of it. I would dream while I could before my heart had to face the consequences. "Rule number one, boyfriends don't shake hands." I slid my fingers through hers. "We hold them."

Chester chuckled. "About time you made a move."

SEVENTEEN

CALLIE

Instead of going back to the house to hang out, we decided to head to Emerson Trails and go on a walk. That was safer than being at home where anyone could have overheard what was coming next. Carson and I agreed that we needed to talk more about how we were actually going to make this work. We'd been best friends for so long, and I'd steeled my heart so thoroughly against dating him, the idea of faking feelings with him seemed as possible as me throwing on a pair of tennis shoes and running a marathon.

We started down the north trailhead at Emerson Trails, which was usually less crowded than the other main paths. That suited me just fine because the fact that I needed to have a pretend boyfriend was embarrassing enough.

As I got out of the car, I glanced over at Carson. He'd somehow secured a bag of gummy worms and had one half dangling out of his mouth.

"Seriously?" I asked. "Are you always eating?"

"Or thinking about eating," he said.

I rolled my eyes and continued toward the path. It wasn't fair. Even when I'd been working out regularly, eating food like that would make me gain weight just by looking at it. Carson practically guzzled high fructose corn syrup and popped a few extra abs after.

Our sandals flopped against the trail as we walked side by side. The trees slowly became more densely packed, and the silence was audible. This was big, what we were about to do. Not only would Carson and I go somewhere our friendship had never gone before, he'd be committing his last summer in Emerson to dating me, closing down the possibility of love. And, no matter how much I hated to admit it, he'd be giving away his chance to spend time with his aging grandparents. Even if I wanted him around, I couldn't ignore what he was giving up.

"Carson," I said, "you don't have to do this if you don't want to."

He shook his head. "I want to."

The surety in his voice was impossible to argue with. When Carson made up his mind, I knew it was better to just go with it than try to argue. Instead, I smiled over at him. "I don't know what I would do without you."

"Probably go hungry." He gave me half a smile and extended a gummy worm my way.

I laughed and bit it in half, chewing over the sweet flavor. There was another downside of all of this that I hadn't considered. "My parents are going to freak."

"You're eighteen," he said. "It's not like they can ground you until college."

"No, but they can say that you're not allowed to come over as much or hang out in my room... or stay in our house."

The corner of his lips pulled down as if he hadn't thought of that yet. "Robert wouldn't turn me away."

"I don't know," I said. "He's pretty protective."

"Well, if that doesn't work, I'll rough it on Beckett's couch. Or maybe Kai will let me stay in one of his fifteen extra bedrooms."

This was all seeming like too much. "Are you sure?"

He nodded. "It's just for a little bit, and then we'll be off to Stanford, right? When the summer's over, we can say it was weird to be boyfriend and girlfriend after being just friends for so long and go back to how things were."

But why did he sound so sad as he said it? Why did I feel so sad about it? "That's a good thing, right?" I asked for both of us.

The way he forced a smile and nodded told me he wasn't saying everything on his mind. But part of me was afraid to know the truth. Maybe a part of me was too desperate to just have someone think I was beautiful. To see me as I was and not what I could do for them.

"Okay, boyfriend," I said, "how are we going to make this work?"

He kicked a rock ahead of us, and it skittered down the dirt trail. "Well, if we want it to seem real, we have to tell everyone."

I raised my eyebrows. "Everyone?" The thought of lying to my parents, Joe, Nick, and my friends made my stomach turn. Maybe this wasn't such a good idea after all.

"We can start by making it official on social media?" he suggested.

"And then get like a million hurt text messages about it? I don't want to keep it secret from everyone anyway. Can't we at least just tell my friends about the arrangement?"

He raised his eyebrows. "Jordan has the loudest voice ever, so no way it'll stay a secret. And Zara is going to say how stupid it is right away, then Rory and Ginger will turn. They totally won't go along with it."

Carson made a fair point. Jordan's voice did carry, and Zara had been rooting for Carson and me to date for months. "But won't they be upset when they find out we lied to them?"

"No one has to know we lied," he said. "Remember, we're going to have a breakup. And we won't be dating long enough for anyone to get that invested in Carsie."

I gave him a look.

"Okay, Callon."

I rolled my eyes. "The issue is not with our 'ship name."

"Then what is it?" he asked, taking another gummy worm from his bag and biting it like this arrangement between us wasn't going to change everything.

"How can you be so laid back about this?"

He stopped and smoothed his hands over my shoulders. "It will just be for the summer, and then we can go to Stanford and have a fresh start where no one knows us as Callon or Callie or Carson. You'll be the best piccolo player in the marching band, and I'll be the hottest guy on the swim team. Our fake relationship will just be a blip in the grand scheme of our lives."

The thought of this major moment being just a blip sent my mind spinning. I shook my head and reached into the bag for another gummy worm. "You're crazy."

"Crazy enough it just might work?"

I shrugged and continued walking. "I still have no idea how we're going to get anyone convinced that we're actually boyfriend and girlfriend and not just hanging out like always."

We came to a big tree fallen across the path, and Carson jumped over it, then extended his hand for me. He looked into my eyes and said, "A little touch goes a long way."

So I placed my hand in his and stood on the

tree trunk. He reached out and picked me up, lifting me and then setting me gently on the ground.

My heart fluttered. Carson hadn't picked me up before, except when he gave me a big hug on graduation day and excitedly spun me in a circle. But I wasn't used to him helping me like that. Or putting his arm around me like he had in the diner. Could I handle this without spiraling back to having a crush on him? "What kind of touch are you thinking about?" I asked, regaining my distance.

He put his hand on my lower back, gentle and soft. "Maybe something like this?"

My stomach swooped at the contact, and I stepped away, unsettled. "You're going to get sticky gummy worm all over me," I hedged.

He laughed and shook his head. "I promise to wash my hands before touching Her Royal Highness."

"Good," I said. But what I was really thinking was that I would have to find a way to smother my reaction to his touch, or find a way to be okay with never having a chance with Nick.

EIGHTEEN

CARSON

Putting my hands on Callie like I had always dreamed of had been the sweetest form of torture. There was probably an extra circle of hell where they punished you with someone you could never— and should never—have.

I was still thinking about what it felt like to slip my fingers through hers when Mom snapped her fingers at me at the hotel breakfast table.

"Earth to Carson," she said.

I blinked quickly. "Sorry, what's up?"

"I was just asking if you'd given any thought to where you wanted to go next. I want to be sure to give Gramps and Grandma plenty of notice if that's the way you want to go. They're not exactly spring chickens anymore."

I snorted. "They've been to thirty states in their RV in the last two years. They would have plenty of energy for me," I said. Then my stomach bottomed out as I realized anywhere I went, I would be a burden. With my mom, she'd have to keep track of me while she moved from job to job. With my grandparents, they would give up the freedom of traveling during their twilight years. With Callie, her family would be supporting me, and with Beckett, I'd be crowding up their living room.

"I'd love to have you come with me," Mom said, picking at her biscuits and gravy. "It might be our last chance to spend time together."

The vulnerability in her voice hit me deep, but I sat, frozen. Would I see her again? Would I choose to visit the woman who kept me under the roof of an abusive father? I honestly didn't know.

Slowly, she sat back and said, "You want to stay here."

There was no denying her statement. I already knew I couldn't leave Callie. No matter how much better for her that would have been. A part of me still selfishly wanted to be near her this one last summer, even if I couldn't call her mine.

Mom nodded. "I'm assuming you'll stay with the Copelands."

"I don't know if that will be an option," I answered slowly.

"Did something happen?"

I shook my head.

Her expression transformed from troubled to ecstatic. "Are you and Callie *dating*? You have to call and tell your sisters! They are going to be over the moon about this."

I smiled along with her and nodded, because I wanted there to be at least one reality where a relationship with Callie was possible.

"I knew it," she said gleefully. "I just *knew* you two were meant to be together."

Her words caught me off guard. I'd heard similar from my friends and hers, but never from my mom. "What do you mean?"

"The first moment you told me about her, I could see it in your eyes." Her expression turned somber. "When Cook men fall in love, they do it for life."

I knew she hadn't meant to drive the stake further through my heart, but she had. She just reminded me why I needed this fake relationship to work for Callie. She deserved better than a life with the curse.

I pushed back from the table and said, "Better get to work."

Up in the room, I put on one of the new suits I bought. The floral one Callie had picked that looked good, even if I'd never admit it. I drove to the pool. Since I was eighteen now, I could use it without a lifeguard present and get my workouts in.

I shucked my shoes at a chair and jumped into one of the lap lanes. I threw myself into the exercises my college coach had given the team, just wanting to escape for a little bit.

Swimming did the trick. My lungs were burning, and my muscles ached, but my mind was blissfully numb. At least for now. Knowing my shift was coming up soon, I got out of the water and went to the locker room to rinse off. Before work started, I needed to get in touch with Beckett and see if I could stay at his place.

Once I finished rinsing off, I sat on a locker room bench and fired off a text to Becks.

Carson: Let's hang out after work?

Beckett: Come to the bakery when you get off. I can take a little break.

After my shift at the pool, I drove across town to Seaton Bakery. They made the best cupcakes, and now that they made donuts, I was pretty sure there was no better place to grab breakfast.

Usually I listened to music as I drove, but today I couldn't bring myself to turn it on. So much was up in the air, and I just felt lost.

Through the big windows, I could see Beckett walking around the dining area with his camera. He took photos for their social media and website and had even started a series on their regulars.

When I walked through the door, he pointed his camera at me, and the shutter sounded.

"No pictures please," I said with an exasperated smile.

He batted his hand at me and said, "That one was already perfect anyway, pretty boy."

I rolled my eyes.

"Grab something to eat, and I'll come sit with you," he said.

I followed his directions and got a cupcake heaping with frosting, along with a donut and a hot chocolate. It was hot outside, but the AC in here was ice cold.

I took a warming sip of my cocoa on the way to the table and sat down. As I peeled the wrapper off my cupcake, Beckett slid into the seat across from me and took a bite of his own cupcake.

"How's it going?" he asked.

I shook my head. "It's a long story."

Through a mouthful of food, he said, "I'm pretty much done here. Tell me."

Raking my hands through my hair, I unloaded everything to Beckett—even the part I was afraid to tell Callie. All I held back was the fake dating part, but finally I had to tell him the truth I hated. "I'm just like my dad, and Callie deserves better."

Beckett swore low, shaking his head. "You aren't like your dad."

The resolution in his voice took me off guard. Made me angry even. "How can you say that? I would have *killed* him."

"You didn't," he said easily. Like we weren't talking about murder.

"But I wanted to," I gritted out. "My mom had to stop me."

"You *let* her stop you." He leaned forward, resting his elbows on the table. "You and I both know your mom isn't strong enough to hold you back. If you really had it in you, if you had really wanted to kill him, you would have done it."

I wanted so badly for his words to be true. But

even if they were and I wasn't as bad as my father, I was close enough to know Callie deserved better. "I just need a place to stay for the summer," I said.

"Done," he replied. "Our couch is yours. Heck, you can probably take Dad's room. He's gone most of the time with football season gearing up anyway."

My chest got that tight feeling again. This time with gratitude. I didn't deserve the wholehearted way he welcomed me into his house, but here he was, just like Callie, giving me all the chances I'd never earned. "Thank you," I managed.

"No problem. Actually..." He reached into his pocket and began fiddling with his keys. "Take this. I'll be out with Rory tonight, but you can make a copy for yourself and let yourself in whenever you need."

I took the silver key and held it tight. I didn't know how, but someday, I'd pay Beckett back for the kind of friend he was to me.

NINETEEN

CALLIE

Carson parked in front of the animal shelter for my first day of work. I usually volunteered here every other weekend, but I couldn't wait to start my full-time summer internship to see what it was like to manage a shelter and be responsible for so many hurting animals.

Every animal in that place had been discarded somehow—neglected or abused, dropped off by a former owner, or in some of the saddest cases, left behind by an owner who had passed away. In some ways, I felt akin to the animals, wanted to pour all of my love into them.

Carson killed the engine and said, "Ready for your first official day?"

I nodded. "I'm excited. You really didn't have to drive me, you know."

"Well, you weren't ready to tell your parents or anyone yesterday. I figured today would be a good way to ease you into it."

"True." I had put off letting my family know, but Lorelei, the shelter owner, already knew Carson and loved him, so it should be simple to just walk in holding his hand. Right?

He opened his car door and said, "Let me come and open the door for you. I'll look like a jerk if I don't."

"So chivalrous," I teased.

With a chuckle, he pulled his keys and got out before walking around the front of the car to my side. He was wearing the board shorts we bought the other day and a white tank that had a plus sign with the word "GUARD" on it. He was already tan, but by the end of summer, his skin would be a deep hazelnut color. Then I realized I'd been staring at him for way too long.

He opened the door and smiled at me. "Hi, girlfriend. I definitely just saw you a minute ago, but I'm really happy to see you now."

Laughing, I rolled my eyes. "So you're the

doting kind of boyfriend? How did Sarah deal with you for so long?"

"She didn't." He took my hand to help me out. "She knew I was in love with you, remember?"

His words kicked the butterflies in my stomach into high gear. I tried to remind them this was all for show. As I got out of the car, I could already feel everyone's eyes on me from inside the broad windows of the animal shelter.

"Remember to breathe," Carson said low.

I realized that I hadn't been and took a deep breath. Carson opened the door to the animal shelter, and I was immediately comforted by the familiar smell of animal dander and the soft song of quiet mews and dogs' paws on the floor. I loved it here.

"So, I see you're holding hands?" Lorelei asked from the front desk.

I grinned at my boss and the paisley bandana she had around her neck. "Grooming day?"

"Of course," she said, "but don't dodge my question."

I looked at Carson, who was smiling wide, playing the part perfectly. "We're together," he said.

"Oh, I am so happy for you two!" she cried, coming to give us both a big hug. Her curly hair itched my cheek, but I didn't mind. I was glad she was happy for me. I didn't think I could handle lying *and* disappointment at the same time.

"Thank you," I said.

She stepped back and looked Carson over. "I'm guessing you're not coming to volunteer today?"

"No, ma'am," he said. "Just dropping off my girl."

"Ew," a voice said from behind us. "'My girl'?"

My eyebrows raised because this was the one safe haven I thought I had away from *that* voice. Away from the person attached to it who ruined my life. But when I looked over my shoulder, there she was. Merritt Alexander.

Lorelei chuckled. "Still a little burned on love after what happened to your brother?"

Merritt shook her head and put a full-wattage grin on her face. "No, I'm just teasing my *good* friends."

Lorelei clapped her hands together. "I was hoping you would know each other!"

"Of course," Merritt said. "We went to school together."

"That's what I thought," Lorelei said, folding her arms over her chest.

I still wasn't tracking. "Are you coming to look

for a cat?" I asked. I didn't add that she had enough cattiness to go around. She didn't need any added to her house.

"No," Merritt said, pushing up her designer flannel sleeves. "I'm here for my first day of my internship."

"Internship?" I croaked.

"Yes," Lorelei said. "My niece needed a summer job that would look great on her resume, and we definitely need the help. It'll be great to take some of the pressure off you and the part-time volunteers."

"Niece?" I asked, still stuck on that word. How did Lorelei and Merritt even live on the same planet, much less share the same blood?

"Yep. On her father's side. Aka my little bro." Lorelei went and put her arm around Merritt's shoulder.

Merritt laughed but gave a disgusted look when Lorelei wasn't looking. "So, *Auntie*, what's on the agenda today?"

Lorelei had a plotting grin. "A little team bonding the old-fashioned way. Nothing makes fast friends like holding down an eighty-pound dog for a shave."

My eyes widened. "A full shave?" We never did

that unless the fur was matted beyond repair, but the animals always *hated* it. Sometimes we even had to sedate them.

Lorelei nodded. "We got a dog in this weekend, and I've tried bathing him and even conditioner, but it's just not happening. We need to shave his coat."

Merritt looked revolted, but I was honestly sad. That poor animal must have been really neglected and scared.

"Well," Carson said, "it looks like you guys have plenty on your plate." He bent and kissed me on the cheek, then whispered, "Call me when you're done." His breath tickled the spot where his lips had been, and I felt a shiver go down my spine. Would I ever get used to Carson kissing me? Even on the cheek?

"I'll see you later," I managed, and he gave a short wave before walking out the door. And then it was just Lorelei, Merritt, and me. I hadn't stood this close to Merritt in a long time. Not since junior high when she started calling me The Thing.

My scalp itched just thinking about it.

Lorelei grinned between us. "I am so excited to have you two working together. My dynamic duo. Merritt, if you don't already, you are going to absolutely love Callie. She is *so* good with the animals.

Callie, I really think Merritt can help us get some of these animals into homes. What did you say, Mer? That you had like a thousand friends on Twitter?"

Merritt closed her eyes like what Lorelei had said had physically pained her. "I have a hundred and fifty thousand *followers* on *Instagram*."

"Even better," Lorelei said. "Cal, why don't you show her around the shelter while I finish getting the grooming room ready?"

"Merritt hasn't been here before?" I asked. I mean, I kind of knew the answer, since I'd been here a ton over the last couple years, but I had to know why she'd gone from having nothing to do with the shelter to working here full-time.

Merritt put on a disappointed face. "I've always been too busy with cheerleading to be able to volunteer, but now that I don't start cheer practice at college until July, I have some free time." She didn't add that the last place she wanted to be was here. I might not have known her the best anymore, but I knew she hated places like this. Too many opportunities to break a nail and no one around to inflate her ego.

Lorelei gave us a wave before walking away, and I started toward the kennels without another word. I couldn't believe I was working with *Merritt*. The

whole reason I loved this job was because I didn't
have to work with people like her. Or people at all,
really. The animals couldn't talk back, couldn't say
anything mean, and if they were acting badly, it was
because they didn't know better.

Part of me wondered if I could find an internship somewhere else. I hated the thought of being
around Merritt's torment, especially since I knew
Lorelei wouldn't be able to supervise every moment.

I fought to keep my voice level as we reached
the back of the shelter. "This is the storage room
where we keep all of the food for the animals. Some
of them have special diets where they can only eat
soft food, and you'll find that in the fridge here." I
knocked on the old white refrigerator.

Merritt leaned against the door frame,
observing her nails. "So, you and Carson? It's about
time."

Brushing past her, I said, "This way." I walked
toward the dog cages to introduce her to the
animals. "Each dog has a kennel with a comfort
item, food, and water. The big dogs have access to
runs outside, and we walk the small dogs multiple
times daily." I glanced at the cage where I'd first
seen Gertie, and my eyes watered. I was glad she'd
found a home with a single older woman who doted

on her like crazy, but I still missed her. Franklin would probably be gone soon, but I couldn't think about that. Not without crying, and I wasn't going to do that in front of Merritt.

I came to my favorite dog in the shelter, an old chihuahua with gray hair and a pink bow tied around her neck. "Hi, Barbie girl," I said. She came closer to the door and let me reach my fingers in and scratch her neck.

"Let me pet her." Merritt pushed me out of the way and reached her fingers through the wires, making Barbie snap at her and bark like crazy.

I did my best not to laugh as Merritt jerked her hand away.

"Terrible animal," Merritt said. "I don't know why my aunt loves these things so much."

I opened the latch on the gate and reached back to retrieve Barbie from the corner she was hiding in. I held her to my chest and gently scratched her ears. "You just scared her," I said, turning back to Merritt. "Here, let her smell your hand."

"She's not going to snap it off?" Merritt asked. "I'm so not losing a finger over this."

I did my best not to roll my eyes. "She's a chihuahua, not a pit bull." I stepped closer, and Merritt extended her perfectly manicured fingers to

Barbie, who sniffed them curiously. Apparently deciding Merritt was okay, Barbie licked her fingers.

Merritt yanked her hand away. "Dog slobber doesn't exactly go with this outfit."

Shaking my head, I pushed forward with the tour. I held Barbie as I led Merritt through the rest of the shelter. There was the cat room, where close to fifteen cats had all the space to play and rest and scratch. They had a big window on the side of the building where people passing by could look in on them. Then there was the operating room, where Lorelei could provide healthcare to the animals. We even had a small room with couches and toys where families could spend time bonding with their potential new pet to make sure it was a good fit.

I seriously loved this place and the thoughtful way Lorelei had set it up to save animals and give them a chance at a family. The shelter hadn't opened for the day yet, but soon we would have visitors coming through and looking at the animals. Helping them find their new homes. And even though I didn't like Merritt, I had to admit, I really hoped she could follow through on her promise and help these animals find the place where they belonged.

"Callie! Merritt!" Lorelei called. "We're ready for you."

By "we," I hoped she meant her and the dog, not her and another Voldemort-esque co-worker to torture me with. But knowing Merritt, her best friends/evil sidekicks, Tinsley and Poppy, would be coming by any moment.

I gently put Barbie back in the cage and promised her I'd be back soon, then led Merritt over to the grooming room.

What looked like a goldendoodle that had never been groomed in its life sat atop one of the tables, clipped to the stand. His hair was so dirty and matted it hung in dark gray tangles. Despite looking worse for the wear, he gently swung his big head toward Merritt and me, then sniffed the clippers Lorelei held.

Since Lorelei was a veterinarian, she was also really skilled at grooming and animal behavior. What I loved about her the most, though, was that she would just jump in and get the work done, no matter how "beneath her" some people might have thought it.

"Look at that sweet boy," I said softly, going up to Lorelei and the dog. "Have you named him yet?"

Lorelei grinned at me. "Roomba. Because I

was having a snack earlier, and he sucked all the crumbs off the floor before I even had a chance to move them away."

I giggled. "It sounds like a good name."

Merritt stayed quiet, standing a few feet behind me.

"I'll go and get the cleanup gear," I offered and went back to the closet in the corner of the room that held the broom, dustpan, and a hand-held vacuum cleaner. As I went, Lorelei flipped the buzzers on and got to work trimming back Roomba's coat.

He became a little nervous when she got near his feet, so I went by his head to practice the hold Lorelei had taught me. But he was so big that I needed a little bit of help.

"Merritt, come over here," Lorelei said.

Her eyes were wide. "I thought I was just watching today."

"No better way to learn than to dive on in," Lorelei said. "Come on."

Merritt cautiously stepped closer, tiptoeing over the dirty hair on the floor, and begrudgingly followed Lorelei's directions. Once we both had our arms wrapped around the dog, Lorelei resumed trimming. In no time at all, it looked like an entire goldendoodle had shed on the floor, and there was a thin animal standing in front of us with close-cropped, curly hair.

"He's beautiful," I said, taking him in.

"And smelly," Merritt grumbled.

"He'll make a fine dog," Lorelei added. "Why don't you two go ahead and give him another bath, and then bring him out to a run so he can get some exercise."

I nodded and helped Roomba down from the grooming table. Taking ahold of his collar, I walked him to the shower stalls in the corner of the room.

The door shut as Lorelei left, and from a few feet behind me, Merritt said, "Are you really doing this willingly?"

Just the sound of her voice was making my psoriasis itch. I gave her a sideways glance over my shoulder. "Yes, I wanted to be here." Until I found out you were coming, I didn't add. "I like helping animals."

She shook her head like I was a lost cause.

As I led Roomba into the bathing stall, I couldn't help but ask, "Why are you really here? Surely there were a bunch of other internships your dad could have gotten you."

Merritt rolled her eyes. "He said I need to be

getting some good PR for our family. Especially right now."

Of course her being here was a chess move in a perverse game of power and control. The shelter wasn't a game though. There were living beings here looking for families, recovering from hurts. The last thing they needed was another person who didn't care walking through their lives.

I couldn't hide the disgusted look on my face, so I turned back to Roomba and showed him the showerhead, just as Lorelei had with the clippers. Then I turned on the water to warm and got to work scrubbing him. He was still so dirty that the water ran brown on the floor. This would take a long time without help, scrubbing his thick coat. "Jump in any time, Merritt."

She looked at me over her cell phone. "I'm not getting wet."

I rolled my eyes. "It's just your hands that are going to get wet."

"No way. You might be used to hanging around shaggy dogs like Carson, but I am not."

Anger welled within me, a practically foreign feeling. I'd been embarrassed before, disappointed, sad, dejected, hurt, but never *angry* like I was at Merritt for insulting Carson. Without thinking, I turned the spray of water at her and completely drenched her, phone and all.

She looked just as shocked as I felt, her hair limp and her mouth hanging comically open as she stared back at me. "What did you do, fish skin?" she wailed.

What *had* I done? My mind was short-circuiting at my actions. I'd never treated anyone like that. Guilt drenched me just as the water had done Merritt. I attempted to sputter out an apology that was basically just the word sorry a bunch of times.

Her eyes narrowed at me, her black mascara streaking down her face. "You are so going to pay for this."

As she stormed away, I looked down at Roomba. He had his big dark eyes turned on me, but I could have sworn he was smiling.

TWENTY

CARSON

Mom asked Dad out to supper. She said she wanted to talk things over with him and give me a chance to get to the house without him being there, but part of me was terrified. Not that he would hurt her, but that she would fall back into her old habits. She'd said she was done too many times before and kept going back to him. Would the same thing happen again?

I slowed my car and stopped along the street in front of the house. I couldn't bring myself to park in the driveway. That was something you did at home, and this was the furthest thing from that. I got out of my car and leaned against it—I couldn't quite bring myself to go into that house right now.

There was so much hurt buried within those walls I could practically feel its aura surrounding the house.

"Hey, Cars!"

I glanced over and saw Joe and Nick walking toward me with a rugby ball.

"Getting some practice in?" I asked. They played on the club rugby team at Brentwood U, and Joe had gotten kind of freakishly buff for how much time he spent playing video games.

"Heading to the park for a pickup game," Joe answered. "Wanna come?"

Nick nodded his approval. "Should be fun."

Just the sound of Nick's voice grated against my ears. But that probably had more to do with the fact that Callie liked him than the way he actually sounded.

"I gotta grab some stuff."

Joe frowned, and he squared his shoulders. "Everything okay?"

I glanced from him to Nick, not sure if I wanted Nick to know about the messed-up family I came from. But then again, there was a pretty good chance Joe had already told him. It wasn't like my parents were great at keeping their secrets. It had taken all of five minutes for Callie's mom to decide I needed a friend, to welcome me into their home.

"I'm moving out early," I said shortly.

Understanding crossed Joe's expression. "We'll help you grab your stuff." He looked over his shoulder at Nick. "Text the guys and tell them we'll be a little late."

"Sure," Nick said, already on his phone.

Joe tossed the rugby ball into his yard and started toward my front door. "Come on, man, I saw your dad leave. Let's get this over with."

My eyes heated, and I cleared my throat, following him. Nick didn't need to see me fall apart.

Inside, I grabbed a box of garbage bags from under the sink. Joe stared around the living room, his eyes landing on a hole in the drywall. That was from the time Dad threw the end table. He had thought Sierra was staying out too late with her boyfriend. He accused her of things that made my skin crawl.

"Come on," I said, heading toward the stairs.

Joe and Nick followed me up the stairs, and I tossed each of them a black bag. "Grab stuff from the dresser."

I went to my closet and started loading shoes and hanging clothes into my own bags, not even bothering to take them off the hangers. I wasn't sure how much time we would have, so we needed to be quick. If Mom stuck to her decision to leave, there was about a fifty percent chance Dad would get pissed halfway through the meal and storm out.

"What next?" Joe said.

I looked around my room, trying to decide what more I needed other than my clothes. There wasn't much in this home for me. I'd trade it all for the kind of life Callie and Joe lived any day of the week.

"The pictures," I said finally.

"I got it," Nick said.

He reached atop my dresser, taking the framed photos of Callie and me. I watched as his eyes lingered on them for a moment longer than necessary.

Suddenly, I felt caught, realizing that my plan would work. That there was something there between Nick and Callie. And even though I should have been happy, I felt sick instead.

"We're good, other than that, Cars?" Joe asked.

Swallowing down acid, I nodded. "Let's get out of here." I grabbed two loaded bags, and the guys took hold of three more before we hurried down the stairs. We needed to be fast.

My heart was racing, terrified of what would happen if Dad came home to this. I knew I could take him, but I didn't want to. Didn't want another reminder of just how alike we were. Especially not in front of the guys.

We walked out the front door, Dad's car nowhere to be seen, and shoved the bags in my trunk and backseat.

Joe looked at the open trunk and said, "Why aren't we bringing them to our house?"

I felt Nick's eyes on me as heavy as the guilt in my chest. "I can't," I said finally.

"Why not?" Joe demanded. "We have that extra room for you."

I was tired of the lies, of the secrets. So I told him the truth. "Because I'm in love with Callie."

Joe's blue eyes were somber as he nodded, but Nick's expression was veiled. What did he think about that? And why did it bother me so much that I couldn't tell?

Tires screeched at the end of road, and my heart dropped into my throat. My dad saw me, and he was on his way.

"GO!" Joe said, shoving me toward the driver's seat, shocking me into motion.

As the car hurtled down the street, I sprinted for

my own and took off. Part of me worried Dad would follow me, bash his car into my own, but I just kept my eyes forward and slammed the gas pedal to the floor. I took our neighborhood streets as fast as I could, and when I hit the main road, I drove even faster until the ocean came into view. Somewhere, I lost Dad, but I kept driving anyway. Sometimes it just felt good to escape, even if you didn't know where you were escaping to.

TWENTY-ONE

CALLIE

Some time with my girls was in order after the kind of week I'd had. From finding out about Carson's mom to having Merritt invade my space, I was having trouble finding my footing. We sat around Rory's studio, using watercolor pencils to make our own creations. Before I broke the news about my relationship, I started by telling them about my new co-worker.

"You're working with who?" Rory demanded, shocked.

I looked away from the mess I had on my own paper. "Voldemort."

"You might as well be," Jordan said. "Why is

she even interested in working at the animal shelter?"

Zara swallowed the caramel-dipped apple slice she was chewing on. "She's probably going to suck their blood."

"You know it's about status," I told them, running my pencil in an arc over the page. "She's just doing it to make her family look good."

Ginger shook her head, just as disgusted by that as I had been. "Are you going to find a different job?"

"I don't know." I sighed. "Zara, big movie producer. Any need for a semi-talented teenage girl on set?"

She laughed, waving her pencil through the air. "We're only the first day in, and it's so much more than I know what to do with. I'm still trying to understand the book we're adapting and figure out how to work with my dad."

"Is everything good between you guys?" I asked. They had been fighting so bad just months ago that Zara had lived with Jordan for a while.

"He's reading a lot of self-help books if that tells you anything."

I laughed and shook my head. "My dad just reads philosophical stuff. Like about how to be a better Christian or improve the world around you."

Ginger snorted. "That's better than obsessively reading food labels. My mom still has to make sure that everything that goes into our house is perfectly organic. Which is weird now that my boyfriend's a cowboy."

"True," I agreed and then sighed. "Maybe I should start reading self-help. Lord knows I'm going to need it if I keep working with Merritt."

Rory set her beautiful water color drawing of a sunset aside. "Why would you need help? You're basically a saint."

"Actually..." I began, and then I told them the story about spraying Merritt.

Each of my friends thought that was the funniest thing they'd ever heard, and Rory was still wiping tears from her eyes when she asked, "Did you get in trouble?"

"No, I told Lorelei it was an accident, and she gave Merritt an extra pair of clothes that they keep on hand for volunteers."

Jordan snickered. "I bet she loved wearing something without a label. That someone else had worn before, no less."

Actually, the sight of Merritt in an extra-large

T-shirt and sweatpants held up by a string was going to be something I remembered for the rest of my life, but I still felt guilty. "I have no idea what came over me."

"Did she say something to you?" Jordan asked, leaning back against the wall.

I looked up at the ceiling, the one blank space in Rory's studio, and groaned because I couldn't tell them what Merritt had said about Carson without telling them that Carson and I were dating. Fake dating, but Carson thought they didn't need to know that. And I wasn't going to do anything to jeopardize Carson's help because I knew I needed it if I was going to have a chance with Nick.

Out of the corner of my eye, I saw Rory lean forward. "What *did* she say?"

I let out a sigh. I might as well tell them now, before Merritt had the rumor going around social media.

"Carson and I are dating," I said. And if I thought that me spraying Merritt with a hose had gotten a reaction, this was ten times elevated. They were each grinning and cheering, and Rory said, "Should I break into my parents' liquor cabinet and get some champagne?"

My cheeks were blushing bright red, partially

because of the lies and partially because of how excited they were. Didn't they see that Carson and I were just friends? That it would be weird for me to think of him as more than that?

Ginger scooted over to me and put her hands on my shoulders. "Callie, we have been waiting for you and Carson to start dating since we all started hanging out together. You guys are *made* for each other."

I shook my head. "You're all crazy."

"But I don't understand," Jordan said. "What does this have to do with you spraying Merritt?"

I closed my eyes, more embarrassed now. "She called him a shaggy dog."

Laughing, Zara snapped her fingers. "No one better mess with Callie's man."

Fake boyfriend or not, I thought.

Ginger patted her lap excitedly. "You know what this means, right?"

"What?" I asked.

"Quintuple date!" she cheered.

Zara grinned, Jordan clapped, and Rory nodded eagerly, leaving me as the only one not completely thrilled by the idea. "How is that going to be any different than normal?"

"Because," Ginger said, "we're all in *love*." She waggled her eyebrows.

"Hold your horses, cowgirl," I said. "We *just* started dating."

Ginger nodded approvingly. "Nice ag pun."

Shaking my head, I said, "It's still so new with Carson and me..." I didn't want them to get too invested in *Callon*, only to get their hopes dashed when things worked out with Nick. He was the one I wanted to quintuple date with.

Jordan put her finger thoughtfully to her chin. "It's not really that new, though. You and Carson have known each other forever."

"Yeah," Rory agreed. "You guys probably know each other better than any of us and our boyfriends."

Zara waggled her eyebrows. "Speak for yourselves."

My cheeks heated as I laughed. "I do know a lot about Carson. Like the fact that he goes to the bathroom at exactly 6:03 every morning." The girls laughed. "*And* that he takes one bite from each item on his plate and cycles through an *entire* meal that way."

Jordan sighed dreamily. "That *is* romantic. You

know each other better than anyone else, and you're still choosing each other, flaws and all."

Which was exactly why a relationship with Carson could never work. On the off chance we were attracted to each other at the same time, we would know too much. There would be no mystery, no excitement. Even if him holding my hand sent my heart into a frenzy.

Of course, I couldn't tell them this because it would break Carson's rule. So my friends and I continued creating art, them thinking Carson and I were in love, and me wondering if they would ever forgive me that we weren't.

TWENTY-TWO

CARSON

After work, I dropped my bags off at Beckett's house. The idea of rolling into their penthouse with garbage bags made me feel like the trash the bags were meant to carry. Thankfully, Beckett and his dad were gone, so I could tuck the bags mostly out of sight. Even with my things here, this place didn't feel like home. To be fair, my own house didn't feel that way either. No one I loved lived there. My mom would be leaving the next morning, and I would be in Emerson, on my own.

I sat down on the couch, the idea of sleeping here for the next couple months both depressing and exhilarating. Beckett's dad didn't throw half-empty beer bottles at the wall. He didn't slug his son's face. I could practically taste the freedom I had been craving.

Except being here, working the twisted plan I'd created, didn't feel like a success. In gaining what I needed, I'd also lose what I wanted. Callie. But like Beckett said, if I loved her, I had to let her go.

My phone vibrated in my back pocket, and I pulled it out, hoping for a call from Callie. The name I saw on the screen was just as good.

I swiped right and held the phone to my ear. "Gramps! How are you?"

"Good," he answered in his low, comforting voice. "Grandma's here too."

"Hi, sweetie," she cooed.

For a moment, I had a flash of regret. I could be far away from this mess in Texas with my grandparents, being loved like I hadn't in years.

"We heard you decided to stay there," Gramps said.

My throat felt tight, so I swallowed to clear it. "I did."

Grandma said, "I was hoping to have a grandchild around to spoil! It's been months since I've seen Clary's sweet babies!"

I scratched at the back of my neck, feeling guilty. Mom and Dad might have moved us here to help our family, but Grandma and Gramps were the truest family I'd ever known. They'd lost just as much in the move as my sisters and I had.

"Maybe I can come for a weekend soon?" I asked, trying to hide the hope in my voice. I missed them on a visceral level.

"We'll do you one better," Gramps replied. "We decided to drive our camper up there for a week before you start college. Kind of a last hurrah. And then we can go wherever you want. Yosemite, Yellowstone, Washington Mountains. You name it, we're in."

My eyes stung at the care in his voice and the prospect of getting out of here. By the time Callie and I would leave for college, she and Nick should be solid, while my heart would be solidly broken. Spending time with my grandparents would be just what I needed.

"It sounds like a plan," I said. "I can't wait."

"Us either," Grandma said. "And you give us a call if you ever need anything. Your mother said you're staying with a friend, but sometimes friends make the worst roommates."

"She would know," Gramps said with a chuckle. "Going on fifty years living with her best friend now."

Their banter just made my eyes sting worse. I rubbed at them, trying to shove back the thought that I may never have the kind of marriage they did. That I may not be capable of one.

"Sorry, I gotta go. Love you guys."

"We love you too," Gramps said, and I hung up the phone.

At least now I had something to look forward to, an escape plan aside from going to the dorms and starting practice for the swim team with Callie on the same campus. I'd have a week, a break, some time to just be with the people who loved me no matter what.

I don't know how long I sat on the couch, but eventually the light outside became weaker, and I decided it was probably time to go before I had to see Beckett and explain why I'd zoned out on his couch for so long.

I went to the elevator and took it down to the parking garage where my car waited. I opened my phone to call my mom and see what we were doing for our last night together, but there was already a text from her.

Mom: Meet me at La Belle? At 8?

I checked the time and saw I had just long enough to get there on time.

Carson: See you then.

On the drive to La Belle, I thought about my family. We *never* went out to eat. Even on the rare nights when Mom was around, we'd order in pizza or make one of those frozen lasagnas that never tasted as good as Grandma's.

Once I was older and had a little spending money, I'd gone out with the football team after games or out to eat with Callie and our friends. But hardly ever with Mom. Was it weird that I was so worried about it? She'd asked Dad out to eat when I went to get my stuff. Was there something off about this?

I shook my head. This was my mom we were talking about.

I finally reached the Italian restaurant near Emerson Shoppes and parked along the street. The main street here was made of bricks, and the twinkle lights hanging in the front patio made the place look peaceful. Maybe I should take Callie here on a date.

Mom waved to me from a bench near the front

door. She still had on her work clothes but had at least shucked the white coat. It was always weird to see her in that.

Once I reached her, she stood and gave me a tight hug.

I swallowed hard as I returned it, knowing it might be one of the last I got for a long time.

"Thought we should celebrate our last night," she said.

The hope in her eyes filled me with relief. This wasn't a set up at all. It was a going-away party.

We went inside, and she encouraged me to order way more than I normally would. Pasta, bread, apps, fancy virgin drinks the football guys would tease me about, and more dessert than I could even dream of finishing.

With cannoli crumbs and half a chocolate cake in front of me, I leaned back in the booth, wishing it wouldn't be strange to unbutton my pants in public. "I'm so stuffed."

"Me too." Mom's eyes lit with a smile.

There was something else about the way her lips lifted. "You're excited, aren't you?" I asked.

It was hard to keep the accusation out of my voice, but I must have managed because she nodded and said, "I am. This will be the first time in twenty-six years that I've done anything without your father."

I couldn't fault her excitement for that, not when I was hoping for some space myself. But still, a little bit of guilt for my father hit me. "What's he going to do? He can't afford the house."

She cut her fork through a piece of cheesecake. "We're selling the house, and he's moving back to Texas."

No matter how casually she said them, her words hit me like a punch to the gut, and that wound just spread anger within me. Here I was with Mom, trying to pick up the pieces of our lives, trying to help my best friend have a chance at love, and my dad could just move on. Go back to where he started and just wash his hands of all of us.

"What, honey?" Mom asked.

I shook my head. "It just doesn't seem fair. He gets to go back to Texas like nothing ever happened, and we have to deal with what he left behind."

Gripping my hands across the table, Mom said, "He is not, and never will be, free of the pain he caused us."

I looked into her eyes. "Neither will we."

Immediately, her gaze shifted to the table, and

she pulled her hands into her lap. She knew I was right, but didn't want to admit she had a hand in causing our pain.

The rest of our meal passed in silence, and when we walked outside, we stood awkwardly on the sidewalk in front of our cars. Mom looked so much younger than she had these last few months. Even the circles under her eyes seemed to be lighter.

She was going on the adventure I was hoping college would be for me, and I was happy for her. I was.

"I hope you find everything you're looking for," I said.

"You're not coming to the hotel?" she asked.

I shook my head. It was time for both of us to move on. She pulled me into a hug and kissed my forehead. "I love you, precious boy," she said and stepped back. "There's something special in you. I can't wait for you to see it."

With that, she walked to her car and gave me a wave before backing out. I couldn't bring myself to leave, not yet, so I began walking the sidewalks around the restaurant. This part of town was well lit and always had a steady stream of activity this time of night. Still, I wandered aimlessly, not ready to face my new situation, the fact that a couch would be my home.

I found a bench across the street from a fancy restaurant and sat down, watching the couples go in and out. They looked so perfect. So happy. And it gutted me that I'd never be that guy walking in there with Callie on my arm, smiling at me like I'd invented chocolate mousse myself.

My phone vibrated in my pocket, and I pulled it out.

Callie: So, day one. A success?
Carson: Definitely.

TWENTY-THREE

CALLIE

Carson agreed to come over the next day after we both got off work. He'd been pretty monosyllabic since we told Merritt about us "dating." To be fair, we hadn't talked on the phone or anything, just texted.

Maybe he was as nervous as I was. Telling my friends was one thing—but my family? Nick? I didn't know if we could pull it off.

I glanced at the alarm clock by my bed. He should be getting here any minute now. Careful not to wake the sleeping dog on my lap, I leaned over my desk and looked in the concave mirror, applying another layer of mascara. When we told Nick, I wanted to look good. Fabulous. At least improve the last memory he had of me in my yellow shower cap.

Footsteps sounded in the hallway, and Carson came into my room carrying a plate of cookies.

Franklin jerked away and gave a warning bark, but the second he saw it was Carson, he settled back down. I absently scratched my neck as I craned to get a look at the cookies. "What is it this time?"

Carson held up an orange triangle that looked somewhat like a carrot. "Vegetables."

I laughed. "I need at least three servings a day, right?"

"They *are* a part of every balanced meal." He handed me a radish and a celery stalk to go with the carrot.

I laughed and took a bite. "Mom's definitely getting out of her comfort zone."

Franklin growled at me, and I broke off a tiny piece of cookie to give him.

"You spoil him," Carson said and sat on my bed.

I scratched Franklin behind the ears. "You don't have a problem with it, do you, boy?"

He snorted happily, his tongue lulling out of his mouth.

"Should I give you two a room?" Carson teased.

"This is it," I said, gesturing around my room.

Carson shook his head, muttering, "Crazy dog lady." While he continued working his way through the platter, I finished putting on my eye makeup. I never wanted to be seen in front of Nick without it again. When I was done, I turned to face Carson and nibbled at my "celery."

"So," he said, "are we doing this thing?"

"You mean lying to my parents?" Why didn't we just call it what it was? Because playing pretend with Carson had my stomach in all sorts of knots.

He swallowed his bite. "Don't forget your brother and the guy you say you're in love with—for whatever reason."

Although he said it lightheartedly, it really bothered me that Carson didn't seem to like the one guy I'd had a crush on. (Other than him, but he didn't need to know that.) Carson's opinion was important to me, and I wanted my first boyfriend to be Carson-approved. "What's wrong with Nick?"

"You mean besides his obsession with killing fictional characters?" Carson shucked his sandals and leaned back against the wall, crossing his legs. "Come on, why do you like him anyway?"

My cheeks felt hot at being put on the spot. My crush on Nick was hard to explain without telling

Carson where it began. That I let myself fall for Nick so I could finally stop falling for him. Nick was no Carson, but he had so many good qualities. Like... "Do you remember when Joe's appendix ruptured last year?"

Carson nodded.

"Nick stayed with him in the hospital the entire time. Didn't leave once, not even when my mom said he should go home and shower or when we had all of our family in there. He stayed, for Joe."

Carson's face stayed expressionless.

"And it's not just that he's a good friend to Joe— like you are to me. He writes poetry, and supports animal shelters, and he has these beautiful dark eyes that—"

"Okay, I get it," Carson said, leaning forward. "But you're telling me there's been no other guy that you've been even remotely attracted to up until now? Because you've never told me about a one."

Instead of telling him the truth, I capped my mascara and said, "It's complicated."

"How complicated can it be?" he challenged.

Complicated enough to ruin our friendship. But I didn't say that. I said, "Do you really want me to get into it?"

"Tell me," Carson said. "Why is it so important

for *Nick* to like you? Why can't you just be yourself and wait for a guy who will appreciate you the way someone should?"

My eyes stung, and I shook my head. "You don't get it. You've always been attractive and had girls all over you. It's not like that for me. I'm The Thing, remember?"

Carson rolled his eyes. "That's just a dumb nickname you got in middle school. You can't tell me you're letting twelve-year-olds determine how you feel about yourself now?"

His words hit home, and I shook my head, blinking back tears. "It's fine. We don't have to do this. I'll tell my friends and Merritt it was all a joke."

The tears were coming harder now, and I wished more than anything they would stop. Franklin nuzzled closer to me, sensing my unease, but it just made me more upset. Even this poor wounded dog was worrying more about me than himself. I kept my eyes closed, trying to stem the flow, to keep my makeup from being ruined, but the tears just seeped through my lashes.

"Callie," he said gently, touching his finger to my chin.

"What?" I blinked my eyes open to see concern

and care on his face, matching the tenderness of his voice.

"I told you I would help you." He gave me a weak smile. "You're my best friend. I'd do anything for you."

I managed a smile of my own. "Same for you, Cars."

With a soft "Come here," he set Franklin on the floor and embraced me. He held me close before pulling back and saying, "Let's do this thing."

I checked my makeup in the mirror while he grabbed the plate, and together with Franklin, we began walking down the stairs. Even though my heart was racing, I knew I needed to do this. To get over Carson once and for all and find my own happily ever after.

I could hear his footsteps fall behind me, and it felt like each step he took matched the pounding of my heart. What would my parents say about Carson and me being in a relationship?

What would Nick think?

When we reached the bottom of the stairs, we looked around and saw no one was in the kitchen or living room, so we continued to the basement to find everyone sitting on the sectional, watching one of my mom's favorite British baking shows.

"This guy's totally going to win," Nick said, pointing at the middle-aged man on the screen.

"No way," Joe argued, "not with that sloppy form right there."

My mom chuckled, and Dad held her hand. It was sweet. Would the moment still be sweet after we told them?

Nick looked up at us first, his dark eyes taking me in. I felt completely bare under his gaze. What did he see? Did he like how I looked? Or would he have to overcome his distaste for my looks based on my personality if we were to have any chance at all?

My mom followed his gaze and smiled at Carson and me. "Want to watch the *Great British Baking Show* with us?"

"Sure," I said. Franklin wiggled in my arms, and I set him down so he could run to his favorite throw pillow.

"Actually," Carson said, taking my hand, "can you guys pause it? We have something to tell you."

TWENTY-FOUR

CARSON

I had to squeeze Callie's hand to keep mine from shaking. Everyone in the living room—Callie's parents, Joe, and the guy she loved—looked back at me expectantly. It felt like all the blood was draining from my face as I prepared to tell them the truth: that I was in love with Callie.

Callie's dad lifted the remote and paused the show. It was frozen on an old lady with her lips bunched up, clearly tasting something. I would much rather be in her position right now, because my stomach was becoming more and more knotted by the second.

"What's up?" Robert asked. "Everything okay?"

I looked to Callie. Everything was always okay with her at my side. For a moment, I stared into her deep blue eyes and found the courage I needed to tell them. "Callie and I are in a relationship."

Callie's eyes slid over to her family, and I followed her gaze to them, holding my breath.

A look of realization crossed Joe's face, and he immediately burst out laughing. Like loud, obnoxious laughter. He pointed between Callie and me. "Carson has been so deep in the friend zone, he might as well be wearing a dress. And he made it out?"

I squeezed Callie's hand tighter, if only to keep me upright. This was everything I'd dreamed of—getting out of the friend zone and becoming more. But this alternate reality was what I signed up for instead, and I needed to remember why. Callie deserved better than me for her future. She deserved more.

Callie's eyebrows came together in that adorable way they did when she was angry. "Why would you say that about Carson?"

Joe's smile faltered. "It's not that; it's just... I've seen you put makeup on him."

I shuddered. Why did he have to bring up that

snow day gone wrong? "Come on, man, that was one time in fifth grade."

"And remember last year when you guys dressed up as Charlie's Angels for Halloween and Callie's foster dog had to be the third angel?" Joe said. "Carson held her in your purse the entire night!"

"Joe, honey," Anne warned him.

I gave Callie a look. "I told you that was a bad idea."

Callie shook her head, then turned back to Joe, speaking forcefully. "Carson is the best friend a girl could ask for, and I'm lucky that he would even *consider* dating me."

Her words sent my heart twisting in all sorts of uncomfortable ways, like maybe she should just rip it out of my chest already, but I just held on to her hand for dear life. I would make it through this. I had to.

Joe seemed to sober. "So this is real."

But it wasn't Joe who Callie was looking at as she answered. She gazed directly at Nick and said, "I'm with Carson."

Her words found their target, as Nick straightened and forced an unconvincing smile.

"Well then." Robert stood up and walked over

to us, clapping my shoulder. "Guess you two aren't allowed in the same room by yourselves anymore."

Callie squeezed my hand, like a silent *I told you so*. She smiled at him and said, "Really, Dad?"

He reached out for a hug and took both of us in his big arms. "No," he said, "I'm happy for you two!"

Finally, I relaxed.

Callie's mom came next, wrapping me in a tight hug. Robert's eyes stayed lovingly on his wife as he said, "Marrying my best friend was the best thing I ever did."

Anne cleared her throat. "Not that we're saying you two should get married right now. That can wait a few years."

My eyes widened, and I looked at Callie, who was also obviously taken aback by her parents' reactions. But their support almost hurt more. Like they thought I was good enough for their daughter and all I'd done was disappoint them and myself. If they knew who I really was, the curse that I carried, they'd be telling their daughter to run as far and as fast as she could.

"Look at the time," Nick said. "I better get going home." He waved at Callie and me. "Congratulations."

I couldn't help but grin as he retreated up the stairs and out the door.

As her parents turned back to the couch, I gave Callie a nudge and mouthed, *It's working.*

She grinned back at me. "Time for our first date?"

The words gutted me with pain and hope, and all I could do was nod.

Callie said to her parents, "We're going out to eat. Can you watch Franklin?"

"Sure. Just be back by eleven," was all her mom said. I could hardly believe it. In all that time I pictured dating Callie, I had never imagined a world in which her parents were *this* supportive. Part of me wondered what could have happened if Sarah had never pursued me like she did, if I hadn't agreed to date her. Would I have followed through with my plans to tell Callie the truth of how I felt about her? Or would I have chickened out like I had the last several years?

I didn't know. All I knew was I had Callie's hand in mine and we were walking toward the door, toward our first date.

We got in my car, and she asked, "Where do you want to go?"

I already knew. I'd planned my first date with

Callie a million and one times, and now was my chance. The only problem was I hadn't been able to plan it long enough in advance for it all to fall into place. "Hold on," I told her and opened up my car door again.

"Where are you going?" she asked.

I held up my phone. "Gotta make a call."

She gave me a curious look but settled on fiddling with the radio. I shut my door and stepped away from the car, calling the place I wanted to take her.

They were open!

I turned away from the car and pumped my fist. Even if this wasn't a "real" date, I still knew Callie would love it.

When I got back in, she gave me a curious smile. "Where are we going?"

"You'll see," I said and put the car in gear. This place was a little bit of a drive, but we jammed out on the way like we usually did in the car. She was a terrible dancer, but seeing her move her body and do corny moves made my heart feel lighter than it had all week.

We were getting closer to our destination, and I peered out the window until I saw the sign that said Brentwood Puppy Rescue.

Callie's mouth fell open as she took it in. "The *puppy* rescue?"

The joy was so obvious in her voice; it brought an excited smile to my lips. "You've heard of it?"

"Of course!" she cried. "They rescue at least a hundred puppies a year, they perform pro bono spay and neuter clinics, they—"

"Okay, you're starting to sound like a brochure," I chuckled.

"But what are we doing here?"

This was the good part. "The owner agreed to let us come in and play with the puppies!"

Her eyes brightened like a kid on Christmas morning, and she fumbled with her seatbelt, rushing to get out of the car. "Let's go! Let's go!"

Chuckling, I got out of the car myself and followed her to the front door. I rang the bell, since it was after hours, and someone dressed in a Brentwood Puppy Rescue polo answered the door.

"Carson?" he asked, making his beard wobble.

I nodded, trying not to laugh.

"Come on back."

We followed him into a brightly lit room with several kennels setting out. There were multiple families of puppies and even a few mother dogs who had been brought in with their litters. Some looked like they had just been born, but he led us back to a kennel that had what looked like a dozen spotted puppies inside.

"Heelers?" Callie squealed.

The guy grinned at her and opened the gate. "Good eye."

The puppies crashed out of the kennel, romping with each other and coming up to lick our feet. Callie sat on the ground, holding them and snuggling them, so much love in their eyes. "I feel like I'm cheating on Franklin."

"I think he'll forgive you," I said with a chuckle.

"I'll leave you two to it," the guy said. "Call me when you're ready to go."

I slipped him a twenty. "Thanks again."

He left us in the room, and I sat next to Callie, rubbing a puppy with red and white spots. "They're so cute."

"They're perfect!" she squealed, hugging two to her cheeks. "Best first date ever."

"And it's not even over yet." I scratched the puppy's soft, squishy belly, and it rolled on its back, blissfully flopping its leg back and forth.

"There's more?" she asked.

"Of course. I'm going to be the best fake boyfriend you ever had."

For the next hour, we played with the puppies, seeing how many we could hold at one time, giving each of them silly voices and personalities, and talking about what kind of dog we wanted when we were out on our own.

"You have to have a golden," Callie said.

"Really?" I asked, frowning.

"Why is that such a bad thing?"

I shrugged, keeping my eyes on the puppy in my arms. "Golden retrievers are just so... typical."

She rolled her eyes. "What kind do you think I should have?"

"Poodle, obviously." I nudged her. "So high maintenance."

Giggling, she said, "No, really. What kind of dog am I?"

"A human one?"

She gave me a playful shove.

"I don't think it matters what kind of dog you have because you have a habit of giving everything more love than it could ever imagine."

Her lips pulled up in a slow smile, and she nuzzled her cheek against the puppy. "Thanks, Carson."

I smiled and nodded. "Any time. But we should probably get going so we don't break curfew."

With a nod, she began picking up the puppies and putting them back in the kennel. At first, it was kind of like herding cats, but she did it with impressive skill. I shut the gate behind them, and we stood up, brushing puppy hair off of us.

We found the guy in an office, and he let us out the door before locking it behind us.

"Where to next?" Callie asked. "Heaven?"

I opened the car door for her. "Almost," I said. "Waldo's."

Her eyes lit up as she sat inside. "Strawberry milkshake?"

"Could you imagine anything better?" I teased.

"Nope." She buckled herself into her seat and smiled contentedly.

"Good," I said and shut her door. The first date was going exactly how I had planned, and it wasn't even over yet.

TWENTY-FIVE

CALLIE

This had already been the best date of my life, and it wasn't even really a date. Even though I knew it was all just for show, I couldn't help but feel sad that this relationship and the way Carson was treating me wasn't real. Would Nick ever be so thoughtful? Ever know me as well as Carson did?

But then again, wasn't that the best part of a relationship? Getting to discover someone and know and love them for who they were? I shoved those thoughts to the back of my mind. Spending time with Carson didn't used to be so complicated.

I glanced over at him. He had one hand on the steering wheel and the other on the center console. His shaggy, sandy-blond hair swept over his forehead, and the evening light hit his green eyes, making them look pale.

Again, I felt a pang of guilt. He could have been dating anyone this last summer before college, having a fun fling or finding true love, and here he was with me.

My heart warmed, making my lips smile. I reached across the console and took his hand. "Thank you. You're an amazing friend."

Gripping my hand back, he winked and said, "Make that boyfriend." Still smiling, he parked in the crowded lot in front of Waldo's Diner and turned off the car. "There's going to be more people in here. Are you ready?"

Nerves sparked in my stomach, but I nodded anyway.

"Let me get your door," Carson said. "People might be watching from inside."

As he walked around to my side, I steeled myself for the eyes that were sure to be on us. Waldo's was always packed with people our age on a Friday night. Even if Nick and Joe weren't here, being seen together in public as a couple would go a long way toward making our relationship look real.

Carson opened my door, and when I got out, he slipped his arm easily around my waist like we'd been doing this for years. "Now," he said, "smile like you're about to get a strawberry milkshake. Because you are."

I giggled and shook my head. "Thank goodness for milkshakes."

He opened the door for me, moving his hand from my waist to tangle his fingers with mine. We walked into the restaurant together, and just like I'd expected, chattering filled the air, and there was hardly an open booth. We waited for one to have the dishes cleared off, and then I slid into the seat. Carson sat right beside me, his muscled leg pressing against my own.

"The same side?" I asked. "Isn't that a little corny?"

Putting his elbow on the table, he turned and locked eyes with me like we were the only two people there. "Is it a crime to want to sit close to my girlfriend?"

The serious way he said it and the way his eyes trailed to my lips made my heart beat faster. "You're really good at this."

A waitress named Betty approached, and Carson ordered for both of us like the guys do in romantic black and white movies. Once she walked away with our order, a high-pitched voice I wanted to forget said, "Beauty and the Beast are together?"

I closed my eyes, knowing wherever Poppy was, Merritt and Tinsley were sure to follow.

Carson gripped my hand under the table and said, "I know I lucked out with this one." He nuzzled his nose against mine, and little butterflies erupted in my stomach.

Merritt came to stand beside our table, along with Tinsley and Poppy, and said, "You know we were calling you the beauty, Carson. How did she finally convince you to date her? Is she paying you?" She leaned forward and whispered. "Holding you hostage? Should we find you a hotline to call?"

Carson rolled his eyes. "Sounding a little jealous, Merr."

She let out a short burst of laughter that was too loud. "So she's drugged you, for sure."

Tinsley and Poppy cackled along with her.

Chester walked up to our table. "Lovely couple. You know when my Karen and I were dating, they put actual drugs in the soda?"

Merritt groaned. "And dinosaurs walked the earth?"

Poppy giggled. "Too bad they missed the asteroid."

They had crossed a line, and I was going from embarrassed to downright furious. I opened my mouth to put them in their place, but Carson said in a deadly voice, "You better watch who you insult."

"Oh yeah?" Merritt folded her arms over her ample chest. "And why is that?"

Betty stepped around the counter with our drinks and stood behind Merritt, saying, "Because we choose who we serve around here."

Merritt's eyes narrowed to slits as she said, "Come on, girls. Just *wait* until Daddy hears about this. He'll have this place closed down in two seconds flat."

The door clanged shut behind them, and Betty stepped forward with our drinks. "Good riddance. You okay, Ches?"

The old man nodded. "I'm more worried about these two." He nodded toward Carson and me. "You shouldn't have to listen to that."

Betty set our cups down, mine an overflowing strawberry milkshake and Carson's a sweating sweet tea. "Kids can be so cruel."

"So can adults," Chester said. "But I better get home for the day. Karen's done with her volunteer shift, and we have a kitty to spend time with."

My eyes lit up. "You got a kitten?"

"We did." He let out an exasperated sigh, but there was still a smile in his eyes. "It's the love of my wife's life."

The waitress chuckled. "Sure it is. Now get home to your girl, kitten."

As Chester and Betty walked away, Carson grinned at me and said, "Looks like we've got some allies for Team Callon."

With a smile, I shook my head and sipped at the strawberry shake. This was just round two with Merritt. Betty brought our food, and as we ate, I told him about round one, spraying her at the shelter.

He laughed so hard tears dripped from the corners of his eyes. "Aw, Callie, you didn't need to defend my honor."

My cheeks heated, and I said, "Hey, it was mine too. I don't want people thinking I'd date a shaggy dog."

He barked at me and pretended to sniff at my shoulder.

Laughing harder, I shoved him away. "You're crazy."

He waggled his eyebrows. "Crazy about you."

From beside our table, Ginger's younger sister,

Cori, stood with some of her friends holding to-go cups and said, "Could you two be any cuter? Ugh."

Her friends echoed her, and I grinned back at them. "Hey, Cori, how's your summer going?"

"Good," she answered with a grin. "Living the life. *Single* life, unfortunately."

Carson smiled at her. "You'll find someone when the time's right. Just like I found Callie."

Her friends awed at him, and Cori covered her heart with her hands. "See? Adorable. I'm going to leave before I get a tooth ache."

She and her friends left in a heap of sighs and giggles, and I gave Carson a look. "Laying it on a little thick, aren't you?"

He lifted his chin toward a couple of guys our age sitting along the counter. "They keep looking back here. Checking you out. I think I'm laying it on just thick enough."

I followed his eyes to the boys, and I almost couldn't believe him. They were cute. "They were looking at me?" The one on the left had some serious back muscles showing through his shirt. I was pretty sure he was on the weightlifting team at Emerson.

"Of course they were," he said. "You're beautiful."

My heart warmed at his words. "You might just be the best boyfriend I've ever had."

"I'm the only boyfriend you've ever had."

With a smile I shrugged and looked toward the ceiling. "Details, details."

"Well, hold the praise until you see where we're going next."

I couldn't wait.

TWENTY-SIX

CARSON

Sitting in the car with Callie, I could smell her perfume, and it was intoxicating. We'd been together before, but it was like I was smelling her for the first time. Maybe it was all this date stuff that was making my mind go into hyperdrive. Whatever it was, I kept breathing it in, savoring it, because I knew this couldn't last.

Then I realized what a creep I was for sniffing my best friend like she was some kind of candle in Bath and Body Works. I needed to get a grip on myself, and fast, before I forgot that this was fake to Callie.

I pulled up to Beckett's apartment building, and

Callie gave me a confused look. "What are we doing here?"

"This is where Beckett lives," I said.

Her eyebrows came together in the cutest way. "We're telling Beckett about us in person?"

With a smile, I shook my head. "Even better. Come on."

We got out of the car, and I led her toward the elevator in the parking garage. Using the key that Beckett gave me, I unlocked the elevator button labeled **R**.

Her eyes widened as she took in the lit level. "We're going to the roof?"

I nodded.

The indicator in the elevator changed from **12** to **PH** to **R**, and the doors opened to a terrace filled with greenery and twinkling lights. It was beautiful up here—I could tell from the way Callie's hands covered her mouth and her eyes shining right along with the lights and stars.

"How does a little stargazing sound?" I asked.

"Amazing," she answered, lowering her hands.

Even though there wasn't anyone around to impress, I took her hand, and she let me. This was our dream date, and I wanted to experience it fully with Callie, even if it wasn't "real," even if it wouldn't last. Even if it was the only time.

With our fingers laced together, I led her around a planter, revealing the nest of blankets and cushions I'd asked Beckett to set up for us. Even though it was late May, the ocean blew cool air over the coast at night, and I didn't want her to get too cold.

The second our fingers slipped apart, I felt her absence, but I tried not to lament that fact as I lay back on one of the cushions. She lay beside me, settling in.

"We can't see all the stars, since there's some light pollution, but we can at least see some of the major constellations," I said. "You like it?"

"I love it," she breathed. "I can't believe you set this up."

When she said things like that, my chest seemed to swell, like I was the strongest man in the world, just because she believed in me.

For a moment, we lay there, the breeze sweeping around us as we stared up at the sky. There were a few constellations I could point out. Orion's Belt was always the first thing I saw when I looked at the sky, but Callie quickly found Cassiopeia and Mars.

"Would you ever live on Mars?" I asked. "I heard they're sending people up there soon."

"They always say that," she replied.

I rolled my head to the side and looked at her. "Would you, though?"

She turned her head toward me, hair falling over her cheek, and smiled softly. "It depends. Would you come with me?"

Her words caught me off guard, and I had to take a deeper breath to reply, "Of course."

"Then sure," she said. "Remember our promise?"

"Wherever you go, so do I," I breathed. If only she knew how much of a bad idea that was for the both of us. That I would someday have to break it for her well-being.

"Exactly." She rolled her head toward the stars. "Besides, if I'm not around, who's going to tell you to get a haircut?"

My lips twitched. "You have a problem with my long hair?"

"Of course not. But then again, I take care of stray dogs, remember?"

"Ha." She was only teasing, but it cut a little too deep. For a little while, I focused on the sky, on the stars and how small I was in this big world. If I remembered I was small, maybe these feelings wouldn't be so big.

We were quiet for a bit, looking at the stars, thinking our own thoughts, and then Callie whispered, "What's next?"

"We make it official." My voice was hoarse as I breathed the words I'd been dreaming of saying for so long. "Callie Copeland, will you be my girlfriend?"

Her breathing was ragged, and then she replied, "Of course I'll be your fake girlfriend."

The response tore me apart, but I forced a smile as I reached for my phone and swiped to the camera. I held it out and took a picture of us, her hair splayed around us as we grinned into the camera. Her smile lit the screen bright enough to hide the light that didn't quite reach my eyes.

Once the image was frozen, saved forever, I went to social media and made it official. The public start of my own personal heartbreak.

TWENTY-SEVEN

CALLIE

When I woke in the morning and checked my phone, my eyes nearly bulged out of my head.

Hundreds of people had commented on my new relationship status, saying they loved *Callon* as a couple, that they'd been expecting this for years, and cheering Carson on for "finally" making it out of the friend zone.

That last one rubbed me the wrong way for so many reasons. First of all, Carson was a catch. Just a year ago, I'd been hoping he'd even consider dating a girl like me. And now that I was trying to be satisfied with our *platonic* relationship, everyone acted like there was something wrong with me? Why didn't anyone think it was possible for a girl and guy to just be friends? If Carson and I were happy with our friendship, why couldn't everyone else be?

I locked my phone screen and got out of bed, dreading yet another day at work with Merritt Alexander. After getting dressed, I padded downstairs and went to the kitchen, pouring myself a bowl of cereal.

Mom was on the phone, talking about plans for a cookie bake-off benefiting Invisible Mountains, the non-profit where Dad was the CEO. From what I overheard, the event sounded fun. They were even trying to get a celebrity chef to make an appearance.

Once she hung up, she set the phone on the counter, then came to sit with me at the table.

"How's planning going?" I asked.

"Good, but I'm worried we won't have enough contestants."

"Carson and I can compete," I offered. "And I bet I can get the girls to join in."

She smiled. "You think so?"

I grinned, nodding. "Maybe we can even get some other kids from the Academy too."

Her eyes lit up. "That's a great idea, Cal!"

My heart warmed from the inside out. Helping

people felt amazing—I loved feeling like I'd made a difference in someone's day for the better. "Want me to put it out on my social?"

Nodding, she said, "That would be great. Let me get you a link to the sign-up page."

She stood and went to her phone, typing in the information, and my phone went off with her message.

While she poured herself a cup of coffee and came to the table, I posted it online, hoping this would get Mom some more volunteers and maybe get people to move on from my relationship news.

"Are you okay?" Mom asked. "You seem a little off."

I glanced up from my phone and tried to gauge her expression. I knew she was busy dealing with the fundraiser, but the idea of going to work with Merritt was weighing on me.

"Is it about Carson?" she asked. "That was some big news last night."

Her question caught me off guard, but now I was more than curious to know what she had to say. "Were you surprised?"

"No." She wrapped her hands around the coffee mug. "But then again, it is hard to see you as the young adults you are and not two kids digging in my flower beds for worms so you could catch some fish in the ocean."

"We never caught anything," I said, smiling at the memory.

"That's not the point of fishing," Mom said. "Your father could tell you that."

I dipped my spoon through my bowl of cereal, letting the milk wash over each piece. "Merritt Alexander is working at the shelter."

Mom's eyes widened in realization. "It's been a big couple of days for you then."

I nodded. "I don't want to have to deal with her. She already insulted Carson, and it's a hundred percent clear she doesn't want to be there. I almost want to quit and see if I can find something somewhere else so I don't have to see her every day."

"Hmm." Mom thought for a moment, drumming her fingertips on the table. "Do you want to vent, or do you want advice?"

"Advice," I said immediately. I could complain about Merritt until I was blue in the face, but it wouldn't accomplish anything.

She nodded and took a cautious sip from her cup. "You know the right thing isn't always the easy thing."

I cringed but nodded.

"I have a feeling Merritt has been through a lot more in her life than she lets on. And you being a friend to her, showing her grace even though she doesn't deserve it, well, it could change her life."

"And if it doesn't?" I asked. "What if she just makes my life miserable all summer?"

"That's her decision. It shouldn't keep you from doing what you love."

The meaning behind her words stung deep. Mom had always been disappointed that I gave up sports, but sometimes I hated to think who I might have become if I kept playing. Would I have turned out to be just another Merritt? Another jock who felt superior because of what I could do on the court?

I glanced at the clock on the stove and realized time was in short supply. "I have to go, or I'll be late."

She patted my hand atop the table. "I'm sure you'll make the right decision."

Mom seemed more confident in me than I did. But I got up, grabbed my purse, and started out the door anyway. On my way to the car, I glanced up to Carson's window on the side of his house. It was dark, just another reminder of how different things truly were.

As I approached Nature, I saw two kittens playing with each other in the windowsill of the cat room. The calico kitten tackled the small black kitten before the black kitten gained purchase and pushed back.

I smiled at them, and then a knock on the window jarred me. Merritt wore a frustrated look, along with a pair of yellow rubber gloves. Lorelei was having her clean the windows in the cat room? Classic. I had to hide a smile—that job was a nightmare with the cats crawling all over you and thinking the rag waving through the air was a toy.

Although Merritt was dressed in what I assumed were designer clothes, she looked about as frazzled as I'd ever seen her. She waved her hand like she wanted me to come in and mouthed, *Help*!

Stifling a laugh, I nodded. I tried to keep my mom's words in the back of my mind. A month ago, I might not have been able to even dream of a flaw in Merritt's absolutely perfect life. Now, I knew better. Her brother was still the talk of the news after a teenage girl turned him down for marriage, and their family was struggling financially. Maybe there was more I didn't know.

As I entered the shelter, I didn't see Lorelei sitting at the front desk, which wasn't that big of a surprise since she was usually working with animals or out trying to gain funding. I hurried back to the kitten room and found Merritt covered in cats. Well, at least her feet were. Four of them circled her, a kitten crawled up one pant leg, and she looked absolutely horrified.

I giggled as I walked closer and began peeling them off of her. "Just keep doing your work," I advised. "They'll get bored of you eventually."

She rolled her eyes. "Is that before or after they maul me?"

I looked down at the kitten climbing her legs and picked him up. "This little guy? I think you'll survive it." I rubbed my nose on him. "You're a big, scary kitty, aren't you? Aren't you?"

She gave me a sardonic look and continued cleaning the windows.

For a second I watched her, struggling with what to say, and then finally, I set the kitten down and said, "Hey, Merritt?"

She continued scrubbing and let out an irritated, "*What?*"

"I, um..." I absently scratched at my arm. "I'm sorry about yesterday."

Her hand froze on the windowpane. "It's okay," she said slowly.

"It's not," I said, "but I promise I won't do it again."

She began rubbing her rag in a circular motion again. "Well, I probably shouldn't have insulted your boyfriend like that. Or said what I did at the diner."

Merritt actually owning up to the fact that she did something wrong? This should be written in the history books, marked as the day everything turned upside down.

Still reeling from her almost apology, I said, "Okay, well, I'm going to go feed the dogs."

She nodded.

And that was that. I went to the dog cages and immediately got Barbie out. She'd been in the shelter for about a year, and even though she was a sweetheart to people she knew well, most visitors could not get over the fact that she had a tough exterior or advanced medical needs. If she didn't have to take daily insulin shots and have to be watched so closely, I would have brought her home to foster myself.

I held her in my chest as I continued doling out the right amount of food and water for each animal according to their dietary guidelines. I was happy to make sure that they had it and that they were in as good of shape as possible when they went to their new forever home.

When I was done making sure each of their dishes was full, I put Barbie back in her kennel and went to see where Lorelei was. I found her at the front desk now with Merritt, training her on the computer system. Roomba lay in a neatly trimmed pile at her feet. I smiled and went to him, scratching him behind the ears. "Looks like he'll make a lap dog yet."

Lorelei smiled down at him. "I'm starting to become very fond of him. But I'm not sure he would like the other four dogs at my house, though."

I shook my head. It was so crazy to me that Lorelei could have so many pets at her house. And she wasn't even mentioning the bird, turtle, mini pig and sugar gliders she owned. She was an animal lover through and through, and it was easy to see why. Sweet Roomba here, turning his big brown eyes up at me, was just one example.

Lorelei said, "Callie, any tips for Merritt before we start having people come in today?"

I tried to think about my encounters with potential adoptive families. "Becoming more comfortable with the animals is really important,"

I offered. "If you act afraid, the families will be too."

"That's a good point," Lorelei said. "But Merritt's not exactly an animal lover. Let's think about ways that she can contribute outside of positioning them or preparing them for adoption."

That made more sense. "Honestly, the paperwork is something I'd love to hand off, but I don't know how Merritt would feel about pushing paper all summer long."

"That's thoughtful," Lorelei said with a proud smile. "Why don't we start out with Callie showing people around, and Merritt completing the paperwork process? That way she can get skills on the back end of things before going more hands-on with the animals."

I nodded, simply because Lorelei was the boss. This shelter was Lorelei's baby, and I trusted that she wouldn't do anything to jeopardize it.

"I'm fine with whatever if I don't have to see the cats again," Merritt said, shuddering.

Soon, we got into the swing of people coming and going. There were plenty of parents looking for animals to keep their children busy during the summer. I loved seeing the smile in the parents' eyes as they looked on at the animal and noticed it bonding with their child. Those are my favorite moments.

We had a few rough ones too, like when someone moved too quickly to pet Barbie without getting to know her first or when a Great Pyrenees got too friendly and sat on a little two-year-old. (The two-year-old was fine, but the parents were shaken.) By the end of the day, we had adopted out three animals, but we had also gotten two more in. One step forward, two steps back.

I walked to the front door and slid the lock shut so we could begin cleaning up for the day.

"This is so slow," Merritt said, drumming her fingers along the countertop.

I shrugged. That was just the nature of this work. Most people didn't want to rescue a cat or dog; they wanted something that they could grow and shape into their own from a baby. As I walked past Merritt to feed the animals again, I said, "Good job today."

She gave me a stifled smile and said, "Thank you." It sounded like she meant it.

TWENTY-EIGHT

CARSON

As I pulled into the pool parking lot for my shift, I couldn't help but look around for my father. The sound of his wheels screeching on the pavement in front of our house and my heart pounding as Joe yelled at me to drive away was still fresh in my mind. My muscles were ready to spring into action at a moment's notice.

What would I do if he confronted me in person? His car was still there and the "for sale" sign was still up, according to Callie, which meant he had to still be in town. It bothered me in a visceral way that I didn't know where my own father was living, that I didn't know if I was safe, or if he was safe from me.

Shutting down that line of thinking, I turned off my car and shoved my keys into the red fanny pack I wore for work. Callie always made fun of me for it, but that thing came in way too handy to ditch it.

As I walked toward the pool building, I saw a mom with three kids trying to get all their floats and toys out of the car while keeping her toddlers reined in.

"Let me help," I said, reaching for one of the larger toys.

"Thank you." She sent me a grateful smile and passed me a couple more life jackets while she held one kid on her hip, grabbed another's hand, and had the third carry their pool bag.

"Mom," the oldest one said, "can we get some ice cream?"

"Ice cream! Ice cream!" the toddler yelled.

"Da da, da da," the baby copied them both.

We traipsed inside the building, a smile on my lips. Hearing the kids interact with each other and their mom made me miss my sisters. Maybe I could talk Grandma and Gramps into a drive to see Clary's family. If not, I'd talk to Mom about getting a plane ticket to visit since I knew none of them were coming back here.

We got through the doors, and Mrs. Mayes

signed the family in. I helped set their stuff at a table and went back to clock in and grab my guard float.

"How's it going?" Mrs. Mayes asked.

I shrugged, adjusting the straps over my shoulder.

"Saw you and Callie made it official. Where's your smile?"

Instead of smiling, my cheeks got hot. She was probably one of the million people who could see how much I loved Callie, and now she was one of the million who would get to watch my heart get split in two.

Mrs. Mayes grinned wide. "Always thought you two would get together. Didn't realize it would take you this long to make a move, though."

"You and me both," I muttered.

The other guard on duty called a safety break, giving me the perfect excuse to get in the pool and swim a few laps. While everyone got out of the pool, I set my float by the chair and peeled off my tank. The same college girls who showed up every shift I worked giggled loudly, but I ignored them as I slipped into the cool water.

I ripped back and forth down the lap lane, working as hard as I could so when my time was almost up my chest was heaving with the force of my breaths. With a couple minutes to spare, I pulled myself onto the side and went and sat in the chair. Several kids lined up along the water's edge, their eyes flitting between the clock and me.

With a chuckle, I made a show out of putting the float strap over my shoulders, clicking on my fanny pack, and dropping the whistle around my neck.

They jumped up and down, antsy to get back in the water. With a grin, I held the whistle between my teeth and blew. They crashed into the pool with cheers and shouts, and I paced the side, making sure everyone stayed safe.

The time passed slowly, but eventually the sky darkened, and it was time to close. Mrs. Mayes and I did all the regular things—checking the filters, putting away toys, locking up the cabana—and then it was time to go.

Was it sad that I felt safer having her walk alongside me to my car? My dad wouldn't make a scene in front of her. No, he'd rather protect his reputation than his children.

But when we reached the parking lot, I stopped, standing stock-still. Someone was leaning up against my car.

TWENTY-NINE

CALLIE

After I got out of the shower, there were several messages on my phone. I held it up, reading through the group chat.

Jordan: Want to come hang out at Kai's pool tonight? He and his dad are out of town, but they said we could use it.
Zara: YES. Ugh I miss having a private pool.
Ginger: Please? I'm so hot right now I'm practically a ginger snap.
Rory: LOL I'm in!
Callie: What time?
Jordan: Seven?
Callie: I'll be there.

I dug through my closet until I found an old swimsuit at the bottom. It wasn't really a swimsuit, more like swimming trunks and a tank top, but it was all I had. Swimming was honestly the last thing I enjoyed doing. Mostly because it meant showing off my skin, especially when I had a flare-up, leaving angry red spots on my skin. But it was just us girls, and after everything we'd been through this year, I knew they wouldn't judge me.

I put on the swimsuit and then walked out to my car. Carson was working now, and I was kind of glad for the break. Even though our relationship was fake, my mind was having a hard time remembering that. Getting out of the house and spending time with my other friends would be good for me.

I got into my car and drove across town to the ritzy neighborhood where Kai lived. His house was enormous. Not that my house was small by any means, but four of mine could have fit into his. I drove around the driveway and parked by the others' cars at the back gate. As I got out, I could already hear sloshing water and the giggles of my friends.

Taking a deep breath, I pushed through the gate just in time to see Rory do a giant cannonball off the side of the pool. I giggled at how carefree she was, especially since she had started dating Beckett. Even though he'd been our school's star quarterback, he never seemed bothered by her size or the fact that she wasn't the stereotypical idea of beauty. That made me like him even more.

As I got closer, I yelled, "Ten out of ten!"

She pumped her fist in the air, bobbing in the water, and then swam toward the edge of the pool where the other girls leaned against the stone lining.

"About time you showed up," Jordan called.

"I couldn't find my swimsuit," I said, gesturing at my shorts and tank and knowing full well it was all I had.

Zara, who rocked a one piece that was just as revealing as a bikini, looked over at me and said, "That can't be it?"

"Well, I don't normally go swimming."

Zara shook her head, clicking her tongue. "Girl, next time I'll bring you a real suit. You gotta show off those curves!"

I didn't think to tell her that there probably wouldn't be a next time. Me going out in public and baring my skin like this just wasn't a thing that I did, mainly because of my size and psoriasis.

Ginger tucked a red curl behind her ear and

asked, "How's work going? Have you murdered Merritt yet?"

Jordan snorted. "She did almost drown her."

My ears heated. "That was so unlike me. We've actually been getting along for the last week."

Jordan pulled herself out of the pool so only her legs were dangling in the water.

Zara did the same, waving her feet through the clear liquid. "You can't be serious. Merritt didn't pull anything?"

I shook my head. "She's not really great with the animals, but she does okay with greeting people for appointments."

Ginger seemed surprised but shrugged. "And how's your *boyfriend*?"

Just the word made my cheeks warm. "He's fine."

Jordan made a kissy face. "What's it like to kiss your best friend?"

I hadn't thought it possible, but my cheeks grew even redder.

Rory clapped her hands together. "That means it's good."

Shaking my head, I sat in one of the open chairs and got some sunscreen from my bag. As I rubbed the lotion into my skin, I asked, "Why is Kai out of town?"

"Business trip with his dad," Jordan said with a frown. "But it's fine because Mom and I have been getting tons of videos out for her YouTube channel."

"Is it still going well?" I asked. Last I heard, it had been making them enough money to actually begin investing in a retirement fund for Jordan's mother.

Jordan smiled and pointed at Ginger. "Thanks to that one."

Ginger's cheeks flushed under her freckles. "I've already told you it's no problem."

I smiled between my friends. If anyone deserved a good home, it was Jordan and her mom.

A small splash sounded as Zara dropped the rest of the way into the water again. She began swimming toward the other side, and Ginger dove after her, yelling, "Race ya!" As she went under the water, her curly hair immediately flattened around her.

They raced to the other side as we cheered for them, and then Zara yelled at me, "You getting in?"

I hesitated and finally shook my head. "I'm going to sunbathe for a little bit."

Jordan pulled her legs out of the water and said, "I'll join you."

"Suit yourselves," Zara said and elegantly dipped under the water, beginning to breaststroke back across the pool.

Jordan and I leaned back in the comfortable lounge chairs, and I closed my eyes, enjoying the feeling of the sun's rays gently caressing my skin. The longer I sat, the warmer I felt, and it was easy to just relax. For the last week, I'd been so tense, lying to my parents, trying to get Nick to notice me, and figuring out this new arrangement with Carson. For the first time in a while, I just felt like me. It had been far too long.

I let out a sigh, and Jordan shifted in the chair next to me so she was lying with her cheek on the backrest, facing me. "What's up?"

As she untied the back of her suit to prevent tan lines, I lifted the corner of my lips. "Have you ever felt like everything's the same, but completely different?"

"Yeah, that's kind of what it feels like to be out of high school. Like I should just be putting on my uniform and going back to Emerson tomorrow, but instead I'm working and getting ready for college."

I nodded and decided to tell her the truth. As

much of it as I could, anyway. "It kind of feels like that with Carson. Like we're dating, but he's still just my best friend."

"Dating *is* like being friends," Jordan said.

Since I'd never dated before, I had nothing to compare this to other than watching my friends and brother date and fall in love. Carson and Sarah never seemed like friends—they seemed more preoccupied with their bodies, with the PDA stuff. But then again, they'd broken up. I wondered if I would ever get to the point with Nick where I felt like he was a friend and not just some unattainable person in my brother's life.

"If you're just not feeling a ton of chemistry yet," Jordan said, "it will come. It just takes time sometimes."

Maybe that was the problem. I was feeling too much chemistry with Carson, and I needed to direct my energy toward something more possible. Toward Nick.

"Did it take time with you and Kai?" I asked.

"Hello," she said, "I hated him when I first met him."

I laughed, remembering how she complained about her now boyfriend the first day she and her mom were working to clean his house. "I'm pretty sure the words 'detestable Emerson rich kid' were thrown around."

She chuckled. "See? You already know you like Carson. You're a step ahead of where I was."

A nagging sense of guilt tugged at me. "He could be dating anyone else."

"But he *chose* to date you," she said. "I know you're so worried about meeting everyone else's needs, but maybe it's time you think about your own."

I lifted a corner of my lips. She was right. My whole high school career, I'd been worried about filling my time with community service, helping my dad with Invisible Mountains, serving with my mom at fundraisers, and doing my schoolwork. Soon, I'd be going to college and participating on campus there, working toward a veterinary degree so I could help animals like Lorelei did.

I had one summer, three months, to use for myself, and I needed to make the most of it.

THIRTY

My sister pushed up from the car and ran to me, wrapping me in a big hug.

I stumbled back from the force of her embrace and said, "Gemma? What are you doing here?"

As she stepped back, I heard the engine of Mrs. Mayes's SUV.

Gemma waited until she drove away to answer. "Dad called me crying, begged me to help him pack."

It had been a year since I'd seen Gemma, but she seemed so much older than me with her hair cut in a short bob and her clothes so much more refined than the T-shirts and leggings she always used to wear. That mixed with her words had me totally off guard.

"Dad was crying?"

She nodded, her eyes wide and pale in the streetlamps. "Said Mom surprised him with news about leaving and you beat him up then stole a bunch of stuff from the house?"

Acid rose in my throat. "Of course he said that."

"But that's not true, right?" she asked.

Her confidence in me nearly tore me apart. Almost as much as the fact that what Dad told her wasn't completely wrong.

"And now you're dating Callie!" Gemma continued, not needing an answer. "Are you staying with her family while the house sells? Is it awkward having Dad next door? Has he threatened you?"

I held my hands up against the rush of questions. "Are you hungry?"

"Always," she said.

"Why don't we grab some food and talk then?" I looked around for her car but didn't see any around. "Did you drive to town? Where's your car?"

She began walking to the passenger side of my car. "I flew in, and Dad picked me up. I told him I was Ubering back to the hotel, but figured I'd catch you instead."

I unlocked the car, and we got in. "And work? They just let you drop everything to come?"

"I brought my laptop to catch up."

"Of course." I smiled. Gemma had thrown herself into work, and I got it. I'd done the same with sports and school.

"Please tell me you're taking us to Waldo's," she said as I started down the highway. "Chester's still there, right? He has to be what? Ninety?"

"Eighty-four," I said with a smile. "And he's still there. Probably won't be this late, though. Gotta spend some time with the—"

"'Love of his life,'" Gemma finished, making her voice sound old and raspy like Chester's. She sighed with a soft smile. "I always liked knowing a love like that was possible."

My throat felt tight as I nodded. "Me too."

I pulled into the diner's parking lot, and I couldn't help but smile as I thought of Callie and her trademark strawberry milkshakes. Honestly, I thought the things were gross—chocolate was way better—but they could change her whole mood in two sips flat.

"You're smiling like you're in love," Gemma

said with a teasing grin. "Things are going well with Cal Pal?"

My lips twitched. I didn't really feel like talking about it. Not with Gemma. Not after being away from her for so long. "Let's talk about you," I said, unbuckling my seatbelt. My throat clogged as I told her the truth. "I've missed my sisters."

Gemma smiled sadly and put her small hand on my arm. "We've missed you too. We just couldn't stay..."

"Here," I finished. I got it—I was a casualty of their escape, but tonight I just wanted to be with my sister.

I opened my car door and got out. She smiled up at the sign written in sweeping cursive. "I've missed this place."

"It's missed you too." I put my arm around her and led us into the restaurant.

As I'd suspected, Chester wasn't in his usual booth, but my waitress from the other night was here—Betty. She welcomed us with a smile and asked if there was anything she could get for us. Gemma ordered a Mt. Dew, and I opted for a sweet tea. With all the swimming I was doing lately and the time spent out in the sun, it was hard to keep my energy up, so I took the extra calories where I could get them.

The TV in the corner of the diner played something completely innocuous about local squirrels and a nut shortage, and Gemma dreamily watched it.

"What?" I asked. "Suddenly take up an interest in woodland creatures?"

She chuckled. "No, it just seems like all the news in Manhattan is extremes, you know? So much good and bad happens that there's not time for anything in between."

I nodded, even though I didn't really get the fascination. I tried to stay away from the news—too much pain and mudslinging for me. I'd rather be out, living my life than hearing about other lives being destroyed.

And speaking of destroyed lives... "So what are you doing at Dad's house?"

She shrugged. "Apparently Mom offered to hire movers to get their things out and sold, but Dad didn't want strangers going through their stuff."

I rolled my eyes. "Typical."

"Yep. So I'm going to help him box up *his* things and get them loaded into a trailer, then let Mom know when the movers can come in to get the rest."

"Very practical."

She smiled, but it quickly faltered. "It was weird being in the house. Like I could feel the aura there."

"Aura? Come on," I teased, knowing I'd felt the same way before.

"Maybe it's just me feeling the memories again. It's like I've been away, created this life for myself, but the second I walked into the house, I was a little girl again listening to them fight."

That tight feeling was back in my chest because I knew exactly what she meant, except I'd never gotten the taste of freedom she had—could only cling to the hope of something more. I couldn't wait to move into my dorm at Stanford and know I had a space that was my own, free of my parents.

Gemma covered her mouth and pointed at the TV. "No way."

My eyes followed her finger, and I read the headline scrolling along the bottom. *BREAKING NEWS: Charles Alexander caught for insider trading.*

"That's Ryde's dad, isn't it?" she asked, but she didn't need to, because soon there was footage from a helicopter of police leading their father out in handcuffs while the family trailed behind, holding on to each other. The news anchor continued speaking. "Charles Alexander is a renowned financial banker on the West Coast, as well as the father of movie star Ryde Alexander and recent high school graduate Merritt Alexander..."

I covered my mouth, realizing one of the small blonde specks on the screen was Merritt.

"Looks like we're not the only ones with a sleazy father," Gemma said, turning to me.

For the first time in my life, I thought I might have more in common with Merritt than I did with Callie.

THIRTY-ONE

CALLIE

I got five texts at almost the same time as I lay in bed with my shower cap on, scrolling through social media. Franklin had nuzzled under my arm and was snoring away. That dog snored louder than my dad.

Carson: You have to check the news.

The next messages were from my friends.

Zara: Guys... Merritt's dad's being taken to jail.
Ginger: WHAT?

Jordan sent a screen shot of a news story saying Merritt's dad had been caught for insider trading.

Zara: The feds froze all of his accounts. Even money that Ryde gave them is tied up.

My mouth was slack as I read the messages, and my heart immediately went to Merritt. She may have had a large network, but that just meant more people had access to her for judgement and shame.

Not sure what I was doing, I pulled up a new text message and entered in the contact information I still had from seventh grade. No matter how Merritt had treated me, she deserved to have at least one kind message reach her eyes.

Callie: Merritt, I'm so sorry about what happened. Please let me know if there's anything I can do.

I hit send and hesitated. When someone was going through a crisis, the last thing they needed was to make extra decisions, to feel more vulnerable by reaching out for help that might get turned down. I typed out another message and hit send.

Callie: We have an extra bedroom if you need a place

to get away. I promise no one here will talk about what happened unless you want them to.

I knew Merritt probably wouldn't see my message amongst the hundreds she was surely getting, much less act on it, but it was the best I could do before seeing her at work. If she would even be there.

I wouldn't blame her for not showing up. I'd almost quit because one person I didn't like would be there, but hundreds of thousands of people knew she worked there now, thanks to her posts on social media. I cringed and sent a text message to Lorelei.

Callie: Let me know what I need to do on Monday in case things get crazy with Merritt.

Within minutes, Lorelei messaged back.

Lorelei: I love your heart. I'll let you know as soon as I do. <3

A new message came through on my Curvy Girl Club group chat.

Zara: That must have been the financial troubles she and Ryde were talking about.

Rory: Is it weird that I feel bad for her?

Ginger: No, but after what she did to you, we wouldn't blame you if you didn't feel bad.

Jordan: Exactly, caring makes you awesome.

My heart lifted. I loved these girls so much. Less than a year ago, Merritt had led our entire high school in throwing cupcakes at Rory during the homecoming game, and after it all, Rory was still kind enough to care for Merritt. Being friends with them was such a blessing.

Callie: I agree with Jordan. Hopefully it will all blow over soon.

Zara: Depends on who her dad screwed over.

The truth in that hit me. I hoped for Merritt's sake it wouldn't be too bad.

Another message came through, and even though I'd been expecting another one in the group chat, it came from Carson.

Carson: Meet me at our park?

My eyebrows drew together. What was he doing around here?

Callie: Even if I understood WHY you're close to your dad's house, I would still say no. I'm in my shower cap! Carson: It's an emergency.

I closed my eyes and groaned, making Franklin stir. He gave me a dirty look before walking to the end of my bed and lying down in a huff.

"I'm upset too," I muttered. Nick and Joe were downstairs playing video games, and the last thing I needed was for Nick to get another view of me looking like a mixture of a rubber duck and a grandma.

Carson: Please?

With a sigh, I got out of bed and rummaged through my closet for a thin sweater. After pulling it over my head and lifting the hood to cover my shower cap as best as I could, I picked up Franklin's leash and clipped it on his collar. I picked him up and started quietly down the stairs. Sometimes the guys got so into the zone they hardly noticed anything around them.

As I rounded the corner to the second set of stairs, I bumped into a hard body and looked up. My breath caught in my throat. "Nick?"

Franklin barked loudly at him before jumping from my arms and racing down the stairs.

Still, Nick didn't back away. Instead, his lips lifted in a smirk. "Going somewhere?"

"Downstairs," I breathed.

His gaze flicked from my eyes to my lips, making my heart hammer in my chest.

"What's the hold-up—" my brother said from behind him, holding Franklin.

Nick stepped back on the landing, finally giving me space to breathe. When Joe caught sight of me, he smirked as well. "Sneaking out to see your boyfriend?"

I glanced behind us toward Mom and Dad's room and shushed him.

He rolled his eyes. "Have fun, lover girl."

But my eyes weren't on Joe; they were on Nick. The smirk had left his mouth, and his dark eyes were watching me intently.

"I'll see you," I breathed, mostly to Nick, but my brother said, "Use protection."

That snapped me out of my trance just enough to grab Franklin and hit Joe's arm before going the rest of the way downstairs. I slid the glass door open and set Franklin down. As I stepped into the cool evening air, I couldn't help but think about Nick and how close he and I had stood to each other, the charge I'd felt in his gaze.

Once Franklin finished his first pee of the walk, I hurried to the park, excited to tell Carson. The second I saw him on the swing, I said, "Carson! You're not going to believe this. Nick and I—"

"Callie!" He jumped out of the swing and wrapped me in a hug. "Guess who's here."

The urgency in his voice made sense as he turned to the side and showed me the girl hiding in the playground equipment.

"Gemma?" I cried while Franklin yapped frantically.

Carson picked him up, instantly quieting the dog while Gemma jogged over to us and gave me a hug. "Callie! Look at you. You are so beautiful! And grown up!"

Even though Gemma was only a few years older than us, she seemed so glamorous, like she had her whole life together. And she was absolutely gorgeous with an ample hourglass figure and clothes that made her look both sexy and polished.

Not like me in my pajamas and shower cap with a scraggly, yapping dog.

"Look at yourself! You look amazing," I said. I could see why Joe always had a hopeless crush on her. "What are you doing in town?"

She and Carson exchanged a dark look, and she answered, "I'm helping Dad pack up."

Ice filled my stomach as I glanced from her to Carson. "Are you sure?"

She nodded. "I'm not the little girl I once was."

Feeling reassured by her confidence, I gave her another hug. "I'm just happy you're back. Carson has missed you and the others like crazy. How long are you in town?"

"Four days, but I want to get together with you and Carson. I have to know how he finally convinced you to date him. You know when you guys were twelve and you went to that party—"

Carson hooked his arm around her shoulders, ruffling her hair, and said, "That's enough of that." As Gemma shoved him off, he said, "I better get this one back to her hotel, but I'll see you tomorrow, Cal."

They began walking away, but I was still rooted to the spot. What had Gemma been about to tell me? I had to know.

THIRTY-TWO

CARSON

All day Saturday, I was on edge knowing Gemma was in the same space as Dad. Even though I was working a double shift at the pool, I kept my phone on Mrs. Mayes's desk so she could let me know if she heard it ring. She thought I was hoping to hear from Callie, but the truth was I just wanted my phone to stay silent. No news was good news when it came to my dad.

My nerves were strung tight by the end of my shift, but when I checked my phone, there was a text from Gemma.

Gemma: I'm riding with Callie to Waldo's. Everything went okay with Dad. Tell you more later.

My curiosity piqued, but I tried to focus instead on showering off and changing into the spare clothes I'd packed. One of the major gifts athletics had given me was the ability to focus on a specific task and block out everything else. I used that skill as often as I could—my mom called it a man's "nothing box." I called it survival.

I stayed in the nothing box until I got to the diner, but when I saw Gemma and Callie in the window, I came undone. The sturdy walls around my fears and worries collapsed, and my eyes got hot just watching them together. I was so thankful Gemma was safe. Thankful Callie would soon be safe from me.

I wiped at my eyes, removing the traces of moisture, and got out of the car. They were sitting at a booth midway into the restaurant, talking to Betty. She greeted me and took my drink order, then left me alone with two of the people I loved most.

I went to sit by Gemma, but she said, "Sit with your girlfriend! I want to bask in this moment."

I rolled my eyes at her and sat next to Callie. Our thighs touched, and the heat from her body warmed me in ways I didn't want to admit. Steeling myself, I took a deep breath and put on a happy face. It was what they both wanted from me.

"How was today?" I asked.

Gemma frowned. "You know, same ol', same ol'. Dad blamed Mom for all of his problems, said it was her fault he got his work injury because she asked for help with you the night before and he was too tired to be safe, and then he threw a bunch of stuff and broke it."

My fists balled, and my muscles readied me to stand, to fight. "He *what*?"

"Not at me," she said. "It was just some of Mom's trinkets, and it was after he'd had a few drinks. I got in with Callie pretty soon after."

Callie gently rubbed my arm, trying to ease my stress, but I needed to get far, far away from her because my rage was too close to the surface.

"I have to use the bathroom." I got up and stormed toward the facilities. Why did Dad have to do that stuff around his daughter? At least Mom was another adult, not someone he'd had a hand in *creating*. Not someone who'd *flown across the country* to help him.

I shut myself in the single-stall room and locked the door. Bracing myself on the sink, I stared at my reflection in the mirror, trying to find something I could recognize, but all I saw was my father. The strong chin. The square face. The fury in my eyes.

I turned away and took deep breaths. This was just another reminder of why I needed to get as far away from Callie as possible and make sure she'd have Nick to cling to.

He might have been a poet and had about as much personality as a post, but he probably hadn't almost killed his dad. Wouldn't flip into a rage every time he heard about his father's actions.

Deciding the only way to get past this was to go through it, I left the bathroom and walked back to Callie and Gemma. The second they saw me, they quieted, which just reinforced the fear that they'd been talking about me.

Callie gave me a concerned look and said, "Everything okay?"

"Peachy."

Gemma frowned. "Callie was just telling me about your workouts for the swim team at Stanford. It sounds intense."

I shrugged. "You need to be in good shape to compete." And I needed to compete to go to Stanford and live independent of my parents. If I picked up a part-time job, I could probably pair that with savings from lifeguarding to cover all of my own expenses without ever needing to call my mom. Right now, nothing sounded better.

Callie leaned against the wall behind her, getting farther from me. "How's work, Gemma? I still don't understand what you do."

She batted a hand. "No one does," she said with a chuckle. "I actually work in supply chain management so it's kind of like really complicated inventory."

"And you like it?" Callie asked.

Gemma nodded. "I mean, it sounds kind of boring, but actually, there are a lot of moving pieces, and I get to work with so many different people. Plus, there's lots of room for advancement. I'm about six months of good work and online classes from a promotion and a pretty decent raise."

"That's amazing," Callie said, her voice full of light and happiness. I tried to feel the same things for my sister as I echoed Callie's words.

"What about you, Carson?" Gemma asked. "Did you decide what you're majoring in?"

"Still upset I can't major in lunch," I said to break the ice in my own veins, not to mention the awkward tension that had fallen over the three of us.

It got the response I wanted as both girls giggled.

"And the verdict is?" Gemma said.

Honestly, I'd spent so much time trying to get out of here, I was still murky on what the plan was for after. "I'm stuck between teaching gym and studying business so I can manage a gym or a fitness program. Maybe even coach." I shrugged.

Gemma tapped her chin as she thought it over. "Business would probably give you more opportunities for growth."

Of course Gemma would want me to pursue the more lucrative career.

"But, Carson would be amazing with children," Callie said, nudging my shoulder.

She had more faith in me more than I did in myself. Honestly, the thought of working with children was terrifying. What if I messed up? It could have implications for the rest of their lives.

Betty brought our food, thankfully relieving me of conversation for a little while. Once we finished eating, I offered to take Gemma to the hotel and waved goodbye to Callie. She smiled and got into her car, then drove away.

I went to get into my car, but realized Gemma was still standing on the sidewalk. Her arms were folded over her chest, and she stared at me with an eyebrow lifted. "Something is off. You need to spill."

THIRTY-THREE

CALLIE

Carson and I decided to find the lowest rated B-list movies to watch on Netflix and make fun of them. Two movies in, Franklin was deeply asleep on *his* throw pillow, and Carson and I were having a ball.

That was, until Nick and Joe came in and we had to stop physically acting out the bad acting. There were some things I could do in front of Carson that were just not flattering in the least. Like rolling around on the floor, pretending to be a tire that exploded things.

That impersonation had us both on the floor, laughing and holding our stomachs. Until the door upstairs opened.

Our laughter stalled as we listened to Joe's and Nick's voices come in. They'd gone to play a pickup game of rugby with some of their college friends, and they must have finished up.

Carson jumped onto the couch and put his arm on the back, waving me over. "Come on, come on," he hissed.

I jumped up from the floor and leaned against his arm as he took the remote and flipped away from the movie. They really would never let me pick a movie again if they saw this one on. My chest was still rising and falling heavily with the force of which we'd been laughing.

As Joe came down the stairs, he gave us a look. "Are we interrupting something?"

"No," Carson said too fast and adjusted his shirt. I knew what he was doing—trying to make it look like we'd been making out...or more.

My cheeks heated, having what I was sure was the intended effect.

Nick's eyes slid over us to the TV, and he asked, "What are we watching?"

Franklin growled at the sudden change in company and walked over to the couch and dropped onto my lap.

"Anything but that last movie Callie picked,"

Carson said. "Still trying to figure out if her bad taste in movies is adorable or a deal-breaker."

Joe flopped down on the couch. "Deal-breaker, obviously. Pass the remote."

I rolled my eyes and leaned back into the crook of his shoulder as Carson tossed him the controller. I'd be lying if I said this wasn't comfortable. I could sleep all night like this.

Nick sat as far away from us as he could on the couch, and I couldn't help but hope my closeness with Carson was making him uncomfortable.

Who was I becoming? Someone who wished for another's discomfort? I straightened in my seat, trying to shift out of the guilt I suddenly felt without upsetting Franklin. I reminded myself this wasn't to make Nick feel bad—it was to help him see me as someone's girlfriend. Someone desirable.

Carson leaned close to me, his lips only inches from my ear. His breath sent shivers down my spine as he said, "Can I talk to you for a second?"

I found it hard to speak, so I nodded.

Carson made a show of taking my hand and leading me to the sliding door while Franklin haughtily went back to his pillow despite its proximity to Nick.

Joe made kissing sounds, and while my cheeks

flushed with warmth, Carson winked back and closed the door behind us.

Since our yard butted up to the green belt, we could hear the sounds of nature even though we were in the middle of the suburbs. Bullfrogs and cicadas scored our walk to the back fence. As Carson led me through the gate, I loosened my grip on his hand, but he held on.

A tingle filled my stomach, and I tried to quiet it. Best friends didn't get tingles or butterflies or whatever I was feeling right now. "What's going on?"

He met my eyes and held my gaze. "We've got to take things to the next level."

"What do you mean?" I asked.

"Why do you think Nick hasn't made a move yet?"

Now I was even more uncomfortable. What was Carson trying to say? That I was hopeless? "There could be plenty of reasons," I argued. "Maybe he's scared to make a move since he thinks we're together or he's worried about what Joe will say or he's still working up the courage to ask..." Or he doesn't like me, I didn't say.

Carson looked down at our linked hands. "All

we do is hang out and watch movies together. We hardly even hold hands or post online."

"But everyone knows we're together," I said, finally stepping back and breaking our connection. "You saw all the comments online. People love us as a couple. They've been expecting it. My own friends are beside themselves about it."

Carson frowned. "They might know that logically, but we look like we have about as much sexual chemistry as a sweater vest."

My cheeks warmed at the mention of sexual chemistry. Here I was trying to fight the ways my body responded to him, and now he wanted me to do more? I didn't know if I could handle it. "Where is this coming from, Cars?"

Turning away from me, he ran his hands through his hair, then faced me again. "Gemma knows we're lying."

My blood ran cold. "How did she find out? We were only around her for an hour!"

With a shrug, he said, "She knows us, and she's a little more observant than your brother. I think the real giveaway was that we just waved goodbye. We got sloppy."

"I need to sit down." I lowered myself to the grass, breathing deeply. "This was a dumb idea. I should just come clean, tell everyone how pathetic I am." My eyes stung, and I rubbed them. I'd been stupid to even think I could con my way into Nick's heart. That was no way to start a relationship.

Carson sat beside me and pulled me into a hug. "Hey, hey, it's not a big deal. We just need to touch each other a little more."

At the word "touch," I realized his arms were around me. I looked up and met his eyes, feeling the charge between us. Those feelings terrified me. I'd been in love with Carson before, and I knew where that path led. It led to me watching while he fell in love with someone else, someone better, and I was staying as far away from that heartache as I could.

He brushed his fingers over my cheek, nearly undoing me, and a chuckle escaped his lips. "Is the idea of touching me that repulsive?"

My heart pounded furiously, terrified he would see just how alluring the idea was. How much I needed to suppress those very urges. But then my lips betrayed me with the truth. "I always imagined when a guy touched me, it would be because he wanted to."

Carson's eyebrows drew together in the deepest compassion, and he tilted his head. "Callie, you're my best friend. I'd do anything to help you. Even if it does mean getting a few cooties."

I rolled my eyes at him, then sighed. "I don't see the point in carrying on for the rest of the summer if it's not going to work."

Carson raised his eyebrows. "Seriously? That boy is *so* uncomfortable."

I rolled my head down and shook it. How could we be seeing such different realities?

Carson reached up and gently touched my chin, drawing my eyes back to him. The gesture made my stomach do weird things, and I swallowed, hoping he couldn't see my reaction.

"Callie," he said, "he can hardly look our way at all. And have you noticed that he's not staying over as late anymore to play video games?"

I shook my head, not wanting to believe him. "Maybe he's just busy writing."

Carson rolled his eyes. "Any guy who would rather look at a notebook than you is crazy."

If I kept blushing like this, the last thing I needed to worry about this summer would be sunscreen. I'd already have a permanent burn on my cheeks.

"Look," Carson continued, "I think we're getting close, but we just need to act like we like each other. A little bit." He gave me a teasing smile, and it loosened the tightness in my chest.

"Okay, we can hold hands more often," I agreed, convincing myself. It wasn't like Carson and I had never held hands before, like when we were walking through a crowded concert trying to stick together. We could make this work. And soon, I'd be with Nick and the way Carson's touches made me feel would be a distant memory.

"Good," Carson said with a grin, and he pulled me into a hug, holding me tight to his chest.

I breathed in his familiar scent, sunscreen and chlorine and fresh air.

As he stepped back, he said, "Are we good?"

I nodded slowly and reached for his hand. "Good."

The twist of his fingers through mine left a gentle hum playing through my skin. I tried to blame it on the breeze or all this talk about relationships. My mind had to be playing tricks on me. Carson and I were best friends, nothing more. At least not in private.

"Think we've 'made out' long enough?" he asked.

I rolled my eyes and began walking toward the

gate. As we slipped through the sliding door, Joe said, "This you-two-dating thing is so weird."

Carson chuckled. "Feels like it's been a long time coming, man."

Joe snorted. "I thought we were the only ones who realized you two were in love."

Carson met my eyes. Just another echo of what I'd said outside.

"Come here," Carson breathed as he took a seat on the couch, his green eyes breathing warmth into me. I tucked my feet under me and curled into his side like I'd seen my mom do with my dad hundreds of times before. Up this close to Carson, I felt comfortable—safe.

I couldn't help the heaviness of my eyes as I leaned into the one person I would trust with my life. He drew small circles on my shoulder with his fingertips, sparking electricity in my stomach. How did my friends focus on anything when they were sitting with their boyfriends like this?

Joe said, "Everything okay, Nick?"

Nick's eyes seemed to focus back in, and he nodded quickly.

Joe snorted. "Thinking of more words to rhyme with love?"

Carson chuckled. "I could give you a few ideas,

but they'd probably stall out after dove and glove. I'm not the greatest writer."

My lips spread into a slow smile as I remembered the gift Carson got me for my fourteenth birthday. I sat up so I could look at him. "That's not true."

He looked down at me, his nose only inches from mine. "What do you mean?"

I put my free hand on his chest, using it to hold myself up. "Do you remember that time you gave me a poem for my birthday? I think it was eighth grade."

Joe covered his mouth, laughing. "He wrote you a poem? You had it so bad, Carson!"

Carson's cheeks had grown almost as pink as mine were earlier, and I might have even caught a hint of red on his ears.

"It was actually really good," I said, defending Carson. "I'm pretty sure I still have it in my room somewhere. I can go get it and read it for you guys."

Carson immediately opened his mouth to argue, but Nick stood up.

"Speaking of poems," Nick said, "I better get home and work on mine. That poetry slam's coming up."

Carson lifted the hand that was still holding mine in a wave. "See you later, man."

Nick didn't give us a second look before he walked out the door, but Carson pulled me into an even tighter hug and whispered, "See? You've got to trust me."

There was no one I trusted more.

THIRTY-FOUR

CARSON

I walked through the green belt to where I had parked my car at the pool. We'd decided that was safer than parking in front of Callie's house. Still, I kept my phone gripped tightly in my hand in case my dad was waiting for me there. As planned, Gemma stood beside my car so I could give her a ride back to the hotel.

"How'd it go tonight?" I asked, hitting the unlock button on my key fob.

She shrugged and opened her door. "I stayed upstairs, he stayed downstairs... Is there anything you want me to save from your room?"

I shook my head and got into the car. "I have everything I need." It felt both good and scary to say that, but it was the truth. I had the things I'd bought for college, like my new computer and bedding for the dorms, and I had built up a good savings account to replace anything else that might come up. My room at school would come furnished, and I had an unlimited meal plan, thanks to my swim scholarship. I would be fine, as long as I could live with a broken heart.

"You know what I miss most about Emerson?" Gemma asked.

I glanced over at her as I started the car. "What's that?"

"The beach. It's not the same in New York, and it takes forever to get there. By the time I get off work and ride on the subway, it's basically time to turn around and go back home."

"I can do something about that," I replied, smiling.

"Good." She buckled herself in, and I began driving the familiar path to Seaton Pier. We could have gone to the more touristy beach near Brentwood, but that didn't feel right for tonight.

"What do you do besides work?" I asked her. All I'd heard her talk about was her job, not any friends or boyfriends.

She shrugged. "I have a cat."

"That just sounds sad," I teased.

She rolled her eyes. "I mean, I catch a movie every now and then or see a play or just walk around and explore. Manhattan's not like here. You don't have to plan things; they're just always happening around you. It's one of the reasons I love living there."

I nodded, but it was still hard to miss the hint of loneliness in her voice. I imagined Gemma in a big city, surrounded by people but all by herself.

Soon, we reached the pier, and Gemma grinned. "You know, I always liked this one better than the uppity beach in Brentwood."

With a chuckle, I nodded. "I get what you mean." Even though we'd attended Emerson Academy, the Catholic school we'd gone to in Texas was way more laid back. We weren't used to the money that ran deep at the Academy.

We got out of the car and walked over the wooden planks to the coarse sand lining the ocean. Even at night, this place felt alive in a way our suburb didn't. You could hear the rolling waves, see driftwood bonfires crackling in the distance, feel the electricity in the breeze. For the first time in a while, my chest felt lighter, and I took a deep breath, savoring the feeling.

Gemma adjusted her jeans and settled in the sand. As I sat down beside her, she said, "Can I ask you something?"

"Didn't you already?" I teased.

She rolled her eyes, then looked over the water for a moment. "Why haven't you made a move with Callie?"

Her question brought all the tightness back in my chest, reminding me of my problems. "How do you know I haven't made a move?"

With all the confidence in the world, she said, "Because if you had made a move, you would actually be dating right now."

Her statement took me aback. "What?"

"Carson," she said sternly. "Come on. It doesn't take a genius to see that you love each other and are just too afraid of getting hurt. It's the oldest, lamest story of all time. Girl likes boy, boy likes girl, they don't do anything because they're 'worried about hurting their friendship' and then they needlessly pine over each other until one of them moves on and gets married. Meanwhile, the other one lives their entire life alone, or sad, until that person's spouse dies and they *finally* get a second chance. By then, they're both mad they wasted all that time

when they just could have said something. It's
annoying."

I raised my eyebrows. "And oddly specific."

She shook her head with an exasperated smile.
"Seriously, Cars. Why *haven't* you made a move?
Don't you think it's about time to be honest with
her?"

Her jab at my character just reminded me of all
the reasons I shouldn't tell Callie the truth.
"Gemma, you don't get it."

"No, what I don't get is why you can't just let
yourself be happy! I've been here three days, and I
can already see you're miserable! *Why?*"

"Because I almost killed Dad! Okay?" I stood
and ripped my fingers through my hair, pacing in
the deep sand. I turned toward Gemma, needing
her to see what a monster I was. "That night Mom
told me she was leaving him? I choked him out,
and I didn't want to stop. He hadn't even touched
her, just threw a bottle at the wall, and I was going
to keep pushing on his windpipe until I watched
the light leave his eyes." I ripped at my chest, at
the part where my heart should have been. "And I
would have killed him, if Mom hadn't snapped me
out of it. Callie deserves *so* much better than me
it's pathetic. I'm no better than Dad. As soon as I

get Nick to fall for her, I'm out of her life for good."

Gemma's face was such an open book I could see the emotions playing across her face. Shock. Worry. Confusion. Disappointment. But I didn't see fear. Why didn't I see fear?

She stayed quiet, processing it all right in front of me, and I stood frozen in the sand, trying to see the moment she realized that if Callie should get away from me, maybe she should too.

I couldn't take the silence anymore, couldn't take not knowing what she thought of me now. "Say something!"

"Oh, Carson," she breathed.

The tenderness in her words made my eyes sting. "Go ahead, Gem, tell me I'm worthless. Tell me to leave. I already know the truth."

She stood and put her hands on my shoulders. Even though I was taller by a good six inches, she held my gaze with all the force of someone much bigger than her. "You listen to me, and you listen to me good," she ordered, her voice firm. She pointed a finger at my face. "You are *nothing* like our father. He hurt you—hurt us—and when you feel so much pain for so long, you'll do anything to stop it."

My jaw trembled, and I shook my head. "But I

would have killed him," I breathed. "Sometimes I get so angry I still feel like I could."

She tapped my chest with her finger, hard. "You have a heart of gold, and you would do anything for that girl. She would be *lucky* to have someone like you."

Tears flowed from my eyes. I broke down, fell onto the sand sobbing and wishing with all my heart that Gemma's words were true. She held me to her chest, rubbing my back, running her hands over my hair.

As my sobs subsided, I sat up and wiped at my eyes. "Some welcome home, huh? Your dad's losing it, and your brother's falling apart."

She held my chin up and looked at me. "My dad is facing the consequences of his actions, and my brother is finally, *finally* getting to stand on his own."

"But the curse—"

"Is nonsense," Gemma said. "It's a way for us to minimize generational trauma and toxic cycles. You don't have to be like them."

"But what if I am?" I asked. Even breathing the question scared me. But not as much as hearing her answer.

"What if you aren't?" she said. "What if everything you've ever wanted is on the other side of that fear, and all you have to do is ask for it?"

I looked at the rolling waves, then turned my gaze back on her. "Do you mean it?"

"Mean what?"

My voice was hoarse. "That I'm not like him? The thought of hurting Callie..." Emotion overwhelmed me, and I pinched the bridge of my nose, trying to stop the swell.

Gemma put her hand on my arm. "This, right here? This is *exactly* how I can tell the curse ends with you. You deserve to have the love you never got to live with, and Callie? She deserves to be loved by you."

With Gemma's words healing the cracks in my heart, I decided. I was going to make my move. I was going to see what lay on the other side of my fear.

THIRTY-FIVE

CALLIE

I'd just gotten home from brunch with my parents when my phone went off with a text in the Curvy Girl Club group chat.

Zara: So, are we ever going to get to go on a quintuple date?

As I was reading Zara's text, more appeared on the screen.

Rory: I've been thinking the same thing! Are you guys free today?
Ginger: We can probably hang out this afternoon?

Jordan: Kai just got back from his trip, I bet he would
love to go out with us!

While my parents went to get changed for a func-
tion, I leaned against the kitchen counter and smiled
at my phone screen. I should have known there
would be no denying my friends a quintuple date, or
the chance at seeing Carson and me as a couple.

I opened up a new texting screen and sent a
message to Carson.

Callie: My friends want to go out on a date with us...
Carson: Like four girls, you and me? Um... I'm not sure
I have enough hands for that.
Callie: LOL no, like all their boyfriends and them and
you and me.
Carson: Oh, so like a quintuple date.

How was everyone coming up with this phrase?
It was totally cringe-worthy to me. Still, if you
couldn't beat 'em...

Callie: Exactly like a quintuple date.
Carson: Count me in. When?
Callie: This afternoon? Are you working?

Mom came out of the bedroom, hooking pearl earrings in her ears.

"You look nice," I said.

She smiled at me. "Thanks, honey."

"Where are you going again?"

Dad came out of the room after her, looking smart in one of his suits. "A mixer for parents at Brentwood U. Figured we could meet someone and talk them into giving Joe good grades next semester." He winked.

I laughed. "He's going to need more than a good word. Better have some cash on hand."

Mom made the shame sign at both of us, even though she was smiling. "Any plans for the day?"

My phone chimed, and I said, "Let me see."

Carson: Sure. I just asked Peter, and he said he'd cover for me.

"Looks like I'm heading to the beach with my friends!"

With a smile, Mom gave me a hug. "I'm so glad you've made such good friends this year."

"Me too." I agreed.

They had to leave, so I waved them goodbye

and took Franklin outside. While he nosed around our yard, I replied to Carson's message.

Callie: The girls will be so excited. They've been 'shipping Callon since before we were a "couple."

Carson: LOL have to please the raving fans.

Callie: So modest.

Carson: I'm the best at modesty.

Callie: *eyeroll emoji*

Carson: You know you love it.

Callie: Of course. :) I'll see you then.

I sorted out the details with my friends, and we agreed to meet at Seaton Bakery. Zara and Ronan had found a small beach along the coast they wanted us to check out. Apparently it was pet friendly, so we could even bring Franklin along. We'd switch cars at the bakery and carpool the rest of the way.

When I pulled into the parking lot, my friends were standing around their vehicles. As I got out of my car, Jordan began chanting, "Callon! Callon! Callon!" Franklin barked from inside the car, joining the din.

My cheeks were blushing hot, but Carson walked right up to me, took my hand, and lifted it into the air like a champion wrestler, resulting in a chorus of cheers from our friends.

They rushed up to us, and Beckett clapped Carson on the back. "I never thought you'd get out of the friend zone."

The realization of what Beckett said hit me full force. Beckett and Carson were friends. Had Carson really liked me as more all this time? Or was Beckett just echoing what everyone had suspected?

I didn't have too much time to think about it, because my friends were surrounding me, and Jordan was whispering in my ear, "You and Carson are such a cute couple."

My cheeks continued burning, and at this point, I wondered when they'd burst into flames. Would I ever get used to people commenting on our relationship?

On our lie, I reminded myself.

I went and got Franklin from my car, desperately trying to come up with something, anything to change the subject, and then remembered something. "How do you guys feel about baking cookies?"

"Good," Ginger's boyfriend, Ray, said, "as long as I get to eat them afterward."

Kai slapped him a high-five, and Ronan said, "Ditto."

"Why?" asked Beckett.

Franklin jumped from my arm's into Carson's, and I straightened, saying, "My mom is having this cookie bake-off to benefit a charity, and I was wondering if you guys would be willing to compete. She really just needs more people to bring in entries." I cringed, waiting for their answers. I hated asking for help—usually I was the one doing the helping.

Zara asked, "When is it? I'd have to make sure it's not when we're trying to film."

"It'll be on a weekend," I said, "I think around one or two in the afternoon."

She nodded toward Ronan. "Things are about to get really crazy for us on set, but I'll make it if I can. Oh, and I almost forgot." She reached into her purse and pulled out two tickets. "Remember when Carson helped us spy on Beckett? I owe him a ticket to Ryde's movie premier, and I figured you'd want to go along."

"*What*?" Beckett demanded.

Franklin barked defensively as Carson cringed at Beckett. "Sorry, dude, but"—he reached for the tickets—"I am so pumped! Callie, you have to go with me. Right?"

Giggling at his exchange with Beckett, I nodded. "You're just lucky Zara's a fancy movie producer."

She rolled her eyes. "Not quite. Just learning."

I shook my head. Zara was confident, but not cocky. Even when she'd been one of the richest kids in our class, she was always low-key about it, not rubbing it in people's faces like Merritt had.

Merritt. A pang of guilt swept through me. She still hadn't replied to my messages, and we had a shift coming up together on Monday. I hoped it wouldn't be unbearable—for either of us. I wanted to tell my friends about my worries, but something called me back. It didn't seem like the right time. Especially not when we're all finally hanging out together for the first time this summer. Our schedules had been so crazy, not like when we were in school. I was worried about college and how we would stay in touch. We needed to soak in every minute we could.

"Let's get this show on the road," Zara said.

Carson extended his hand for a high five. "Already using show-biz talk."

She begrudgingly slapped her hand against his

and headed for her car. Carson, Franklin and I got stuck in the back, which was too small for his long legs. I ended up giving him my leg space and draping my calves over his thighs.

Zara looked at us in the rearview mirror and grinned. "You are so cute back there."

Carson smiled at her. "Easy to look cute when you're sitting next to someone like Callie."

The compliment seemed genuine, and I needed to remind my heart not to flutter so excited. This was all a show to him, even if it didn't feel like it.

In the middle seat, Rory sighed dreamily, and Beckett said, "You are head over heels, Cars."

"How could I not be?" Carson said. He was so good at pretending we were in love. I needed to take notes on him so that I can play it up, especially in front of Nick.

Rory asked to hold Franklin, and he was more than willing to get her and Beckett's attention while Carson and I lounged in the backseat.

Zara cranked the music, and even though this vehicle wasn't quite as expensive as the one she used to drive, the sound quality was still amazing. I could practically feel the bass vibrating my body. I looked down at my lap and saw the music jiggling my thighs. Feeling self-conscious, I put my hands over the dimpled skin and tried to stop the constant shaking. It was just Carson, so he knew what I looked like, but it was still embarrassing. I should have worn pants until we got to the beach at least.

He took hold of my fingers and looked me in the eyes. "Callie," he said low so only I could hear him, "you are *perfect* just the way you are."

My knees felt weak under the force of his words. Under his gaze. His eyes were wide open and light green and completely earnest. I could tell he was being honest, but I had to know if it was real. "Do you mean it?"

He lifted my hand to his chest and said, "With all my heart."

THIRTY-SIX

CARSON

Callie seemed to relax once I had ahold of her hand, and I held it the entire way to the beach. I'd always thought it was kind of lame when girls talked about hands fitting perfectly together, but Callie's and mine did.

She had the softest skin, and her fingers slipped so easily around mine. I could fold my fingers back to cover her knuckles, almost reaching the brown birthmark on the back of her hand. I could hold her hand forever, just take it in, because when I held on to her, I felt like I was holding on to greatness.

Zara slowed the SUV and turned off the road. There wasn't a parking spot or anything—we just had to grab the coolers from the trunk and then the surf and boogie boards strapped to the top of the car.

The girls started ahead of us, Franklin leading the way on his leash, and I'd be lying if I said I wasn't pleased with the view of Callie in her shorts. I'd worked so hard to suppress my attraction to her over the years, but now that I was going for it, I wasn't holding back. Not anymore.

Once we hit the bottom of the path, it opened to a flat beach area with coarse sand and plenty of waves. Watching Callie take it in was even better than seeing it for myself.

"How did you find this?" Callie asked Zara, bending over to free Franklin of his leash.

Zara sent Ronan a flirtatious grin. "Oh, just a ride on a motorcycle up the coast." He put his free arm around her waist and pulled her close to drop a kiss on her cheek. A pit of jealousy grew in my stomach at the easy way he could just touch the girl he loved—just be with her. I hoped I could have that with Callie, and soon.

Just ahead of me, Callie slipped off her sandals and held them between her fingers. As she leaned over, her hair swung to the side, revealing a patch of her psoriasis. It was better than it had been, but I hurt for her. She'd told me how uncomfortable it was, not to mention how many painful memories it brought up. Still, she stood up like she always had and kept going. Even if I wished she had continued with sports, she'd gone on her own path and made the most of a hard situation.

We reached the middle of the small beach, and Ginger spread a couple of sheets for all of us to sit on while Ray and Beckett set coolers and bags on the edges to hold it down. Jordan began passing out beach towels, and I just set down the surfboard and took it all in. With that crazy dog running around in the sand like he was a child on a playground and all my friends so happy... this would be one of the days I remembered for the rest of my life, the kind of day I told my future children about. And yeah, I might have been young, but I knew what I wanted. I wanted Callie, and I hoped she'd feel the same.

Kai picked up a board and said, "I'm heading in." He had on a wetsuit, but the rest of us were just in shorts. These girls had brought such different guys together, but I didn't mind. I'd never been the kind to turn away good people from my life. There were already enough bad ones.

Ray came next to Beckett and me and clapped our shoulders. "How about a surf lesson?"

"I'm down," Beckett said, picking up another

board and walking toward the water. Ray picked up the other one, and I followed them to the water. The girls were already spread out on the sheet, giggling about Franklin and applying sunscreen and laying out like their sole mission in life was to roast their skin another shade darker.

As I glanced back at Callie, her position brought a smile to my lips. Her knees were in the air, her hands rested on her middle, and her lips formed a soft smile. What would it feel like to kiss those lips? Would I find out soon?

My stomach disintegrated into a nervous puddle as I followed my friends deeper into the cool waves. We were about waist deep when Beckett flattened his board against the water and began explaining the mechanics of surfing—how to get on the board, when and how to stand up, and the best ways to catch a wave just right.

Back on the sand, I heard the girls giggle louder, and I glanced back. "What do you think they're talking about?"

Ray shrugged. "What an idiot I look like trying to get on this dang thing."

Beckett chuckled. "No way, they're talking about how *dreamy* Carson's eyes are."

I rolled my eyes at him. "Not Ronan's tattoos?"

I glanced at the spot where he and Kai easily surfed farther out in the water.

"Oh lord." Beckett groaned. "If I hear one more time from Rory how hot I'd look with a tattoo…"

"Same for Ginger," Ray said with a grin. "But they're *definitely* staring at my farmer's tan. Chicks dig it." He waggled his eyebrows.

Laughing, I swiveled my head around like I was searching for something. "Where's my T-shirt? I need all the help I can get."

Beckett shoved my shoulder. "Yeah right. Why would you need help, *Callon*?"

My nerves spoke for me. "Maybe because I'm telling Callie I love her for the first time today."

Their eyes widened.

"That's huge," Ray said.

Beckett's eyebrows drew together though. "You haven't told her yet?"

Heat crept into the tips of my ears. "It took me eight years to ask her out—you don't think saying I love you might take a while too?"

With a reassuring smile, Ray said, "It'll go great. You just have to quit stalling and tell her already."

"Yeah," Beckett agreed. "I've been telling you to make a move for *six years*, man. Let's get it over with!" He began pushing me toward the beach, and I dug my feet into the sand.

"Whoa, whoa, whoa!" I said. "I can't just tell her."

"And why the hell not?" Beckett asked, pausing his assault.

"Because... I've waited this long. What if I mess it up? It's not just our relationship hanging in the balance—it's *eight years* of friendship."

Beckett put his hand on my shoulder. "Exactly. Don't you think she deserves to hear the truth?"

I nodded. And this time, Beckett didn't need to push me. I started out of the water. I started toward my fears. I started toward everything I wanted and hoped like hell for a miracle.

THIRTY-SEVEN

CALLIE

Zara nudged my arm. "Check out who's walking this way."

I propped myself up and saw Carson breaking out of the waves like some kind of Greek god. His muscles glistened in the light bouncing off of his dripping body, and he shook his hair out around him, ridding it of all the water that had been there.

Ginger giggled. "It might be a good idea for you to close your mouth, Cal."

I snapped my mouth shut, my cheeks heating. They'd caught me staring at my best friend, and even though they expected that of us as a "couple," I knew the truth. I shouldn't be checking him out like that.

Rory inclined her head toward the water as Carson got within earshot. "How are lessons coming, Carson?"

"Good," he said. "Ray's picking it up quick. But speaking of lessons..." His eyes simmered on me. "I seem to remember a certain someone promised to let me teach them to boogie board last year."

"Oh, no, no, no." I shook my head quickly. "I am perfectly fine sitting here with the girls. Right?" I turned to my friends, but those traitors were clearly on his side.

"Go!" Jordan said, pushing me toward Carson.

Ginger nodded enthusiastically. "Show us how it's done."

Zara waggled her eyebrows. "And have fun in the water."

I turned to Rory, my last chance, but Rory simply scratched Franklin behind the ears and said, "We'll take care of Franklin. Have fun!"

Groaning, I got up and walked with Carson toward the water and the rolling waves. "I can't believe you're making me do this."

He shook his head in mock disappointment. "I can't believe you're making me make you."

I rolled my eyes. "Please. There's a reason I didn't let you teach me last year."

"And that reason is?" he asked.

"Maybe I thought you'd forget?" I said with a shrug.

"Come on. It's so easy. And fun."

"Fun," I said drily, "like embarrassing myself in front of all my friends is fun."

Kai and Ronan passed by us, heading toward their girlfriends, and now there was just Ray and Beckett out farther, trying to surf. As Carson and I stepped into the cool water, I realized no one would be able to hear us over the crash of the waves or the trill of the birds.

We were about waist deep in the water, and even though the sun was hot, the water made me shiver. I folded my arms over my chest and said, "Let's get this over with."

Carson's eyes flicked from my arms to my eyes, and he swallowed before saying, "Okay, so what you have to do is hold it like this." He held the boogie board to his muscled chest, making his biceps flex against the board.

I realized I was staring and focused on doing the same with my board. The waves pulled against its flat surface, nearly knocking me over. Carson instantly reached out and steadied me, his hand warm through my thin tank top.

It had been so long since I'd been in the ocean, always coming up with an excuse not to go with my family and risk getting picked on for my sores. Right now, there was a long red patch trailing down my neck, and it felt nice knowing that Carson wouldn't judge me for it, wouldn't worry that it was contagious or shy away from me. I refocused on the task at hand and resituated the board.

"Not bad," Carson said, "but it needs to be more like this." He slipped his hand from my waist to my lower back and pressed the board closer to my chest. Whether it was the water or the sun or Carson, my nerves went haywire under his touch. I clenched the board, trying to clear my mind, to keep my thoughts from going where they didn't need to go.

"Too tight?" he asked. "You should be able to breathe."

I forced myself to take a breath and said, "It's fine." I didn't want to make eye contact, but I could feel him watching me, taking me in, and I caught his gaze. His eyes were fire on mine, and I could hardly find the words to say, "What next?"

He cleared his throat and said, "You wait for a wave, and then try and flatten your board against it so it can carry you to the shore."

I nodded and hurriedly tried to catch the next wave to get away from the heat I was feeling, but my attempt only resulted in me completely face-planting onto the board and then rolling into the water. When I came up, sputtering saltwater, Carson was laughing.

More than a little embarrassed and with the disgusting taste fresh in my mouth, I hit his arm. "Don't make fun of me!"

He caught my hand and held it to his chest. "I'm sorry. Will you forgive me? And stop maiming me?"

The smile on his lips and his skin on mine had my heart pounding. "Sure, but only if you show me how to do this."

"Okay." He released my hand, and the spot where he had held it suddenly felt cool. He followed the break of a wave. Timing it perfectly, he lay flat on his board and easily held on as it carried him almost all the way to the shore.

I cheered for him, and when he stood, he pumped the board over his head, shouting for himself.

"So modest!" I shouted.

His grin was obvious even from here. "You love it," he called back.

I did. But I wouldn't tell him that. When he came back out, he said, "It's your turn."

"Can we do it together?" I asked, worried.

"Always," he said gently.

We both looked over our shoulders, and when the perfect wave came, Carson said, "One, two, three!"

We positioned our boards on the water, and the wave carried us all the way to the shore. It was exhilarating and exciting and so much more fun than I ever imagined. I stood with my board and gave Carson a hug. "I can't believe I did that!"

He lifted me and spun us in a circle. "You could always do that."

As he set me down, I slid against his chest. My shirt tugged against his muscles, exposing a patch of my stomach that skimmed over his abs. My skin was on fire, and my lungs burned as I gasped for air, looking into his eyes.

They were deep and green like the ocean. Intense, deep, captivating.

My gaze flicked to his lips—they glistened in the sun.

Carson inched closer, so close I could feel his breath evaporating the saltwater on my skin. His eyes flicked from my lips to my eyes. "I love you, Callie. I always have."

So many emotions crashed over me, stronger than the ocean around us, but none of them were negative. Tears stung my eyes as I realized something I'd wanted for so long, something I'd been too afraid to hope for, was coming true. "This isn't just for show?"

He nodded, his nose brushing mine. "Do you...feel the same way?"

The worry in his voice, the vulnerability of it, undid me. Knowing words wouldn't be enough, I answered him with my lips. I pressed mine to his, and the sensation running through my body took my breath away just as surely as his confession had.

His arms wrapped around me, pulling me tighter to his chest, and he tilted his head, deepening our kiss. Each second of his skin on mine was pure pleasure like I never could have guessed. It sent fire dancing over my skin and electricity shocking everything underneath.

I'd always wondered if I would know what to do in a kiss, but this—it was more than thinking—it was acting, feeling. My hands went around his shoulders, and I knotted my fingers in the fringe of hair at the back of his neck.

His teeth nipped my lip bottom, creating sensations I didn't even know I could feel, and our mouths tangled, tasting, discovering further. I could have kissed him forever, learning all the ways my best friend could become even more. Breathing raggedly, Carson parted our lips and rested his forehead against mine. I slowly opened my eyes and found his gaze on mine. His green eyes searched mine, seeking the truth I'd shared in our kiss.

"Us?" he breathed. "It's real?"

I nodded, my lips spreading into a smile I couldn't contain. "I love you, Carson," I breathed. "You're my best friend."

THIRTY-EIGHT

CARSON

The joy ripping through me was powerful, indescribable. Callie had just answered my wildest dreams and made me happier than I'd ever been in my life. It was like all the hard things I'd been through, all the struggles I'd faced, had led me to this very moment when I could call this beautiful, amazing, kind, wonderful girl mine.

And now that I had her, I knew I'd never let myself get so close to that destructive edge of anger again. I never wanted to let her go, because when she was close to me like this, I felt like I could take on the world. Like that rage had been completely shut out, leaving behind only the love I had for her.

Our friends' cheers broke through my fog, and

we both turned toward them, grinning. I kept my arm around her though; I was never letting Callie go.

She giggled and said, "Maybe we should get back?"

"Anything with you is okay with me."

We walked back toward them, our fingers linked together, and I had never felt more *right* in my life. Even the sun's warm rays hitting us seemed to approve.

Franklin ran to us the second we crossed the water's edge. I held him in one hand, his fur tickling my bare chest, while Callie walked right by my side. Our friends gave us our fair share of teasing, but Beckett gave me a silent smile that said he understood just how much this meant to me. For the rest of the afternoon, Callie and I lounged on the sand while our friends went in and out of the water. It was like after all this time of running from each other, we just needed to *be*.

As the sun sank low, we all packed up our things and headed back to the car. This time, instead of worrying about her legs or how she looked, Callie leaned into me and rested as Franklin snored in her lap. I was convinced her head belonged on my shoulder almost as much as her lips belonged on mine.

I kissed the crown of her head, right where her forehead met her delicate blond hair, and she smiled up at me.

In that moment, I realized just how much I had to lose. How careful I had to be so I would never repeat the Cook Family Curse. Not on my girl. Not on Callie.

"I love you," she breathed.

Fear gripped my heart, and I selfishly asked, "No matter what?"

She nodded, full of confidence. Full of love. "No matter what."

I held her tighter, breathed in her scent that lingered through the saltwater. Each breath seemed to bring me closer to calm, closer to the man I wanted to be.

When we got back to Seaton Bakery, I got in the car with Callie and Franklin. I didn't know where we were going, but it was just automatic. Now that I knew I wanted to spend the rest of my life with her, I wanted it to start right now. No more wasted time.

"Do you want to come to my house?" she asked, biting her lip.

The way her perfect pink lips caught between

her teeth nearly undid me. "Yes. A thousand times yes."

She giggled, a balm to my soul, and put the car in reverse. "That can be arranged. And I'll ask Mom if we can put my car in the garage. That way your dad won't see you coming inside or anything."

A fear I hadn't even known I'd had was just relieved, and I could breathe even easier. As we got out on the road, I reached for her hand, and she held it tight.

"I can't even believe this," she said with a grin.

My smile was just as big as hers. "I can't either."

"It's crazy, right? Like, you've seen me in my shower cap. That doesn't weird you out?"

I gave her a sideways glance. "Please, it's cute as hell."

She raised her eyebrows. "And what about my taste in movies? You're going to be watching bad ones from here on out."

"You know I secretly like your romcoms."

She smiled and squeezed my hand. "Then it's settled. You're stuck with me."

"That's exactly what I want," I said honestly. But there was still something holding me back, keeping a pit of fear in my chest. I almost didn't want to ask the question, but I had to, before I got in even deeper than I already was. "What about Nick?"

I held my breath as I waited for her answer. More like I couldn't breathe because I knew her answer could crush me. But she made me wait. She pressed the garage door opener on her visor, and I realized we were already at her house.

Franklin barked at the door, demanding to be let inside. With the car off, she unbuckled and said, "One second."

My heart raced as she took the dog to her house and let him in, saying something to whoever was inside. When she got back to the car, she sat down and turned to me, reaching for both my hands. This was it, I thought. The part where she told me it couldn't happen after all. That this afternoon had been a mistake and she wasn't feeling the same way as me.

"Do you remember when you started dating Sarah?"

My head pulled back. "Yeah?" But what kind of question was that?

She ran her soft thumb over the back of my hand, and I tried to focus on that, not on the gut-wrenching pain I feared would come next.

"That day in the mall? I was going to tell you

how I felt. I had a crush on you, but when you started flirting with her, I kept it to myself."

We could have spent the last two years dating? "Why didn't you tell me?" I asked, devastated.

"Because I thought you deserved to be with someone like her," Callie said. "Someone who felt at home in her own skin, who wouldn't cause you to get made fun of for dating The Thing or the Loch Ness Monster or whatever mean things people said about me. You deserved a girl good enough for you, and when you went for her, I realized I wasn't it."

The pain in her voice took away my own words. I wanted to tell her she was wrong, that no girl in the world could hold a candle to her. Not in the way she looked or in the incredible heart beating in her chest. But Callie continued, "Around the time you guys got serious, Joe brought Nick over, and I just... I think I needed to fall for someone else, so I wouldn't remember how much I'd fallen for you."

My jaw twitched as I realized what an idiot I had been. How might things be different if I'd come clean when we were twelve? Fourteen? Sixteen? So many years had slipped by, but I promised myself I wouldn't do that ever again, not when it came to Callie.

"I'm here for you now," I promised. "And what

I feel for you is realer than anything I ever had with Sarah. I'm in this."

Her eyes were bright in the garage lights. "Really?"

I leaned forward and pressed my lips to hers, answering her in the same way she had answered me earlier. "No more fake dating. What I want with you…it's everything." I cupped her cheeks and laced my fingers through her hair. "I want to be here for you in the morning, when your breath smells terrible and you walk around the house half awake, bumping into things. I want to take in every single foster dog with you and kiss away your tears every time you have to say goodbye. I want to see you become a mom and love a child the way they deserve to be loved." My voice got tight. "And I want to become a better man every day with you by my side, because that's what you do for me, Callie. You make me the man I want to be."

Tears slipped over her cheeks, and I wiped them away with my thumbs.

"Do you want that?" I breathed.

She nodded. "More than anything."

I pulled her into my chest, holding on to her for dear life, because she *was* my life. She was my everything.

"I love you," I whispered.

My phone went off with a text message alert, and Callie smiled at me tearfully. "Let's go inside?"

I nodded, and as I got out of the car, I checked my message.

Gemma: Come get me please.

Gemma: Hurry.

My heart sprang into action almost as fast as my legs. "Callie, get the car ready in the driveway."

"What—?" She stalled by the door to their house, but I didn't have time to wait. "Gemma's in trouble." I started running out of the driveway toward my house, toward the place I never wanted to return.

My footsteps echoed on the pavement, pounding just as loudly as my heart. I sprinted to the front door and ripped it open, but Gemma was already on her way out. The crash of something being thrown hit my ears harder than any of my opponents ever had on the football field.

I took Gemma's shoulders firmly in my hands and pulled her away from the porch, asking, "What happened, Gemma?" My voice was forceful, but I needed to know. "Do I need to call the cops?"

"No," she sobbed, her voice shaky.

"Then what is it?"

Another crash sounded, closer this time, and she shuddered. Her lips trembled. "I'll tell you when we get to the hotel. Let's get out of here."

My eyes swung around, looking for any hint of our lowlife father. I didn't see him coming toward us. Yet.

"Let's go," she said.

"Get in Callie's car," I ordered, trying to take deep breaths. To shove down the rage spitting acid in my stomach and fire in my veins.

Callie had backed her car out of the garage, and it sat running in the driveway. She had the driver's side window open, watching us carefully. When it became clear Gemma was rooted to the spot, I put my arm around her shoulders and marched her to the passenger side, opening the door and helping her get in.

She wrapped her arms around her waist and folded over, sobbing. I knelt and ran my hand over her hair, trying to comfort her and failing miserably. My compassion for her warred with my anger at my father. How could he dismantle my strong, beautiful sister into this crying, broken heap?

"What happened?" I asked again.

She sat up, fruitlessly wiping at her nose. "He said all the things I worried were true about myself." Her sniffles started again, and she took a shaky, forceful breath, rolling her eyes. "All I care about is work, I'm worthless just like Mom, I'll never find anyone who loves me, we turned our mother against him, on and on. I just came here to help!"

"And you stuck around?" I immediately knew it was the wrong thing to ask, but how had Dad managed to get in so many blows without her leaving? Without her walking away like she finally had?

"You don't get it," she cried. "He's my dad. One of the only two people on this earth who should be programmed to love me, and he doesn't. What's *wrong* with me?"

Callie met my eyes over Gemma's sobbing form. I held my sister tighter to my chest. "Nothing is wrong with you." Time for Gemma to listen to her own words. "You are strong and kind and driven. His behavior has *nothing* to do with you. Remember?"

She looked up at me with wide green eyes, and like a punch to the gut, I saw the bruise forming on her cheek.

"He hit you?" I hissed.

She took my hands in hers, squeezing too tight. "Thank you for coming to get me. I know I don't deserve to count on you, but I do."

A rush of rage threatened to consume me, but I clenched my jaw and forced a breath through my nose. I had to be strong for Gemma. For Callie.

"Carson!" Callie screamed, but not fast enough.

Rough hands grabbed my shirt and shoulder and ripped me away from my sister. My father had me on the ground, punching me in the gut, in the side, anywhere he could get his hands.

"Get away from my daughter!" he slurred. "Get out of my life!"

I quickly rolled away and sprang to my feet. I had a fraction of a second before he came at me again, tackling me back to the hard cement. He pinned me down, his elbow pressing into my throat, and I scrabbled at his arm before bucking my hips to throw him off.

This time, I was on top, and I wasn't going down again. I crushed his windpipe just as he'd done mine, but he didn't have the strength to push me off.

"Carson," he wheezed, but I only pressed harder. This man needed to get out of my sister's life. Out of this world.

A hand tugged at my shoulders. "Carson! You're killing him!" Gemma screamed.

The first thought in my mind was *good*.

"Carson!" she screamed.

But I didn't let go. "If you ever touch my sister again, I'll *kill* you."

His eyes drifted shut, and I backed away, my chest heaving from the force of my breath. Gemma knelt next to our dad, shaking his shoulders, feeling for his pulse, shouting his name, despite his chest rising and falling.

"Carson," Callie breathed. Her eyes were wide, and they flitted from me to my father. There was something in her gaze I'd never wanted to see. *Fear*.

"Callie." I stepped closer to her, but she backed away.

My heart froze. No. No. This couldn't be happening. I stepped toward her again, and she stumbled backward.

Her actions said everything her lack of words didn't. She saw me as the monster I feared I was, and that was worse than heartbreak. Worse than living my life in the friend zone.

She didn't want anything to do with me. And I couldn't blame her. Neither did I.

Gemma could call a cab, Callie could drive her,

but the best thing for all of them was that I ran. As fast and as far as I possibly could.

I took off in a sprint, losing my sandals somewhere along the way, and I kept running until my lungs burned and my feet seared with pain and I couldn't physically go any farther. And then I collapsed into a heap on the sidewalk, lying back, not worried about someone coming by or a car hopping the curb and flattening me. I had no idea where I was, but it didn't matter, because no matter how far I ran, I'd never get away from the Cook Family Curse. I'd never escape myself.

THIRTY-NINE

CALLIE

The second Carson and Gemma's dad began stirring, we got into my car and drove away. He would be fine, but the two of us? That was questionable.

She sat ramrod straight in the passenger seat, only speaking to give me directions right or left until I was under the entrance awning of her hotel. Even when I got my car in park, Gemma didn't move. She stayed still for a moment, her eyes reflecting the hotel's green and blue neon sign.

Slowly, she rolled her head toward me, and her eyes were haunted—pools of horror I couldn't imagine—accented with a patch of purple mirroring the one I'd seen on Carson's face at the start of the summer.

"Please don't be mad at Carson," she said. "He was just trying to protect me."

"I'm not mad at him," I breathed. I was terrified. The Carson I'd seen in my driveway was not the friend I thought I knew. The Carson I knew never would have gone further than defending himself, never had the cold-blooded rage I'd seen in his eyes and in his actions. Who was that person I'd seen watching the life leave his dad's eyes? Would he come back?

Gemma nodded. "You know when you guys were twelve and there was that party at that snobby girl's house...Meredith?"

"Merritt," I said.

She gave a tired smile. "Merritt. Carson asked all us girls for advice before the party on how to get you to like him." She laughed softly. "We told him to pretend he wasn't interested, and he said he just ate all night."

The memory of him and the snack bar was still fresh. It made my lips turn up and my eyes water at the same time.

"He'd do anything for you," she said and peeled herself out of her seat. The action seemed to require all of her strength, and I asked, "Do you need me to walk you up to your room?"

She shook her head. "We Cook women learn how to deal with the bruises."

There was a bitter irony in her voice that sent an ache straight to my heart. "I'm sorry." I didn't know what I was apologizing for. I couldn't fix their situation. Couldn't change the family they were born into.

With a slight wave, she walked through the hotel's sliding doors.

After her form had disappeared around a corner, I reached for my phone. Part of me was hoping to see a text from Carson. Some kind of explanation for what had happened or why he hadn't let up when he'd clearly won against his father.

No new notifications waited for me. I even got on social media, hoping against all hope there would be a message there. Instead, I found something worse. An update showing Carson's relationship status had changed to single.

My heart shattered all over again, but I couldn't even cry. I was numb, in shock maybe, about what had happened. And even worse, I was a tiny bit relieved. I knew I should have been able to love Carson through what I saw, been on his side, but how could I give all of myself to someone, trust someone entirely, when I didn't even know all of who he was? We'd been best friends for eight years, and he'd hidden a part of himself so well I'd only just now seen it. What else lay beneath the surface?

I drove home, not even a single tear slipping down my cheek, but when I found myself in the safe place of my bed, looking at the closed curtain and knowing I'd never see my best friend through it again, I fell apart.

I sobbed until there was nothing left of me but tears and pain, and then slowly, mercifully, that pain led me to sleep.

I woke in the morning to a soft shake on my shoulder. My eyelids scratched over my dry eyes as I rolled over to see who'd come. Joe stood by my bed, one arm across his chest.

"Hey, Cal," he said softly.

He knew. I wasn't sure how, but I could see it in his stance, hear it in his voice, and it brought moisture to my eyes all over again.

Slowly, he sat on the edge of my bed and put a hand on my shoulder. "How are you holding up?"

I gave him a look. My puffy eyes could tell him all he needed to know.

"I'm so sorry," he said. "Is there anything I can do? Do you need me to beat him up or something?"

The comment was too close to home, knowing Carson probably had bruises to match Gemma's right now. "No, it's fine."

"Is it?" he asked.

Slowly, I shook my head, blinking quickly to hold back another flood of tears.

He rubbed my shoulder. "Should I have Mom call into work for you?"

"No." Because the only thing worse than going on with my life and acting like everything was okay would be sitting here and focusing on all the ways it wasn't.

"Okay," Joe said and paused. "I know I made fun of you two, but I really thought—I don't know. I thought you would make it."

"I did too," I breathed. And now it was over before it even really began.

He stood, and I got off of my bed too. The only way I knew to survive the break in my chest was to move. I got dressed, put on my makeup, and left for the shelter that had always been my safe place. I hoped it would feel that way today.

When I arrived, Lorelei told me the plan for the day—exercise the animals and give the dogs practice being on leashes. That sounded good to me. I'd be able to keep moving.

"Merritt can help you walk them," Lorelei added. "Could be a good chance for her to bond with the animals."

"Great." Just what I needed. Extra time with Merritt while I was vulnerable. Her surgically altered nose could smell weakness from a mile away and then somehow know exactly what to do to capitalize on it. The only thing I had on my side was that she had a weakness too.

Last I'd heard on the news, her father had been let out of jail on bail, but the Feds still weren't unfreezing his bank accounts. I wouldn't have been surprised if the Alexanders had to move to a less extravagant place. Or if Pam would have to find a job outside of volunteering as Emerson Academy's cheer coach.

Trying not to think of Merritt, or anyone else for that matter, I went to the dog room and pulled out a walking list. I could pair some of the animals together to do more work at one time, but some of the animals hated being around other dogs or cats at all.

I'd already leashed up a couple of dogs, but Merritt was still nowhere in sight. Leashes in hand, I walked to the kitten room and didn't see her there, nor in the storage area. The grooming room was the last place to look.

I pushed open the door and found her sitting with her back to me. "There you are."

She sniffed and turned toward me, revealing a small cat sitting on her lap. "Go away," she said.

Feeling the hurt in her voice, and recognizing my own, I stepped closer. The cat jumped out of her lap, and she said, "Great, look what you did," all the while, wiping the tears and running makeup from her face.

"What's going on?" I asked.

She narrowed her eyes at me, and then her entire hard exterior shattered, showing how broken she was on the inside. "You've seen what happened with my dad."

"I did," I said honestly. "I'm so sorry. I sent you a text, but it probably wasn't enough."

She wiped at her eyes, which were still leaking profusely. "Do you have any idea what it's like to wake up to helicopters flying over your house and reporters standing at your gate, finding out you're living off of money your father made by ruining lives?"

A fresh wail escaped her lips, and she leaned over her lap again, shaking with the force of her sobs. I didn't like Merritt, had been tortured by her, but I couldn't stand the pain she was in. I went to her and put my arms around her shoulders. Even though she stiffened, she didn't push me away.

Comforting someone else made me feel more like me. Like if I couldn't fix my own problems, at least I could help Merritt with hers.

The cat she'd been holding was now working its way around my legs, purring, and I picked it up. "Cats are great comfort animals," I said. "Do you have one at home?"

"No, my parents would never allow it. We're gone too much."

"I mean, that's kind of ideal for a cat. If you could hear the thoughts going through their minds." I raised my eyebrows. "Whew."

She laughed, and then glared at me. "Stop making me laugh. I'm sad."

I managed to smile myself and sat on the ground next to her. "Do you want to talk about it?"

She shook her head. "Not really." Then her

eyes landed on the leashes in my hands. "We're supposed to be walking the dogs, aren't we?"

I nodded. "But I can go and take care of the first round if you need some more time to yourself."

"No, it would be good for me to get some exercise. Maybe the endorphins will help."

The idea of exercising with Merritt brought back a flood of memories, along with new pain. Carson had always protected me from their ridicule back then, but now? I was on my own.

I pushed myself up from the floor and continued toward the door. The soft tap of Merritt's work shoes came behind me, blending with mine and the dogs' footsteps. We walked out the door and into the warm summer morning.

"Where do you want to walk?" Merritt asked, her voice still raw.

"There's a dog park not too far from here where we can go. These two should be pretty good with other animals."

She nodded, and for a while we walked side by side along the sidewalk that led toward the dog park. The hot summer sun beat down on our backs, making sweat bead on my forehead and neck. Some of the saltwater slipped into my psoriasis scabs, and I cringed against the pain.

"What's up with you?" Merritt asked.

I shook my head. "Just hot."

"Well maybe you shouldn't have worn a long-sleeve shirt," she said with a sense of superiority that rubbed my frayed nerves entirely the wrong way.

I glared at her. Did she even know what she was saying?

"What?" she asked, raising her hands in defense.

"Well, I can't exactly wear short sleeves or tank tops around you."

"Why not?" she popped off, and then realization crossed her face. "Oh."

Her words sparked a fire of anger within me. Not just at her but at this entire situation. Not only was I fat because I'd given up on sports, I'd been betrayed by her, a person I thought was my friend, just like Carson had betrayed me now, breaking up with me one day after promising me forever.

The more I thought about it, the angrier I got. "You know what, Merritt? You had the perfect life. You were petite and cute and your parents were rich and you had friends, and you still found a way to make me *miserable*. It wasn't good enough to just enjoy your own life—you had to crush mine to make yourself look even better. And I'm the dumb one who let you do it." I shoved through the dog park gate to let the dogs off their leashes. My hands shook I was so angry, but I finally got them unclipped, and they immediately ran to play with the other animals.

I sat on an open bench, trying to calm the rush of emotions in my mind. I'd lost everything back then, and it felt like I was going through it all over again, except worse. Because now I didn't even have my best friend at my side.

Slowly, Merritt sat on the opposite end of the bench. "I'm sorry about that, Callie. It was wrong."

I almost didn't believe what she said. I glanced over at her to see if she was joking, if there was a punchline coming, but Merritt had tears streaming down her cheeks. Still in disbelief, I said, "What?" I had to have misheard her.

"I'm sorry I hurt you, okay?" she cried. "I'm a mean girl. That's why Beckett broke up with me, that's why my friends will turn on me at the first chance they get, and that's why nothing I do is ever good enough for my parents." She dropped her head in her hands and sobbed.

My mouth parted, and then I pressed my lips together. "I get not feeling good enough."

"Can you stop being such a saint?" She stood and let out an exasperated groan. "Callie, I terrorized you for a skin condition you have no control over, and you're still trying to empathize with me. Stop." She folded her arms over her chest, shaking her head. "Maybe that's why Carson left you! Because no one can ever measure up!"

Her words were a dagger through my heart, but she was so, so wrong.

"I am so far from perfect. Remember? I sprayed you with a hose!"

"I insulted your ex. I deserved it."

"You didn't deserve that any more than I deserved to be picked on." The words hurt, but it was the truth. Being kind was a choice, and we'd both made some bad ones. "It's not easy to be a good person. And sometimes you fail, and it eats at you." I still didn't know how to make sense of what Carson did. How I felt about it. But I was still guilty for my reaction. My best friend had come toward me for comfort, and I'd stepped away. "We all make mistakes."

Even Carson. Especially me.

FORTY

CARSON

Beckett shook my shoulder roughly. "Carson." Fear filled his voice. "Carson! You okay?"

I slowly pried my eyes open. I felt like I'd been run over by a truck. My muscles ached, my feet burned, and holy hell this headache was making it hard to think.

But my thoughts were there, at the ready to attack me with every passing second.

I'd lost everything last night. My best friend. My girlfriend. My future. And for what? To teach my dad a lesson? That low life didn't deserve any of my time, but I'd fallen into the trap of my family curse, hook, line, and sinker.

Beckett gripped his hand underneath my arm,

hauling me to a sitting position. The light streaming in through their penthouse windows burned, and I squinted against it. "What time is it?"

"Noon," Beckett answered, his eyes dark. "What the hell happened? You look terrible."

I rubbed my forehead, then raked my fingers through the knots in my hair. His question, and my answer, made my eyes sting. "I lost her." Emotion heaved at my chest, and I sobbed, falling over my knees.

"What happened?" The fear was still there in Beckett's voice, but I couldn't tell him part of last night's event without telling him all of it, and I couldn't even think about speaking over this massive boulder growing in my throat.

Every time I thought I was close to being able to talk, the sobs came harder, so hard I dry-heaved until Beckett got me a bowl and I lost acid inside it. He tried consoling me, but when he failed, I heard him talking to Rory on the phone. I assumed it was Rory, because I heard him muttering Callie's name, thinking I wouldn't hear him say it.

I fell back on his couch, throwing my arm over my face to at least shield me from the light. When did light get that bright? When did just being awake hurt so much?

I didn't know when, or how, but I passed out again. My brain must have known staying awake was too much to bear. When I woke again, orange light came through the windows and Beckett was handing me toast. Telling me to sit up and get something in my stomach.

There was a drink too. Something sugary that went horribly with the cardboard I was trying to stomach.

After I'd finished half a piece, Beckett said, "Rory told me what happened."

The stake in my heart twisted, because that meant more people knew how horrible I was. That I'd almost killed my dad, not once but twice. That the Cook Family Curse was alive and well inside my body, and falling for someone just meant saddling them with it too.

Beckett patted my back. "I'm so sorry."

His words made my throat tight, and I swallowed, hard. "I lost her." I choked out.

"It doesn't have to be over, does it?" he asked. "Rory said you were the one who called it."

I shook my head and shoved my drink away on the coffee table. "You didn't see the way she looked at me. She's *afraid* of me."

"She was surprised!" Beckett argued. "Can you blame her?"

"No. That's the problem. She's better off with someone else—anyone else."

"You can't let your fear get in the way of your relationship with her," Beckett said, rubbing his palms over his jeans. "Being in love is hard—no one said you had to be perfect."

I gripped at my chest, over the spot where hollowness had replaced my heart. "And that means I'm not going to risk her."

"But you are!" he argued, standing up. "You're running away scared."

I narrowed my eyes at him, ready to punch him too. If he couldn't see that Callie needed to be protected—that I was a danger to her—he was part of the problem. "You might be fine with girls rolling the dice on a guy like me, but I'm not. She deserves so much better." I shook my head at him and began grabbing my things to leave.

"So that's it? You're just going? You're not even going to try?" Disappointment dripped from his voice and landed on me like acid.

"I've been trying." I hauled two garbage bags over my shoulders and walked to the elevator. The second I pushed the button, the doors dinged and opened.

As I stepped inside and jabbed the button to the parking garage, Beckett looked at me and shook his head. "I thought you were better than that."

I lifted my chin. "I did too."

The metal doors closed on my view of him, and I sagged back against the wall. Everyone was disappointed in me, which just reassured me I was making the right decision by leaving. But I wasn't really sure where I'd go.

I'd planned on life-guarding the rest of the summer and saving my money, but I couldn't stay here anymore. The pool—the town—carried too many memories of Callie. It turned out when you spent your whole life loving someone, it was hard to know what to do, who to be, when that relationship stopped.

I thought about calling Mom, asking if I could bum it with her in her hotel where I wouldn't know a soul, but that didn't feel right either. I'd just be around another one of the women who suffered at the hands of the Cooks. I needed to go somewhere different, somewhere safe.

I got out my phone and typed in my grandparents' address, and then I left Emerson and my old self behind.

The farther I got from Emerson, the emptier I felt. I was leaving my past, but I was also leaving my future. My phone kept ringing as calls from Gemma and my mom came through. Gemma had surely told Mom, but there wasn't a great way to say the apple didn't fall far from the poison tree.

I needed my GPS to get to my grandparents' house, though, so I finally bit the bullet and picked up the phone. Before I had a chance to say anything, my mom's voice came through the speakers, saying, "Carson! Thank God you're okay."

My lip curled at her concern. Was she really that worried about my safety? My well-being? She raised four children in a home with an abuser, and now she wanted to make sure I was okay?

"I'm not okay, *Mom.* I have a bruise on my face the size of your husband's fist and one in my side the size of his shoe. My sister's going back to work with a shiner, and the girl I love is terrified of me." My vision blurred, and I pulled off onto the shoulder. A semi blew past, careless to the turmoil happening alongside the road.

Suddenly, the car felt too small, too tight, and I stepped into the hot, dry air, staring over the desert scrub. I crossed the front of the car, pressing my eyes to keep the tears at bay. When I lifted the phone back to my ear, my mom's sobs came through the speaker.

"I'm so sorry," she cried. "I'm so, so sorry."

I'd dreamed of the day my parents would realize they'd made a mistake—the day they'd apologize for what they put my sisters and me through, but this didn't feel like what I'd imagined. Mom's words didn't change the last eighteen years, didn't make the bruise go away, wouldn't make me a safe person for Callie.

I didn't need Mom's apology. I needed my grandparents. Someone to love me no matter where I came from.

I got back into my car and drove until I reached my old hometown. Until the brick bungalow came into view. And then I walked down the sidewalk and I stared at the bright yellow door to my grandparents' house. It looked exactly the same, but incredibly different. They had the same porch swing out front. The same old truck sat in the driveway, but now they had a massive carport beside their house for their RV. Their doormat read *Home Is Where You Park It*.

Now that I was here, I felt like a little kid again,

running over from my parents' house to avoid their arguing. To get some freshly baked cookies and a glass of milk and a solid hour of cartoons. The same sense of security wasn't there, though. Because I knew no matter how far I ran, I couldn't escape the curse. Couldn't escape myself.

I wasn't even sure if I should knock. As a kid I used to walk right in, but it had been a long time since I called Texas home.

My question was answered as the door swung open and my grandma pulled me into a hug. She was shorter than me—only coming up to the base of my chest—but she made me feel small wrapped inside her arms. Safe.

I dropped my head on her shoulder and sobbed.

FORTY-ONE

CALLIE

When I walked into the house after work, my dad was in the living room watching the news. At the sight of me coming inside, he hit the mute button and twisted on the couch. "How was your day, kid?"

"Long." I dropped my purse off my shoulder and set it by the door. Thank goodness Mom was at her book club because she would have called me on it.

"Want to watch some *Bake Off*?" he asked. "That always cheers your mom up."

"Definitely," I answered. Honestly, it didn't matter what was on. I just needed to be around the one man who'd never let me down. "I'm just going to go upstairs and shower off real quick, then I'll be back."

He nodded and flicked the sound back on. I went up to my room, dropped my dirty clothes in the hamper, and rinsed off, tying my hair in a knot above my head. Hearing from Rory earlier about Carson had really caught me off guard.

Apparently, Beckett had told her that Carson was really torn up—blisters all over his feet, a massive welt on his face, and eyes red from crying. He'd just left Beckett's house with his things and no explanation of where he was going or when he'd be back. But he still hadn't texted me. Still hadn't told me why he'd ended things without saying a single word.

Not knowing where he was felt like having a piece of myself missing. I worried if he was okay...if he was thinking of me. My eyes stung with unshed tears, and I blinked them back, busying myself with applying my psoriasis cream instead. How long could I cry over someone who left me without a second thought? A second chance?

Forever, the pain in my chest told me.

Which meant I had to learn to live with it, because my dad was waiting for me, and I didn't want him to see me fall apart then blame Carson.

Part of me still felt protective over Carson, wanted my family to love him like they always had.

When I finished dressing and had some semblance of composure, I went downstairs. Once I settled on the couch next to my dad, he put his arm around me, and I cuddled into him like I always did when I was younger.

We decided to watch an episode on cookies, and he set the remote down as it played. The lump in my throat grew, but I swallowed it back, overwhelmingly grateful to have the dad I did. Living next door to Carson and seeing how much he and his sisters struggled with their own father made me appreciate mine that much more. I never had to worry about him ignoring me, much less endangering my mom or brother in any way.

I looked up at him, at his clean-shaven face and bushy eyebrows. "I love you, Dad."

"I love you too, kid." He smiled softly and placed a kiss atop my head. "How're you doing?"

"I've been better," I said honestly.

He nodded. "Want to talk about it?"

"Not really." I pointed toward the TV. "Who do you think's going to win the first challenge?"

He pointed at a guy on the right side of the screen. "That one has great flavor, but that one has excellent presentation. If you put them together, they'd be as good as your mother."

I smiled and shook my head. My mom definitely was not bake-show material, but I loved the way Dad supported her behind her back and teased her to her face. That was the kind of love I wanted to have someday. The kind of love I thought I'd had with Carson.

"I heard you found your mom some contestants for her cookie fundraiser."

I shrugged. "Some of my friends agreed to help out. No big deal."

"Maybe," he said, "but you didn't have to, and that makes it that much more special. I'm proud of you, Cal."

"If you keep being nice to me, I'm going to cry," I replied, half-joking, half-honest.

After squeezing me, he lifted the remote and turned the volume up a couple notches so we could get lost in the show. As I sat with him, I thought about Carson, and no matter how much I tried to focus on the mouthwatering food on the screen, or that my dad had praised me, I just couldn't get him off my mind. Couldn't stop seeing the glazed look in his eyes as he towered over his dad.

I wanted to remember Carson as my friend, not as the guy who broke my heart.

But how was that possible when my chest ached with every breath? When my hand felt empty without his holding it?

Dad offered me the remote, and I blinked at the screen, realizing the show was over. Rather than sit in front of the TV and not watch another episode, I kissed my dad on the cheek and went up to my room. Which was completely pointless because I just ended up lying awake in bed, hoping for the thoughts of Carson to stall.

They did. Hours later when sleep finally came.

The doorbell rang, and Franklin danced around my feet, barking loudly.

"Can you get the door?" Mom asked me Friday afternoon. I was making a test round of cookies for the bake-off with Mom's supervision. She had just shown me how to roll out the cold dough, and she had grease and flour on her hands.

All week, I'd found ways to occupy my mind— to avoid my friends. I couldn't handle the thoughts of Carson that always plagued me, especially with his absence so palpable. His name always used to top the messages in my phone, but now it wasn't even on the opening screen. His spot on the couch had remained empty. And my heart? Still broken.

I wiped my hands on my apron and walked to the door with Franklin on my heels. I tried to shush him as I swung it open, but there was no need once he saw Rory and the other girls.

He gave a final yap before running to Rory and jumping on her legs.

Me on the other hand? I was less than thrilled. "What are you guys doing here? I told you I was cooking with my mom."

Jordan narrowed her eyes. "Callie, how long do you think you can avoid us?"

My cheeks heated as I bent to gather Franklin. "I'm not avoiding you. I'm just busy."

Zara pursed her lips together. "So your schedule just *happened* to get slammed the week after you broke up with your boyfriend."

"That's right." I began stepping backward and closing the door. "Sorry, don't want my cookies to burn."

From behind me, my mom called, "I've got them!" at the same time Ginger's hand stopped the door.

I closed my eyes and sighed.

"You can't ignore us forever," Ginger said softly. "Or your feelings."

"Come inside," I finally said.

Rory stepped forward and took me in a hug that almost had me falling apart. I'd only really dated Carson for an afternoon, but every time I closed my eyes, I could see him. Carson hurting his dad. Carson kissing me so tenderly. Carson laughing. Carson running away. How did the same person hold so many emotions in my heart?

Franklin yapped at us, and we broke apart, Rory smiling gently and me wiping at my eyes.

Franklin jumped into her arms, and I turned back toward the kitchen, where my mom was watching it all unfold. Before I had a chance to speak, she said, "Why don't you girls go upstairs? I'll teach you another time, Cal."

I nodded and thanked her before heading to my room with my girls. But now that we were all spaced around with Franklin happily dancing between us for extra pets and cuddles, I had no idea what to do.

I told them as much, and Zara said, "That's fine. We're here for you, whatever you need."

I looked toward the ceiling, fighting tears. "Tell me about your jobs? Life? Anything?"

Jordan jumped in first, telling me she signed up for CNA classes to get hands-on experience in patient care. She would start in the next couple of weeks. Rory had met her college roommate online, and they'd been video chatting to get to know each other. Ginger was hard at work, creating marketing videos for Ray's family's ranch, and Zara had already handled difficult actors on the set of her film.

The summer was halfway over, and they'd already accomplished so much. Meanwhile, I had a heartbreak under my belt and nothing to show for it.

A soft knock sounded on my door, and Franklin ran to it, yapping.

"It's just me," Mom said, poking her head in. She swung the door open wider, revealing a full platter of cookies. "Thought you girls might like a snack." Mom set the platter on my desk, along with a stack of napkins.

Ginger stood from her spot on my bed and went to the desk. "These are adorable, Anne."

Mom smiled so wide her face almost looked like it could split in two. "You think so?"

Ginger took a bite and through a mouthful of crumbs said, "Yeah, and so delicious."

Jordan picked a cookie from the platter and added, "You're definitely winning the cookie competition."

"I'm not entering," my mom said. "That would definitely be a conflict of interest, but I'm excited to see what you girls come up with."

Zara gave her a wink. "Is it too late to get your secret recipe?"

Mom waved her finger in the air. "That is between me, God, and Pinterest."

I laughed. "So, check your Pinterest boards. Got it."

Mom gave me an amused smile and said, "I'll let you girls hang out." She shut my bedroom door behind her, leaving the five of us alone. We were quiet for a little bit as she plodded down the stairs.

Ginger broke her cookie in half and took a big bite of it. "These really are good. Ray's mom makes the best chocolate chip cookies, but these might have them topped. Actually..." She reached into her big purse and pulled out a container of chocolate chip cookies. "I thought you might need some comfort food."

My heart ached at how spot-on she was.

Zara laughed. "Great minds think alike

because..." She got five small frosting containers out of her purse.

"No way!" Rory said. She took out a big bag of fancy chocolates.

We all turned our eyes on Jordan, who blushed and reached into her own bag. "I brought some donut holes from the bakery."

I couldn't help but laugh. My friends knew me well, but they didn't understand that this wasn't a breakup like the movies, where you could stuff your face with ice cream and move on. Carson had been a part of my life since I was ten years old. We rode to school together, attended our first party together, sat at lunch together—he'd been my everything, but he'd made me his nothing.

My laugh turned into sobs, and I put my face in my hands. Each of my friends crossed the room, trying to comfort me, but nothing could change the way my heart constantly felt like a ball of broken glass. Every breath I took only made the pain worse.

As my sobs subsided, Zara asked gently, "What happened? We were all at the beach, and then I'm seeing online that it's over. You two seemed so happy."

"We were," I agreed. But I was tired of lying—

tired of hiding. These girls had been here for me through it all, and it was time I told them the truth. They listened quietly as I told them how my relationship with Carson actually started this summer. That it was a ploy to get someone else. I kept my eyes on the tan carpet as I spoke, hating to think of the betrayal that would show on their faces.

"But somewhere in the pretending, it became real, for both of us," I said shakily. "I gave him my whole heart." Tears spilled over my cheeks, and Ginger rubbed my shoulder.

"So he broke up with you after you said you'd be with him?" she asked. "That doesn't make any sense. Why would he do that?"

My throat was raw as I said, "Because when he needed me, I backed away." If I could go back and do it over, I'd have called the cops, would have punched Carson's dad myself for hurting Carson and Gemma. How could I blame Carson for fighting back and taking out his anger against someone who had caused his family so much pain? I'd just been surprised, scared at the side of Carson I'd never seen before. But deep down, I knew his heart was good. He'd been my best friend for eight years. After all that time, I *knew* him. Knew that he would never do anything to hurt the people he loved.

As I told them about Carson's home life, their mouths fell open in mirroring images of shock and horror.

Zara covered her mouth with her hand. "I never would have guessed... He was always so happy."

My heart broke even more, seeing their initial reaction. Carson had suffered so privately. "He was always the light for everyone else that he needed for himself."

Ginger shook her head, rubbing my shoulder. "What are you going to do to get him back?"

"He made it pretty clear," I said, staring at the wall across from me. "He doesn't want to be with me anymore. I should have just followed through on my plan to be with Nick."

Rory tilted her head toward me, making her dark curls spill over her shoulder. "You know it wouldn't work. You don't feel for him like you do for Carson."

"Maybe that's good," I said, picking the icing off my cookie. "Because if caring about someone like I do for Carson makes me feel like this, I never want to feel like this again."

"Come on, Callie." Jordan pursed her full lips. "You're the most caring person I know. You're practically a saint, for crying out loud."

"I'm not though!" I argued, standing. They each looked at me in shock, but I didn't care. "Everyone thinks I'm so perfect, but I'm not. I sprayed Merritt with a hose. I lied to you. Made up a fake relationship to manipulate a guy. Broke my best friend's heart. Can't you see that I'm...I'm..." My voice cracked, and tears flooded my eyes. "I'm nowhere near good enough for my best friend."

Jordan stood and pulled me into a hug, holding me together. "We're here for you. Whatever you need."

"I need to stop thinking about him," I said through my snivels.

Full of purpose, Zara nodded. "Let's go out tonight then. Do you guys know of anything going on?"

I put my chin in my hand. "I was going to go to Nick's poetry reading tonight, but..."

"But what?" Zara asked. "No matter how much it feels like your heart is coming out of your chest, you've got to live your life. Maybe going to this reading will be exactly what you need. You have to *try*. Life's too short to give up now."

Knowing how much Zara had lost in her short life made her words mean that much more. I reached out for her hand, and she gripped mine back.

"I'll do it on one condition," I said.

"Anything," Zara agreed.

"Will you guys come with me?"

They all nodded, and with a grin, Zara said, "Of course."

FORTY-TWO

CARSON

The week passed by in a blur. Grandpa had me help him with some projects around the house he'd been putting off. Grandma made three-course dinners for every meal and homemade favorites for desserts, loving me with her food. When my thoughts got to be too much, I threw on a pair of tennis shoes and ran as far and as fast as I could until my muscles gave out and my mind gave in. I took different loops around town, making sure to never go by my old house, by the place where all the suffering began.

For three generations, Cook families had lived in that house, each one just as bad as the one before it, and I didn't need to see the physical reminder of all the turmoil in my life. Especially not right now. I was a week into my stay with my grandparents, and I felt just as lost as I had the night I arrived.

Tonight, I walked the last half mile back to Grandma and Gramps's house, cooling down. Last night, Grandma saw me collapse on the porch in exhaustion and got scared. I never wanted to make her worry.

With my breathing steadied and sweat dried into patches of salt on my skin, I walked inside. Grandma and Gramps looked at me from the living room.

A hint of relief crossed Grandma's eyes. "Good run?"

I nodded, going to the fridge to get a bottle of water.

Grandpa chuckled. "Gotta run off all that good cooking, right?"

I laughed and took a swig of my drink. "Not possible." Truthfully, having good meals three times a day was making it to where I could push myself harder than ever.

A baby's cry sounded from somewhere in the house, and my eyebrows drew together. "What was that?" They only had a TV in the main living room as far as I knew.

Grandma and Gramps exchanged a look, and Grandpa gave me a soft, weathered smile. "We found someone we thought could help you." He leaned his head over his shoulder and yelled toward the back bedroom. "Clary? He's back."

My lips parted as my oldest sister came into the living room carrying her youngest child. The little boy, James, was almost a year old now, and he already looked so different than the pictures I'd seen on social media.

I froze at the island and braced myself on the granite top. "Clary?" I asked her as much as them. "What are you doing here?"

Grandma crossed from the couch to me and took my cheek in her hand. "We might not know exactly what you're going through, but we knew someone who did."

Clary gave me a tentative smile and nodded.

"But how?" I asked. Surely a last-minute flight wasn't in my grandparents' retirement budget.

"You know your grandma," Gramps said with a teasing smile. "Always getting those credit card points." He rose from the couch and gently took James from Clary's arms, and he snuggled into Gramps's chest, closing his eyes. He must have felt Gramps was safe, just like I did.

Clary nodded toward the door. "I know you're probably tired, but can we go on a walk?"

Slowly, I agreed. I set my bottle down on the island and moved toward the door without my brain telling me to. Then I stepped into the cool night air with a sister I hadn't seen in years.

FORTY-THREE

CALLIE

Joe sent me the address of the coffee shop in Brentwood, and I plugged it into my phone's GPS. The girls and I each rode separately, but knowing they were coming with me made me feel better.

We met in front of the coffee shop, Espress Yourself, and Ginger chuckled. "Nice one."

I half-smiled before opening the door. It felt weird not having Carson here. He and I did everything together, and I was coming to learn how much I depended on him. How much I truly enjoyed having him around. The thought of going to college and living on the same campus as strangers...it made it hard to breathe.

"Let's get some drinks, then scope the crowd,"

Zara said as if sensing my unease. "Everything's going to be just fine."

Shoving aside the thoughts, for self-preservation more than anything else, I walked alongside my friends through the crowd of people. Even though it was warm outside and the space was packed, the air conditioning in here was ice cold. Probably part of their strategy to keep college kids from hogging the tables all day.

As we waited for the barista to make our drinks, I looked around, wondering where my brother was.

"Hot chocolate and a mocha?" the barista called.

Zara and I thanked her and took our drinks, telling the other three we'd grab seats for everyone. We parted from them, walking the perimeter of the room. Finally, we found my brother sitting with a couple of his friends. And there were still a few empty seats at their table. When he saw me, Joe lifted his chin and said, "Hey," then did a double-take. "Are you wearing makeup?"

My cheeks flushed hot. That had been Zara's idea. "Do you mind if we sit here?"

He shook his head. "I saved it for you." He lifted his chin toward my friend. "Hi, Zara."

She smiled back and said hello before offering

to grab a couple extra chairs. When the rest of us had adjusted to make room, I realized we had the perfect setup. The way these chairs were angled, we would be able to see the stage when Nick was performing.

Callie, Ginger, and Rory sat down, and with my brother here, I felt a little more whole.

The person with the microphone began introducing the poetry night with the theme of missed opportunities.

This had been a bad idea.

Why had I come to a place bursting with emotions when I could hardly contain my own? I clapped along with everyone else, but made my own personal exit plan as he began talking about the poets and how each of them had five minutes to perform an original piece of work.

I leaned over to Joe first, saying, "I need to use the bathroom." With all the people in here, I could slip out without being noticed and send my friends a massively apologetic text.

"Wait," Joe said. "Nick should be up soon."

I shifted in my seat, uncomfortable for other reasons than the lame excuse I'd given him. "Okay, just until he's done."

The first poet came on, and she waved her

hands about as she delivered a short and enthusiastic poem about sunshine and how you didn't appreciate it the right way until it was dark outside. It was cute—a little cliché—but cute. Beside me, Joe snorted.

I hit his arm. "Don't make fun of her."

Pressing his lips together to repress a smile, he shook his head. "Wait until you hear Nick's."

The way he said it made me feel like there was something I wasn't getting. "What do you mean? Have you heard it already?"

Joe's lips formed a half-smile. "I have, because he wrote it for you."

My mouth fell open, and my stomach bottomed out like it had jumped out of an airplane. Nick had written a poem for me? He'd asked Joe about it? I was so confused and curious and in awe. Did this mean...

Nick walked onto the stage to a smattering of applause. Today, he wore dark-wash jeans and a white tunic shirt that clung to his narrow frame. Logically, I knew he looked handsome, soulful. But I couldn't help comparing him to Carson. Thinking about how well Carson filled out a pair of jeans or how the smooth muscles of his arms would look holding up the paper.

Nick glanced at me, a soft smile on his lips, and began reading. "This poem is called 'Fade.'

Zara took my hand. "Is he doing what I think he's doing?"

I couldn't speak because I was too busy listening to the next lines of the poem.

Something's right in front of you,
    It's just as plain as day,
    but when you see it so often,
    it tends to fade away.

No amount of beauty nor grace
    could ever take her place,
    and no type of replacement
    could hold regret at bay.

I've watched her close up,
    never seeing more than from afar,
    and now my heart must stay inside
    a tightly sealed up jar.

. . .

I wonder if I've missed my chance or if
she'll stop and see
that the guy she really should be with
is here and that it's me.

Cheers erupted around me, and for a moment, I was disoriented. I blinked, trying to focus on Nick. He tilted his head toward the door and then disappeared behind the stage curtains.

Joe leaned over and said, "He'll wait for you on the patio—if you want to go." His tone was gentle, and I realized this was his way of helping me and his best friend, but my heart felt like stone inside my chest.

I turned toward my friends, my eyes wide. Their expressions were a melting pot of shock and sympathy.

"Wow," Zara said, squeezing my hands. "This is huge...right? It's what you've been wanting all summer?"

My heart twisted at her words. "Yeah, it is." But was it still what I wanted? I would love to be in a relationship that didn't result in the kind of pain I'd felt for the last week. "But is it too soon?" I looked at my friends. "I have to see him, right?"

Rory smiled sadly. "You don't have to do anything, Callie."

As I realized what they were doing, I nodded. They wanted to give me the space to make my own decisions. The mark of a true friend. And I was lucky enough to have four. I smiled at my friends and left my seat.

Mechanically, I walked toward the double doors at the back of the shop. Through the windows, I could see Nick leaning against the railing around the deck, looking out over the parking lot.

Slowly, I crossed the weathered wood and stood next to him. Beyond the parking lot, other shops lined downtown Brentwood. It was a cute area, and my first thought was that I wanted to show Carson. Reeling from the pain that thought created, I said, "That was a nice poem."

He lifted a corner of his lips and turned his dark eyes on mine. "I had hoped you'd think so."

"Why now?" I asked. After months of pining for him from afar, I had to know. Why had my heart had to get caught up in this mess for him to notice me?

"Because it was better than tomorrow," Nick said. "If the last month's taught me anything, it's that I need to make a move while I still can."

My eyes felt hot, and I blinked back the tears.

Oblivious, Nick slipped his fingers through mine. His hands were smaller than Carson's. Softer. "Watching him hold your hand made me realize how much I wanted to do the same thing." With his free hand, he tucked a curl behind my ear. "It should have been me holding your hand. Kissing your lips." His gaze went from my eyes to my mouth, and I completely froze.

Time seemed to slow and move in years instead of seconds as he closed the gap between us and put his wet lips on mine. I wanted to like it, begged my body to give in to the kiss and forget the boy next door. Forget my best friend, but I couldn't.

Tears streamed from my eyes and a sob escaped my lips. I pulled back from Nick's concerned face. "I'm sorry," I said and left Nick and any leftover hopes of a relationship with him behind.

FORTY-FOUR

CARSON

I still didn't understand what Clary was doing here. For the last six years, she'd been out of my life, busy creating her own. And now, here she was, walking down the sidewalk with me like she had nowhere better to be.

"It's nice outside," she said, tucking her hands into her jacket pockets. "It never cools down at night like this in North Carolina."

I stopped in the middle of the sidewalk, and after a few steps, she realized I wasn't walking with her. I was frustrated, confused, and exhausted beyond measure. I didn't feel like talking about the weather. "Clary, what's going on?"

She bit her lip and looked toward the empty

street. "Gemma called me and told me what happened."

My stomach roiled. "Great, so now everyone knows what a monster I am."

"Carson," she admonished.

"What?" I demanded, spreading my arms at my sides. "Gemma was there. She saw. You think this bruise just came unprovoked?"

Her lips pressed together. "I talked to Mom too."

So she knew the whole story. Heard about my spiral to shame. How I'd lost everything that mattered to me. "And our grandparents called you down here to fix it? You can't." I dropped onto the curb and sat down, lacing my fingers behind my neck and hanging my head between my knees. "No one can."

After a moment, Clary's softer footsteps sounded beside me, and she sat on the curb as well. We sat in silence for a long time—minutes, hours— while all the things I'd ruined ran through my mind.

Finally, I said, "Don't you have a baby to go back to?"

"He's fine with them for a little while," she said. "I pumped extra just in case."

"He needs his mom," I said finally.

"And my brother needs his sister."

Her words struck me. For once, she was choosing to stay. She was choosing me in a way no one had.

"Come on," she said. "I want to show you something."

Even though she was half my size, she extended her hand and helped me up.

"Where are we going?" I asked.

"You'll see." She began walking down the sidewalk, and I followed her, taking in the neighborhood that was the same but so different. People had landscaped their lawns differently, the street had been repaved, but maybe the most different thing was my sister and me.

My breath caught as I realized where she was taking us. "Clary?"

"Yeah?"

"Why are we going there?"

"You'll see."

My heart beat faster as she walked down the sidewalk that led to our old house, the one where we'd endured so much pain, where, when we were on the brink of falling apart, Mom up and moved us to California. This place held so many bad memories, and even though I missed my grandparents, I'd be lying if I said staying away from this house wasn't part of what kept me away from them.

But as the two-story farmhouse came into view, it looked completely different. The new owners had planted beautiful bright flowers along the walk, and there was a giant wreath of flowers hanging on the door. A porch swing, not too unlike the one my grandparents had, set on the porch with plush pillows.

But the most stunning thing? Through the front bay window that showed the dining table, we could see a family with three children, playing a card game. They laughed and smiled and looked like the genuine picture of love.

Clary put her arm around my shoulders, and I felt her eyes on me.

I looked over at her, my eyes moist. "They look so happy." It was everything I'd wanted for myself as a kid and everything I dreamed of for my future —the one I wanted to have with Callie.

"They do," she agreed. "You know, three generations of Cooks lived in that house. Each one worse than the last. And look at it now. It's an entirely different place because of the heart that's inside it."

Her words hit me one at a time as she turned

and put her hands on my shoulders, making sure I was looking at her.

"Gemma left and started a career. Sierra is in love with an incredible guy and having the adventure of a lifetime in Europe. I have the kind of family I always wanted. My kids never go to bed wondering if I'll be hurt in the morning or if there will be glass on the floor when they wake up. They never have to worry if their siblings are taken care of." She blinked quickly, her eyes shining. "And now, you have a choice too." She brushed back the hair falling into my eyes with the tips of her fingers. "Are you going to let it end with you?"

Her eyes searched my face for the answer, and finally she said. "I need to get back to my choice."

And I needed to make my own.

FORTY-FIVE

CALLIE

As I pulled into my driveway, I saw a moving truck outside Carson's house. The sign had been covered with a **SOLD** banner.

I put my car in park and covered my mouth, feeling like a giant door had been slammed on my heart. For the last ten years, I'd looked through my window to see Carson, and this just made it that much more real that I wouldn't be able to do it again.

Carson's dad walked out the front door and down the sidewalk toward the moving truck. Seeing him made the hairs on the back of my neck stand up. Even the stance of his shoulders was predatory, brutal.

Despite growing up next to Carson, seeing him every day after the devastation, I had no idea what he'd really been through. What it would feel like to know the blood that ran through a monster's veins also ran through yours.

My stomach clenched with guilt. I should have been more understanding. More patient. More curious just to sit with him and hear what had been going through his mind after knowing his dad hurt his sister. I couldn't imagine what I would do if anyone ever put their hands on Joe.

His dad crossed the front of the truck, got in, and fired it up. Exhaust flew behind the truck and blurred the taillights as he took off down the street, leaving this place forever. Although I was relieved for Carson that his dad was gone, I felt a deep sense of loss too. Deep inside, I had a need to say goodbye to this house, the one that had kept my friend for all these years.

Getting out of my car, I walked to the fence alongside the house and to the back door. I'd never really been in Carson's house—it was always more comfortable to hang out at mine—but I still remembered the path to his room.

I twisted the knob they always left unlocked and stepped inside, not sure what I would find. A cleaning company must have come through, because the living room and kitchen had been entirely wiped clean of any hint that the Cooks had lived there.

A surreal feeling came over me as I walked up the carpeted stairs, imagining what it must have felt like for Carson seeing this for the first time. For the last.

I turned right at the top of the stairs and walked into Carson's room. It had been left bare. Not his corkboard with the *Star Wars* pins, nor his bed, nor the navy-blue curtains at his windows remained.

I walked to the window that faced mine and took in the white blinds I could see through the glass. Was this what Carson had been looking at through all his struggles since he started dating Sarah? A closed window and a friend who shut out anything uncomfortable?

Feeling a stinging in my eyes, I sat on his floor and cried. I promised to myself I would be there for him from here on out. He would never have to face his demons alone, not with me at his side believing and seeing the best in him.

When my tears were spent, I got up from the floor and left the house behind. It was time to move forward.

Once I was in the safety and privacy of my own room, I got out my phone and group called my friends.

"I need your help," I said.

Equally big grins filled the screen, and Zara said, "Whatever it is. We're here."

"I need Carson. This heartbreak's gone on long enough."

"Yes!" Jordan cheered. "Let's stop this nonsense and get you your happily ever after, once and for all."

Rory nodded. "It's time to get your best friend back."

Truer words had never been spoken.

FORTY-SIX

CARSON

As I walked back to my grandparents' house, I felt like a different man. Clary was right. I had no obligation to continue the curse, and I'd be damned if I let a line of abusers decide my life. I was stronger than that. Had been through too much to repeat the cycle. I had too much to lose. I just hoped it wasn't too late to repair my relationship with Callie. She was everything to me. Ever since I was a little kid, her friendship, support, and guidance were exactly what I needed. I just hoped I was what she wanted.

When I entered the house, the smell of cookies greeted me. The smell of *home*. Grandma, Gramps, and Clary were at the kitchen table, nibbling at a batch of Grandma's famous chocolate chip cookies.

Cautiously, I stepped toward them, feeling vulnerable in a way I hadn't before. Grandma smiled at me and extended her arm. I leaned into her hug, then sat down between her and Grandpa. He patted my back.

Feeling more at home than I ever had before, I looked between them and my sister. "I need to go back and make things right with Callie."

Clary's smile couldn't have been bigger. Grandma looked just as excited, her light blue eyes shining. "Your neighbor girl?"

Clary scoffed. "*The* neighbor girl. Carson's loved her since he was ten years old."

Grandpa chuckled. "What's been the hold up, then?"

Closing my eyes, I shook my head. "I don't know, but I'm done being too afraid to tell the love of my life how I feel and who I am."

Clary reached across the table and took my hand. "I'm proud of you, Cars."

"Don't be proud yet. It might be too late." I shuddered thinking of what moving on looked like for Callie. I had seen the way Nick looked at her.

He wouldn't wait long to make his move, to get his chance, especially with me out of the picture. I couldn't blame him.

"For true love, it's never too late," Grandma said.

My eyes stung, and the lump in my throat got even harder. I swallowed back the emotion and said, "I hope so. Because she's the one."

Gramps and Grandma exchanged a look, and Gramps nodded.

"In that case," Grandma said and began slipping a ring from her weathered finger.

My mouth parted as she took off the gold engagement ring and extended the delicate band encrusted with jewels to me. "Grandma?"

"Your grandpa and I met when we were sixteen years old. I knew then just like I know now that he's my soul mate."

Gramps's eyes shined with love across the table as he nodded. "If this girl is the love of your life, we want you to have this, for when you're ready. Whether it's now or ten years from now."

"Just don't wait too long," Grandma said. "We only get today to tell someone we love them."

I held the ring in my hand, and maybe it was

my imagination, but I swore I could feel the love it held. Forty years of a loving, successful marriage, and I promised myself that I would never break that tradition. *That* was my choice.

FORTY-SEVEN

CALLIE

According to Rory, Carson was no longer staying at Beckett's place. He'd left and took all of his things. He wasn't answering Beckett's calls. When I was finally brave enough to dial his number myself, he didn't answer me either.

I tried to think of all the places he could be staying, but each one came up empty. No one had seen or heard from Carson in a week. The more people I called, the more worried I felt until finally I called Gemma.

I leaned on my open window—letting Dad's cold air out—and prayed for her to answer.

She picked up on the fourth ring, and I could

hear the noise of a bustling city in the background. "Callie? I only have a few minutes."

"I just need a second," I rushed out. "Where's Carson? I haven't seen him all week, and I'm worried about him."

The line was silent for a moment, and I heard Gemma whisper something to someone, but I couldn't make out the words. "Callie?" she finally said.

"Yeah?" My stomach was tied in knots, waiting for her explanation.

"He's okay. He's at my grandparents'."

The wave of relief her words sent over me had me backing up and collapsing into my bed. "Thank God he's okay."

"He is," she said, a smile in her voice. "Or, at least, he will be."

I wanted to ask her what that meant, but she told me she had to go and hurried off the phone. I lay back in my bed, holding my phone to my chest and thinking about my next move. Carson's grandparents lived in Texas, which wasn't as simple as driving across town to find him.

Checking the GPS on my phone, it told me the drive was eleven hours from here. If I got in my car and drove, I could be there by Sunday afternoon.

But I wasn't sure how my parents would feel about that. They'd been pretty lenient this last year, but I also had never asked them to make a cross-country road trip.

If Carson wasn't answering my calls and wouldn't come back to Emerson, I might have no choice other than to track him down on the Stanford campus. That would mean waiting an entire month before seeing him again, and who knew how much could change for him in that time.

Feeling defeated, I dialed my friends on our group video chat, and their faces filled the squares on the screen. I told them about my call with Gemma. "He's eleven hours away, and there's not a chance my parents will be cool with me just picking up and driving there. Not to mention I have work." I rubbed my face with my free hand. "What do I do?"

Rory was the first to speak. "Let me call Beckett, and then I'll text you guys. Maybe he can get in touch with Carson."

We hung up and I stared and stared at my phone, willing her to tell me that it was a huge misunderstanding. That Carson was in town and would walk through the door any time now, but so far, that didn't seem to be happening.

Finally, my phone chimed with a new message alert, and I tapped into the text at hyper speed.

Rory: Beckett's trying to find a way to get in touch with Carson. Let's meet at the mall and brainstorm? I'm dying for some cookie dough.
Zara: I'll be there in 30.
Jordan: Same.
Ginger: Getting my keys now. :)
Callie: I love you guys. See you soon.

A flurry of hopeful butterflies kicked up in my stomach as I drove to the mall. I'd seen my friends overcome an entire school's judgement, break down class barriers, change long-standing beliefs, and shake down cultural norms. If anyone could help make this happen, it was my friends. I had to have faith that Carson would see the real me underneath my fear and insecurities. That he would let me see and love the real him.

I pulled into an empty spot near the mall entrance and began walking inside. None of my friends' cars were in the parking lot, but maybe one was behind the massive RV that had taken up at least five spots.

I couldn't help smiling as I walked into the mall

and got closer to the cookie shop. We were going to figure this out. We *had* to.

I scanned the seats for my friends, but didn't see them, much less hear their characteristic laughter. Sliding my purse down my arm, I found a table that would fit all of us and sat down.

Getting out my phone, I swiped it open and went to my photos. There were so many pictures of Carson and me. Even when I didn't know it, we were writing our love story.

"Callie Copeland?" My name sounded over the speaker they used to call orders. The only problem? I hadn't bought anything.

I looked toward the stand, my eyebrows drawn together, and the guy at the mic repeated, "Callie Copeland."

Picking up my purse, I slid out of my seat and walked to the counter. When I reached the guy, I said, "I'm sorry, I haven't ordered anything yet."

"We have something for you," he replied.

I tilted my head to the side, confused, until I watched my best friend walk out of their kitchen.

FORTY-EIGHT

CARSON

Callie's mouth fell open, and her eyes went wide. She brought her hands to her mouth, shaking her head in disbelief as she said, "Carson?"

My friend Justin stepped to the side so I could walk around the counter to the love of my life. "I'm here." Gently, I took one of her hands and led her to a table. She might not have remembered, but it was the same one we sat at two years ago, the day that Sarah talked to me and I did the idiot thing and gave up on Callie.

I'd known there was no girl for me but Callie then, and I knew it even more certainly now.

As we sat down, her eyes traced my body like

she didn't believe it was really me. "Carson," she breathed. "Why—how are you here?"

Her words, the hurt and hope in her eyes were a punch to my gut. I never should have left her here to deal with the blowback of what she'd seen. I should have stayed for her, but I couldn't change the past; I could only lean into my choices of the present.

I reached across the table, and her hands slipped into both of mine, fitting just right. I looked from our intertwined fingers up to the depths of her beautiful blue eyes, wondering if I would sink or swim.

"Carson," she began, but I shook my head.

"I have something to say," I told her, and she nodded, pressing her full lips together. What I would give to kiss her again. But that would have to wait until I said what I needed to.

"Callie..." I'd practiced a thousand times on the drive here, and I still didn't know how to begin. I rubbed my thumbs over the base of her palms and built up the courage to look her in the eyes. "When I saw my dad hurting my sister, my mom, I lost it, and I thought that anger meant I would be just like him. I would never want you to live a life like my mom and my sisters have." My throat clogged with emotions, but I powered through because I had to get this out. "I promise, if you give me a second chance, I will always keep you safe. I will keep you and me as far away from my dad as we need to be. I'll love you and cherish you the way you deserve, because you're the one, Cal. You always have been."

Watching her take in my words, waiting for her to respond, was the longest few seconds of my life. It was like standing on the edge of a cliff knowing a single gust of wind could send me hurtling to the end. But Callie wouldn't let me go.

She held on to my hand tighter and leaned in closer. "I was wrong, how I reacted. I should have understood. Because I know who you *are*. For eight years, I've seen you do everything to make other people happy. You've been the light of my world, Carson. I don't know how I could have done middle school—high school—without you. And there's no way I'm doing life without you either."

The meaning behind her words hit my heart before it registered in my mind. My chest swelled with joy, with love, with hope, and I crossed the table, pulling her from her seat and crushing her to me in a hug. For the first time in a week, it felt like I could *breathe*. "I love you," I said into her hair.

"I love you too, Carson, more than anything."

I took her face in both of my hands because I couldn't stand not kissing her anymore, not feeling her lips on mine. Our mouths met somewhere in the middle of needing and wanting, and the way she relaxed into my arms made me feel like we had both fallen into place exactly where we needed to be.

This was what strong was, loving a girl well enough that she felt safe with you, that no matter what, you'd be taking on the world together.

I wound my hands through the soft strands of her hair and held her close, adoring her just the way she was. She laid a hand flat against my chest, right over my heart, and I hoped she knew it was beating just for her. Maybe it always had, knowing one day I'd meet a girl who set my world on fire and my heart at ease.

Callie smiled against my lips, and as she broke the kiss, I could hear the cheering around us. Our friends stood a few tables over, along with my grandparents, sister, and nephew, celebrating the love of my life.

Callie giggled sweetly, making my heart melt. "Looks like we have an audience."

I kissed her temple. "I have some people I want you to meet."

FORTY-NINE

CALLIE

Clary had to get home to her family early in the week, but Carson's grandparents parked their RV at a campsite near Seaton Pier. Carson and I spent the week showing them all the things we loved about Emerson. The more time I spent around his grandparents, the more I could see where Carson got his kindness and grace. He didn't need to worry about being like his dad when he was already so much like them.

On Friday morning, their last day in Emerson, we decided a going-away meal at Waldo's Diner was in order.

We all got into Carson's car and drove to the diner that held so much of our history. I couldn't wait for his grandparents to see how many friends Carson had in the restaurant or to taste the food that was clearly made with love.

When we walked inside, nearly all the tables were full for breakfast, except the one where Chester sat. Carson and I exchanged a look, and I nodded.

He walked up to the old man and asked, "Chester, is it okay if we sit with you?"

With the happiest grin I'd seen on his face, he nodded and scooted over. "I'd be thrilled."

We sat down, and Carson introduced his grandparents to Chester. For the better part of an hour, we just talked, enjoying conversation about Emerson and life and next steps. But one topic hadn't been touched on.

"How's your kitty doing?" I asked Chester. "Karen still in love?"

He chuckled. "That cat's been the best thing ever. Gives us something new to talk about, some companionship for Karen while I'm here, and plenty of reason for the neighborhood kids to come by. It's as spoiled as they come."

Gramps chuckled. "I've been thinking about getting a pet. A dog, not a cat though. But I don't think I have the energy for a puppy."

A slow grin spread across my lips, and I said to Carson, "You thinking what I'm thinking?"

His mouth fell open in an excited smile. "That would be perfect!"

The older people looked at us, intrigued, and Carson said, "Callie's been fostering a dog. He's a bit of a grump, but he's also the sweetest dog ever. He's house-trained and loves lying around. He would be perfect for you."

Grandma's eyes lit up. "It must be a God thing. I'd love to meet him, but I need to find the owner of this place first and tell them how special it is."

"You're looking at him," Chester said.

My mouth fell open at the meaning behind his words. "*What?*"

A sly smile grew on his face. "There's a reason I'm always here, you know."

Carson shook my arm. "No freaking way!"

Chester nodded. "But keep it to yourselves." He straightened. "I don't like making a big fuss about being the boss, you know."

I zipped my lips, then said. "Now we know why it's so special."

Chester positively beamed, and Gramps extended his hand to the man sitting next to him.

"Looks like a thanks is in order, for giving my boy here a great place to be."

Chester shook his hand. "Anything for a friend, old"—he winked at Carson—"or new."

As we drove to my house for Carson's grandparents to meet Franklin, I still couldn't believe Chester owned the restaurant. It made sense though; like he said, he was always there. And he did love his wife so much, that came through in how the place was run.

Carson pulled up along the curb. Since my parents were at an event, I ran inside to get Franklin so they could meet him in the yard. My heart raced, hoping that Franklin would find his happy ever after too.

I found him lounging on the couch downstairs, and he lifted his eyebrows lazily when he saw me. I scooped him up and carried him to the front door, my eyes hot as I said, "I think I might have found the ones for you, Frankie. They're the sweetest people I've ever met, and they travel the world in this comfy trailer. You'll be a traveling doggo. Doesn't that sound nice?" My throat got tight as I stalled with my hand on the doorknob. "And I'll still get to see you once you go with them. You'll *always* be my family."

His dark eyes took me in like he heard every word, and he licked my cheek. I let out a half-sob, half-laugh and pushed through the doors. Franklin leapt from my arms and ran straight to Carson, who picked him up and showed him to his grandparents.

Grandma folded her hands at her chest and simpered. "He's just the most precious thing."

Gramps chuckled and scratched Franklin's ears. "Good, solid thing. Not too big for the trailer but can hold his own."

My eyes watered as I watched them fall in love. When Franklin jumped from Carson's arms to Gramps's, I knew it was over.

Grandma looked at me and said, "We'll take him." Franklin licked her cheek in approval.

He rode in Grandma's lap on the way back to the RV, but when it was time for him to go, I took him aside for one final hug. I held him close to my chest and petted his ears and did everything I could to stem the flow of tears streaming down my face.

"Franklin, you've been the absolute best dog a girl could ask for." I curled my hand around his head, scratching his ear just like he liked. "You even warned me about Nick before my head could accept what my heart really wanted. No matter where you go, I know you'll be just what they need."

Like he understood, he nuzzled his head to my chest, and I took a deep, shaky breath. It was time to move forward, with Carson at my side.

FIFTY

CARSON

As we drove away from the RV campsite, Callie had tears streaming down her cheeks. I hated that she was in pain, but she had no idea how much that little dog meant to my grandparents. That was just another one of the things I loved about her. Even though she knew fostering dogs was bound to break her heart, she did it anyway.

I reached across the console and took her hand. "Hey, I'm here for you."

She smiled tearily at me. "Thank you."

If I was being honest, I was going to miss Franklin too. Him leaving with my grandparents felt like a bookend to the summer. "Can you believe we only have a few weeks until it's time to leave for Stanford?"

She shook her head. "Not at all."

The last two months had flown by and hadn't gone remotely how I'd expected. I'd be grateful for that always. Not only had Callie fallen in love with me, but I'd gotten closure with my family I'd never anticipated. My mom apologized. My dad moved away. Gemma and I had rekindled our relationship, and even Clary made me promise to visit them for Thanksgiving. It was like I'd gotten my family back. My *life* back.

Now all there was to do was enjoy it with the love of my life. I wondered how I could make these last few weeks in Emerson ones she would remember. We had her mom's cookie competition, which we'd obviously blow the top off of, and she would be working. Mrs. Mayes even let me back on the schedule despite my last-minute exit.

Callie's phone began ringing, and she moved her finger over the screen. Zara's face came into view as Callie showed both of us on the screen.

"Hey, Zara," I said.

"Hey, Callon," she replied. "So I had an idea. Do you guys want to get ready for the premiere here? We could make it a fun group hang. Everyone else already said they were free."

"Premiere?" Callie asked.

And then it hit me. "Crap! Callie, the movie premiere."

"Oh my gosh," she said. "I totally forgot."

"Well, good thing I called!" Zara said. "Do you guys want to swing by in an hour or so then?"

Callie and I glanced at each other and wordlessly agreed.

"We'll be there," she said.

I grinned as she hung up. This would be the perfect thing to lift our moods. Not to mention, I couldn't wait to see Callie in a dress. I hoped she'd wear one that showed off her curves.

"I have a crazy idea," Callie said.

I turned to her, just a little terrified. "If you try to talk me into sneaking a dog into the dorms again—"

"It's not that," she said, laughing. "No, what if we invited Merritt to get ready with us?"

A sly smile lifted my lips. "Look at you, Callie, trying to be the bigger person."

Blushing, she rolled her eyes. "It's not that... it's just... Her friends dumped her when she lost her money. I can't imagine not having my friends."

This, right here, is why Callie was *my* best friend. After the way Merritt had treated her, I honestly wouldn't have blamed Callie for just going off to college and pretending Merritt never existed. But here she was, opening her heart to even the most unlovable.

"Call her," I said with a smile.

She bit her lip nervously. "What will the girls say?"

I shrugged. "Probably that you're crazy. It'll be awkward, but it's the right thing to do. I think we should all be ready to move on from high school, Merritt included."

"Right." She lifted her phone and slowly tapped her fingers over the screen.

FIFTY-ONE

CALLIE

When Merritt picked up, she said, "Did I forget to close a gate again? I swear—"

"No, that's not it!" I said with a giggle. That had been a challenge getting all the cats back into their room. "I actually had a question for you…"

"What is it?" she asked suspiciously. "I need to get back to getting ready."

"Actually, it's about that," I said. "Some of my friends and I are getting ready for your brother's premiere together, and we thought you might like to come."

The line was silent for a moment as she took in the question. If she was anything like me, she was still reeling.

"With Rory?" she asked finally.

"And Zara, Ginger, and Jordan," I answered.

"Do they know I'm coming?"

"They're excited," I lied.

"Liar," Carson hissed.

I hit his shoulder, still waiting on Merritt's reply. After a moment of silence, I said, "Come on, Merritt, just say yes. I know you need friends, and we're ready to move on if you are."

She let out a long breath. "I'll come."

Before she had a chance to back out, I told her we'd be by to get her in half an hour, although I half expected her to back out. But when we pulled down the winding driveway in front of her house, she was outside with a big duffel bag and a garment bag surely carrying a designer gown.

Carson reached behind him and popped open the back door for her, and she got in, a distrusting look in her eyes.

"If this is a setup, you're going to pay," she said.

I rolled my eyes. "That's so high school."

Shaking her head, she said to Carson, "Let's get this over with."

"That's the spirit," he said.

I noticed the smile she tried to hide. We drove in mostly silence to Zara's townhouse. Merritt stared at the building. "We're going to have to move at the end of the month."

My heart ached for her. "What about your dad?"

"Jail," she said. "For three years."

I turned in the seat and put my hand on hers. "We're here for you, remember?"

With a sad smile, she wiped at her eyes and nodded.

"Let me go make sure everyone's ready," I said and got out of the car, my guilty conscience weighing on me.

When I walked inside, the guys were sitting in front of the TV with Zara's dad, watching baseball. How they always found a sport to watch, I had no idea. They were practically oblivious to me as I walked up the stairs to Zara's room.

The girls were sprawled around the space, talking, and when they saw me, they greeted me warmly. But there was no time for greetings.

"Guys, I have a surprise," I said.

"You're engaged?" Ginger blurted.

"No!" I cried. "Way too soon for that. But um..." I shifted on my feet. What had I been thinking? Merritt didn't need to come. She could have gotten ready just fine at her house.

The door opened behind me, and Merritt walked in, her chin held high. So much for waiting.

"Merritt's going to get ready with us," I said. "She's ready to move past high school, if we are." I gave each of them a look, begging them to be kind. The other girls looked to Rory, knowing she'd been the most hurt by the girl standing beside me.

Rory stood up and extended her hand. "I'll move past it." She smirked. "But maybe we should hide the cupcakes?"

Merritt's cheeks heated, but her lips formed a bashful grin as she gave Rory a hug. "I'm sorry."

The other girls and I watched in awe as Merritt stood back and said, "I shouldn't have done what I did, but Callie's shown me what it means to be a true friend." She reached out and took my hand. "I'd like to be one too."

I squeezed her hand back and smiled at her encouragingly.

"In that case," Zara said with a grin, "welcome to the Curvy Girl Club."

FIFTY-TWO

CARSON

As I walked into Zara's living room, I half expected to hear crashing and banging upstairs. Instead, there was silence. And some laughing. But not the malicious kind. With a shrug, I walked closer to the couch, and the guys noticed me approaching.

Ray stuck out his hand from where he sat on one side of the couch, and I slapped him a high five. Kai nodded at me, and Ronan did the same. Finally, Beckett stood from the couch and faced me. Before he could say anything, I said, "I've been meaning to call, but turns out there's not a great way to say sorry for being a jerk."

Beckett chuckled quietly. "No, but that was

pretty good." He pulled me into a one-arm hug and patted my back. "Welcome home."

I grinned at him. "Thanks." There was so much more to say, but we'd been friends long enough, I felt like he got it.

"Are you coming back to my place?"

"Nah," I answered, dropping onto the couch beside Ronan. The other guys seemed to have their mind back on the TV. "Callie's family is letting me sleep in their guest room again."

"Whoa, seriously?" Beckett raised his eyebrows. "I thought her parents were stricter."

I shrugged. "They said we were about to be on our own in college, so they wanted us to practice 'setting boundaries.'"

From beside me, Ronan smirked. "That should be fun."

The tips of my ears felt hot as I realized what he'd alluded to. Not that I had anything against *that*; we just were taking things slow. In some ways, it felt like we'd been together all our lives, but in others... Callie and I were still getting used to being more than friends. Not that I'd ever get used to the fact that she was mine. That still seemed too good to be true.

I leaned back in the couch and half-watched the

ballgame on the TV, just thinking about the last few months. So much had changed, and I couldn't even be mad about it. I'd go through it all over again if that's what it took to get to Callie. To get to myself.

About an hour later, I grabbed one of my bags from the car and dug through it until I found my suit from prom. It wasn't the thousand-dollar tuxes I was sure everyone else would be wearing, but it was fine for a dark theater.

The game had gone into extra innings by the time I heard giggles at the stairs. Zara came down first, then Ginger, Jordan, Rory, Merritt, and finally...

I stood up and watched in awe as my girl came toward me. "Wow," I breathed. She wore a light silver dress that clung to her waist and draped around her hips. Even more stunning was her face framed with curls so soft I wanted to wind my fingers through them. Her lips were bright pink, making me want to kiss them that much more. "You look stunning."

She bashfully batted her long eyelashes, but she had no need to be insecure. Callie in this dress was...everything.

"You don't look so bad yourself," she said, smiling up at me.

I kissed the smile right off her lips.

"Okay, lovebirds," Merritt said. "We have to get out of here."

Callie looked at me, concerned. "I completely forgot to ask. How are we getting there?"

Merritt waved her purse over her shoulder like we should follow her. "You're riding with me."

FIFTY-THREE

CALLIE

I'd been in limos before—to prom or hanging out with my friends—one of whom was dating a billionaire. But I'd certainly never ridden in one with Merritt.

We got inside, and I sat beside Carson. He put his arm around my shoulder and held me close. It was like we wanted to make up for all the time we spent ignoring our hearts.

"You two are so cute together," Merritt said, almost annoyed.

I smiled and shook my head. "Don't sound so happy about it."

She let out a quiet laugh. "Do you remember

that time we stuck you two together for Seven Minutes in Heaven?"

Carson snorted. "Like I could forget."

"Yeah, he had to put his food down," I teased him, remembering how much he'd eaten that night. And how sweet he'd been.

Merritt shook her head. "I was so sure you two were going to get together then."

Carson's eyes smoldered on me. "If I would have had my way, we would have."

My cheeks warmed, and I leaned my head on his shoulder. "Maybe we needed to be friends first so we could see how much there was to lose."

His lips spread in a stunning smile, showing his straight white teeth. "I think you might be right."

"Well then," Merritt said, walking to the small refrigerator at the front of the limo. "We might as well celebrate." She pulled out a bottle of champagne and three glasses, then popped the cork.

It flew and hit a window, making us all laugh. Grinning, she poured three glasses and we all held them up.

"To friends," Merritt said, her eyes shining.

"To friends," Carson agreed.

"To friends," I said. And as I tasted the sweet liquid, I thought about how grateful I was for mine, whether they were new, like Merritt, constant, like the girls, or forever like Carson.

The limo slowed, and the driver opened the door for us. As we stepped out of the car, cheers ripped through the crowd, but they weren't cheering for us. At the end of the red carpet, Ryde Alexander and Ambrose Welsh were locked in a passionate embrace.

"What?" I screamed. "Your brother loves Ambrose!"

Merritt whooped, her smile shining brighter than the cameras flashing all around us. "I wasn't sure if they would tell anyone," she yelled to me over the noise. "I'm glad they did." She scurried down the red carpet toward the couple, and as I went to follow, Carson took my hand.

He spun me back to him and held me against his chest. Breathless, I looked into his sea-green eyes, and he held my gaze.

"Are you ready?" he asked me, his breath heating my lips.

"For what?" I breathed.

He brushed his thumb over my bottom lip, sending shivers down my spine, and said, "Happily ever after."

EPILOGUE

CORI

Why was everyone at this going-away party coupled off? Mom and Dad were having a going away party for Ginger and all of her friends before they left for college. Except Ray—he'd be staying at his family's ranch and running it like he'd planned to all along.

But everyone here was a couple. There weren't even any cute guys I could chat up. There were a couple of kids from my class here, like Aiden Hutton, but his girlfriend stood with him. They'd been dating for like three years. And my sister? Ray hadn't left her side all night.

Callie and Carson were the cutest out of them all. He'd pulled her away from their group of friends and was slow dancing with her in the middle of the grass like no one around them existed.

I sat on a chair around the perimeter of our yard, wishing I hadn't worn a dress. Maybe if I'd put on some pants, I could go out front and shoot hoops with the kids playing in our driveway goal. But then again, sweaty redhead in summer didn't exactly say *date me* to passersby. Even less so to people I knew.

"Hey, cane sugar," Mom said to me. "Would you go inside and grab some ice? We're running low."

"Sure," I sighed, getting up from my chair. It wasn't like I had anything better to do.

I passed Aunt Rosie and her new boyfriend, Ben, and walked inside to get a bag of ice for the punch like Mom asked.

I still couldn't believe Ginger had pulled off the impossible and made our parents come around to seeing things her way. And while she was changing our parents' firmly held beliefs, I was... well, doing nothing.

I'd had the driest summer in the history of summers, even though I was going into my last year of high school. My friends were having flings, going on vacations, and I'd been working at my parents' store, stocking shelves alongside a totally hot but completely taken college guy. And when I wasn't working at the store, I was practicing my shots in the basketball hoop in our driveway.

There had to be a way to make my senior year better. I wanted to have the kind of year Ginger had—great friends, a great guy, and heading off into the sunset to the college of my dreams.

I had at least one of those things—my friends were amazing. That, I was thankful for.

I bent into the freezer and pulled a bag of ice onto the counter top, flipping it and dropping it until the cubes had formed more manageable chunks.

"Hey, Cor," Ginger said.

I looked over and smiled. "Liking your party?"

"Of course." She took a drink from her red plastic cup. "You know, other than the punch being hot."

I rolled my eyes. "Did Mom send you in here to rush me?"

"No," she said, laughing, and leaned back against the island, resting her elbows on the granite. "I can't believe I'm leaving tomorrow."

I couldn't either. Even though she'd practically started packing her room the day after graduation, it was still hard to believe I'd have the room to myself. That I wouldn't hear her snoring at night, no matter how many times she tried to deny the fact that she did actually snore.

"Are you excited?" I asked.

She nodded. "Yeah, but it will be different. I'll be farther away from Ray. Have a new roommate who I don't even know that I'll like."

"Well, we've already established that you can't top me."

Laughing, she said, "Obviously."

I picked up the bag and started to head outside, but Ginger put her hand on my shoulder. "Hey, do you mind if we—I mean, if I... Can we talk?"

Half confused, half concerned, I set the bag on the counter. "What's up?"

She shrugged, getting onto one of the bar stools. She patted the one next to her, and I joined her. "Is this the part where you tell me you're not actually leaving and I won't actually have my own room? Because if that's true, you can't have it back. You'll just have to take the couch."

She rolled her eyes. "You talk a lot."

"And?"

Her curls fell over her face as she leaned forward, looking at her linked hands on the bar top, then looked back at me. "I don't know. I'm going out tonight and leaving for college tomorrow, and just in case we don't get the chance to talk tonight, I wanted to talk."

My heart constricted with that painful feeling I got when I forgot to avoid thinking of Ginger leaving. "What did you want to talk about?"

"I guess I had a hard time in high school, and I know you're doing better than me, but it wouldn't be right to leave without passing on my...wisdom, right?"

I cringed. "This is going to make me cry, isn't it?"

"Maybe." She laughed, but her eyes were already shining. "Okay, I've narrowed it down to three things I think you need to know."

"Three? I can handle that." My eyes were starting to burn too.

"One, you need to hold on to your friends. They can seriously get you through anything."

"Check." My friends were everything to me, and they knew it. "Number two?"

"Pick the right guy. Don't go dating some jerk like Dugan. He might be hot, but it's totally not worth it."

"Right," I said, "like I'd date the guy who

bullied you for the last three years."

She lifted her hands. "Not him, just his type."

"Sure. Easy," I replied.

"And three." She took a breath, blinking quickly. "If you ever need me, if you ever feel alone, if you ever feel like you're not absolutely beautiful inside and out, call me." Her voice cracked, even though she smiled. "I'll always be here for you."

My throat clogged with emotion, and instead of making a blubbering mess of myself by trying to talk and losing it, I closed the gap between us and held her tight.

"I love you," I said. "And I promise, I'll do my senior year right."

Want to read about Carson's **PROPOSAL** to Callie?! Grab your copy of Carson's Proposal, completely free.

Use this QR code to access the bonus
story!

Keep reading Cori's story in the Curvy Girl
Club by grabbing Curvy Girls Can't Date Bullies
today!

Use this code to discover Cori's story!

ALSO BY KELSIE STELTING

Abi and the Boy Next Door

Abi and the Boy Who Lied

Abi and the Boy She Loves

The Pen Pal Romance Series

Dear Adam

Fabio Vs. the Friend Zone

Sincerely Cinderella

The Sweet Water High Series: A Multi-Author Collaboration

Road Trip with the Enemy: A Sweet Standalone Romance

YA Contemporary Romance Anthologies

The Art of Taking Chances

Two More Days

Nonfiction

Raising the West

AUTHOR'S NOTE

Friendship is one of the most important gifts we can give or receive. My junior year of high school was a really dark time for me. I'd been hurt by a girl with no recourse, lost many of my friends because of that, and I spent night after night praying that God would send me a friend. A best friend I could share life with. Who would be there in the hard times and help me celebrate the good.

Soon after, I met a guy with a sunshine smile who became my best friend. And my husband.

Sometimes what we long for, though, isn't always delivered in the way we expected. With my husband, I've had to practice the delicate art of forgiveness. Grow in self-respect. Lean into some stubbornness.

In this story, Callie is blessed multiple times over with all of the friendship in her life. Her parents are some of her best guides, showing her how to give friendship to others. Her brother is there for her and his roommate when they need it. The girls all lift each other up and demand they each have the self-respect they deserve. And then Carson shows Callie what it means to truly love.

When it comes down to it, isn't that what friendship is? Love?

Beckett wasn't wrong when he said that sometimes love tears us apart, but it can also hold us together. Sometimes it drives us to do incredible things driving across the country to keep someone safe from a perceived threat or reaching out to the mean girl no matter how many times you've been wronged.

Wherever you are today, I hope you'll extend some of that love to those around you, and especially to yourself.

ACKNOWLEDGMENTS

Writing the five books in this series has been an incredible adventure with so many people helping and contributing along the way. Of course, my husband gets first kudos because he has patiently heard me angst and fret and stew and think over these characters for more than a year. He urged me to push Carson in a direction I didn't want him to go and made the story that much better for it. Don't let his accounting career fool you—this guy is a romantic at heart.

My children have been so loving and supportive and have helped me lean into life more than they'll ever know. I hope you'll see some of the wonder and love they've taught me through these words.

Special shout out to our oldest who repeatedly reminded me to have Carson and Callie get married. (Check out the bonus story for that!)

Siblings are the best friends that you don't get to choose, but I wouldn't have it any other way. They are my best supporters and firmest friends. I love them more than air.

Thank you to my mom who even read the ROUGH draft of this book and didn't tell me it was awful.

Sally Henson is a jewel of a friend. Not only has she helped me with my writing, but she's continually pointed me back to God. That is *true* friendship.

It might be a little unorthodox, but I feel like I need to thank Florida. Sally Henson, Yesenia Vargas, and I took a writing retreat there, and I can't tell you how much clarity and hope the beach gave me. At a rough point in my life, the waters cleansed my soul and lifted my spirits. This story and its happy ending are undoubtedly better for that trip.

The sweet people in my reader's club have made the group the best place on the internet. I always know I can go there for a pick-me-up, friendship, and amazing bookish conversation. Speaking of friendship, I'm thankful for theirs.

And you, sweet reader. Thank you for spending time with these friends. I hope each story felt like being welcomed back home. I can't wait to see you again in the next story.

GLOSSARY

LATIN PHRASES

Ad Meliora: School motto meaning "toward better things."
Audentes fortuna iuvat: Motto of *Dulce Periculum* meaning "Fortune favors the bold."
Dulce Periculum: means "danger is sweet" - local secret club that performs stunts
Multum in Parvo: means "much in little"

LOCATIONS

Town Name: Emerson
Location: Halfway between Los Angeles and San Francisco

Surrounding towns: Brentwood, Seaton, Heywood

Emerson Academy: Private school Rory and Beckett attend

Brentwood Academy: Rival private school

Walden Island: Tourism island off the coast, only accessible by helicopter or ferry

Main Hangouts

Emerson Elementary Library: Where Rory tutors Anna, open to students K-7

Emerson Field: Massive park in the center of Emerson

Emerson Memorial: Local hospital

Emerson Shoppes: Shopping mall

Emerson Trails: Hiking trails in Emerson, near Emerson Field

Halfway Café: Expensive dining option in Emerson, frequented by celebrities

La La Pictures: Movie theater in Emerson

Ripe: Major health food store serving the tri-city area

Roasted: Popular coffee shop in Emerson

JJ Cleaning: Cleaning service owned by Jordan's mom

Seaton Bakery: Delicious dining and drink option in Seaton where Beckett works

Seaton Beach: Beach near Seaton – rougher than the beach near Brentwood

Seaton Pier: Fishing pier near Seaton

Spike's: Local 18-and-under club

Waldo's Diner: local diner, especially popular after sporting events

Apps

Rush+: Game app designed by Kai Rush and his father

Sermo: chat app used by private school students

Important Entities

Bhatta Productions: Production company owned by Zara's father

Brentwood Badgers: Professional football team

Heywood Market: Big ranch/distributor where everyone can purchase their meat locally

Invisible Mountains: Local major nonprofit - Callie's dad is the CEO

ABOUT THE AUTHOR

Kelsie Stelting is a body positive romance author who writes love stories with strong characters, deep feelings, and happy endings.

She currently lives in Colorado. You can often find her writing, spending time with family, and soaking up too much sun wherever she can find it.

Visit www.kelsiestelting.com to get a free story and sign up for her readers' group!

 facebook.com/kelsiesteltingcreative

twitter.com/kelsiestelting

instagram.com/kelsiestelting

Made in the USA
Columbia, SC
27 January 2024

30412860R00276